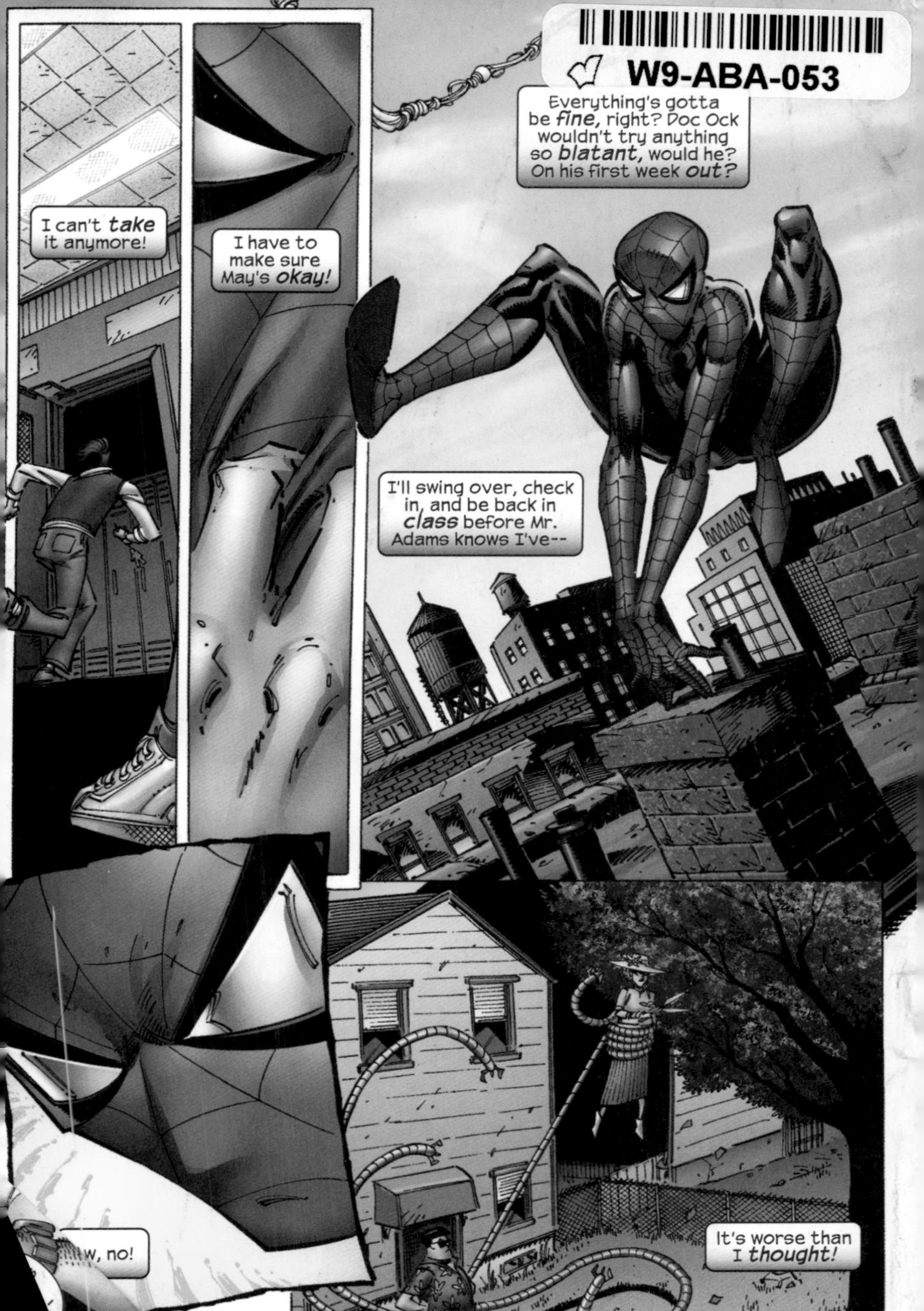
I can't *take* it anymore!
I have to make sure May's *okay!*
Everything's gotta be *fine,* right? Doc Ock wouldn't try anything so *blatant,* would he? On his first week *out?*
I'll swing over, check in, and be back in *class* before Mr. Adams knows I've--
w, no!
It's worse than I *thought!*

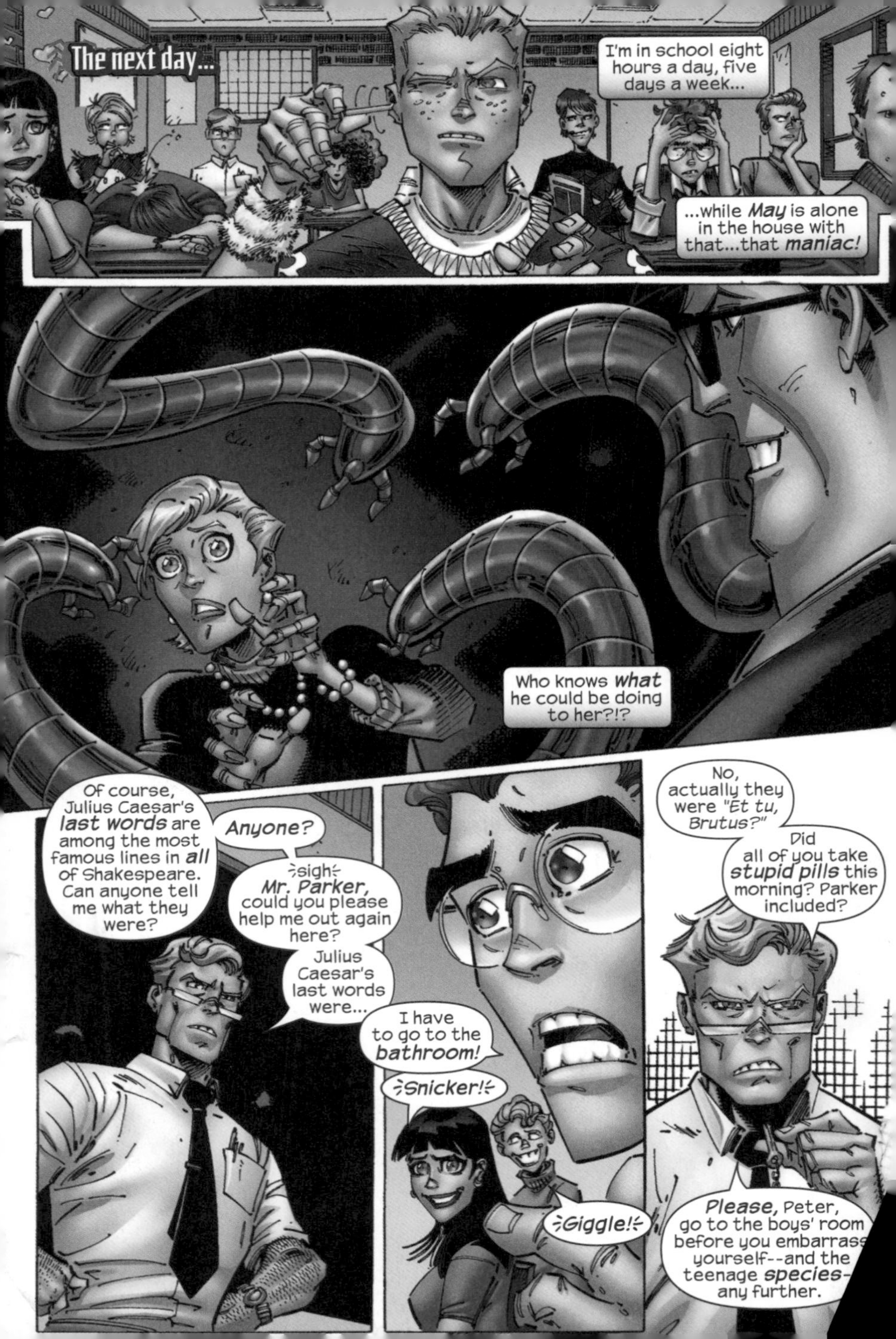
The next day...
I'm in school eight hours a day, five days a week...
...while May is alone in the house with that...that maniac!
Who knows what he could be doing to her?!?
Of course, Julius Caesar's last words are among the most famous lines in all of Shakespeare. Can anyone tell me what they were?
Anyone?
sigh
Mr. Parker, could you please help me out again here?
Julius Caesar's last words were...
I have to go to the bathroom!
Snicker!
Giggle!
No, actually they were "Et tu, Brutus?"
Did all of you take stupid pills this morning? Parker included?
Please, Peter, go to the boys' room before you embarrass yourself--and the teenage species--any further.

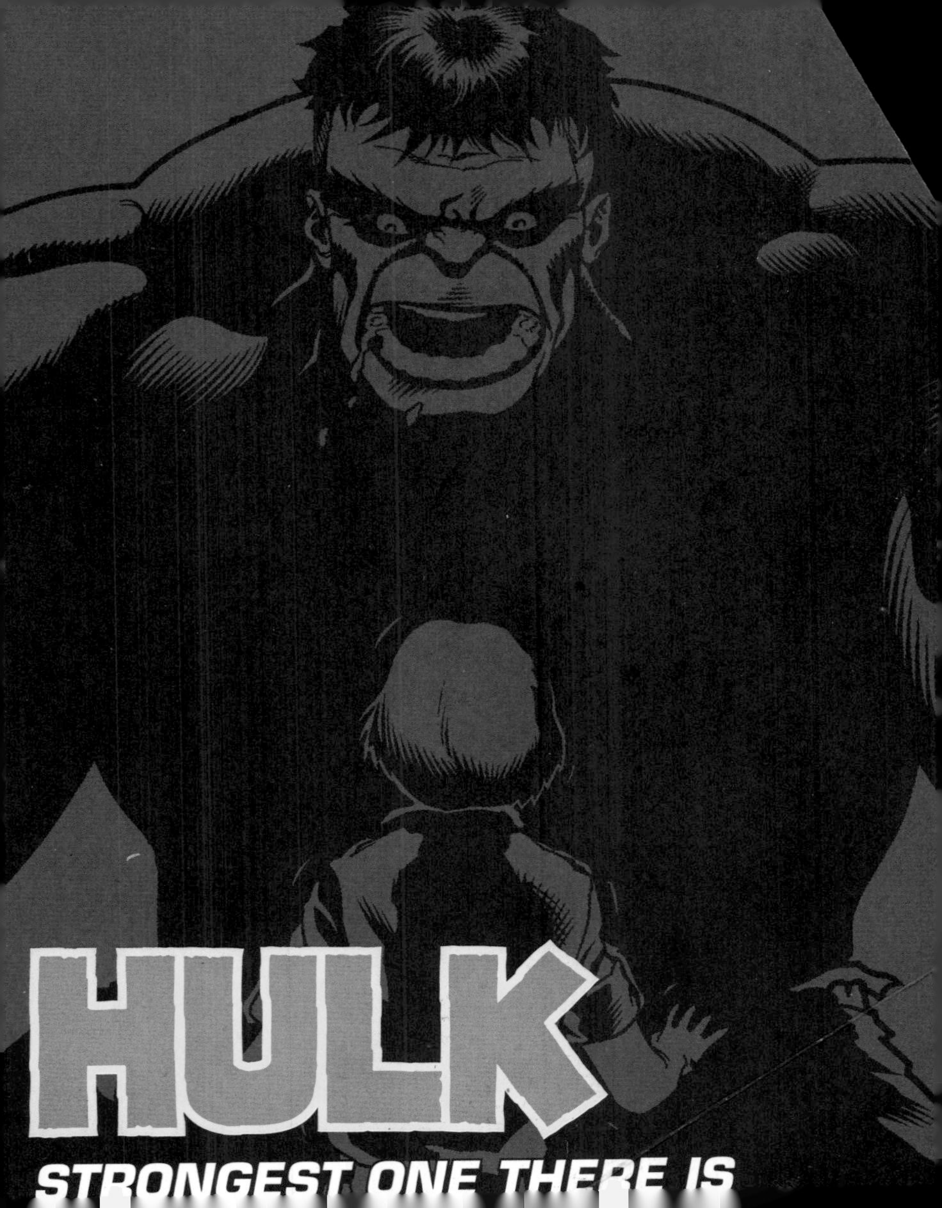
HULK
STRONGEST ONE THERE IS

HULK
STRONGEST ONE THERE IS

WRITER: PAUL BENJAMIN
PENCILER: STEVE SCOTT
INKERS: NATHAN MASSENGILL & TERRY PALLOT

COLORIST: SOTOCOLOR'S A. STREET
LETTERER: DAVE SHARPE

COVER ARTISTS: STEVE SCOTT, JAY LEISTEN, SEAN GORDON MURPHY,
MOOSE BAUMANN, DAVID NAKAYAMA & GURU EFX

ASSISTANT EDITOR: JORDAN D. WHITE
EDITOR: MARK PANICCIA

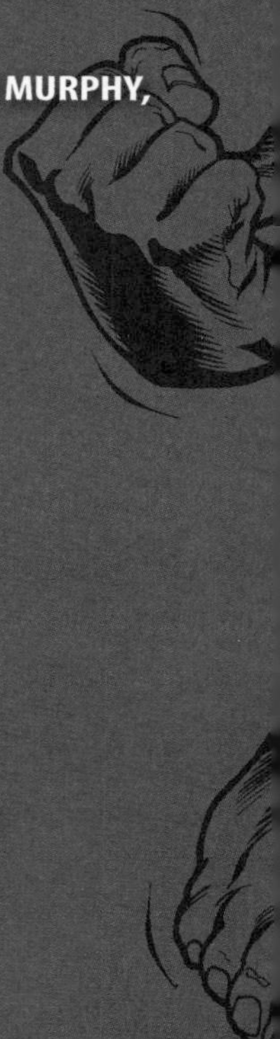

COLLECTION EDITOR: JENNIFER GRÜNWALD
EDITORIAL ASSISTANT: ALEX STARBUCK
ASSISTANT EDITORS: CORY LEVINE & JOHN DENNING
EDITOR, SPECIAL PROJECTS: MARK D. BEAZLEY
SENIOR EDITOR, SPECIAL PROJECTS: JEFF YOUNGQUIST
SENIOR VICE PRESIDENT OF SALES: DAVID GABRIEL

EDITOR IN CHIEF: JOE QUESADA
PUBLISHER: DAN BUCKLEY

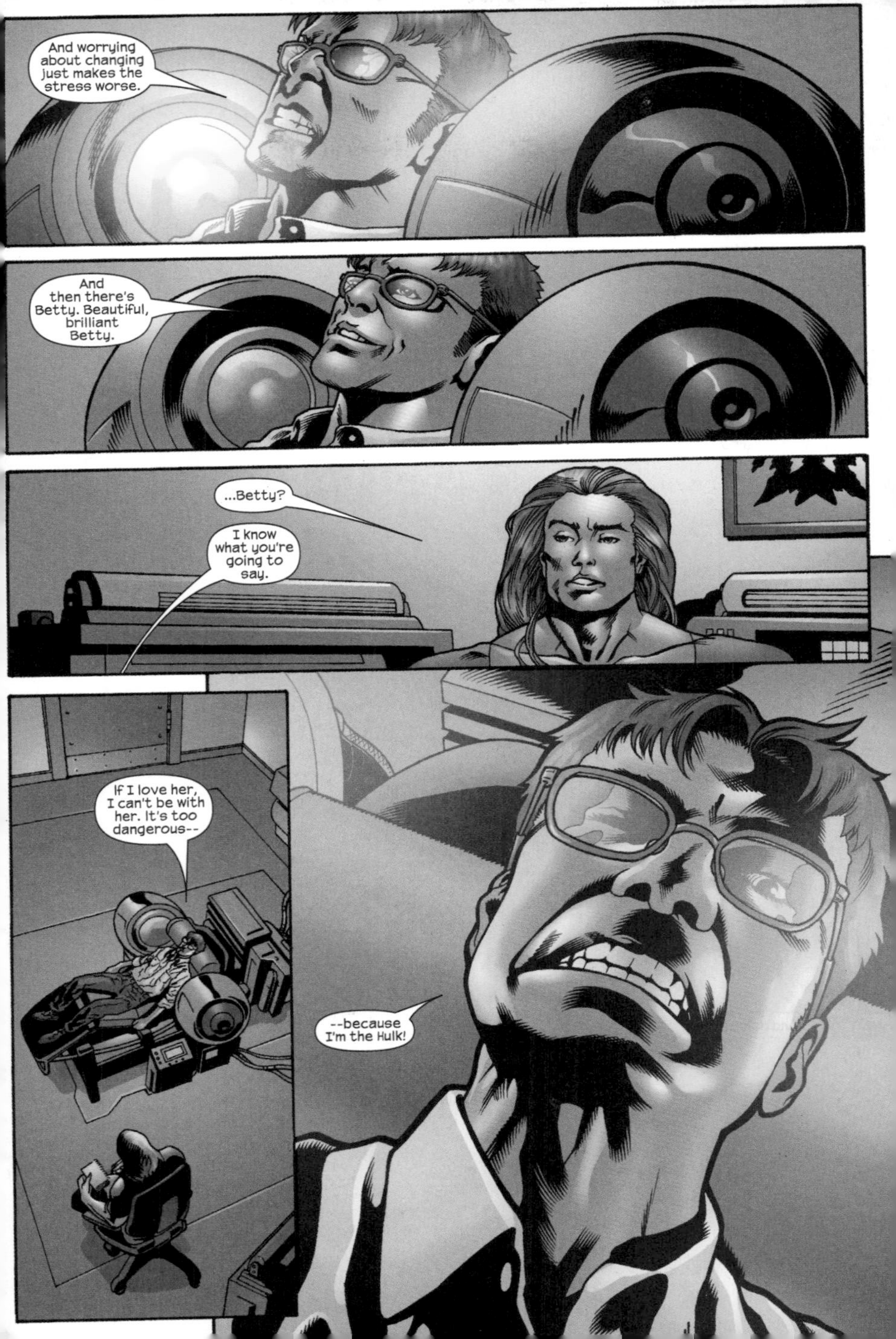

And worrying about changing just makes the stress worse.
And then there's Betty. Beautiful, brilliant Betty.
...Betty?
I know what you're going to say.
If I love her, I can't be with her. It's too dangerous--
--because I'm the Hulk!

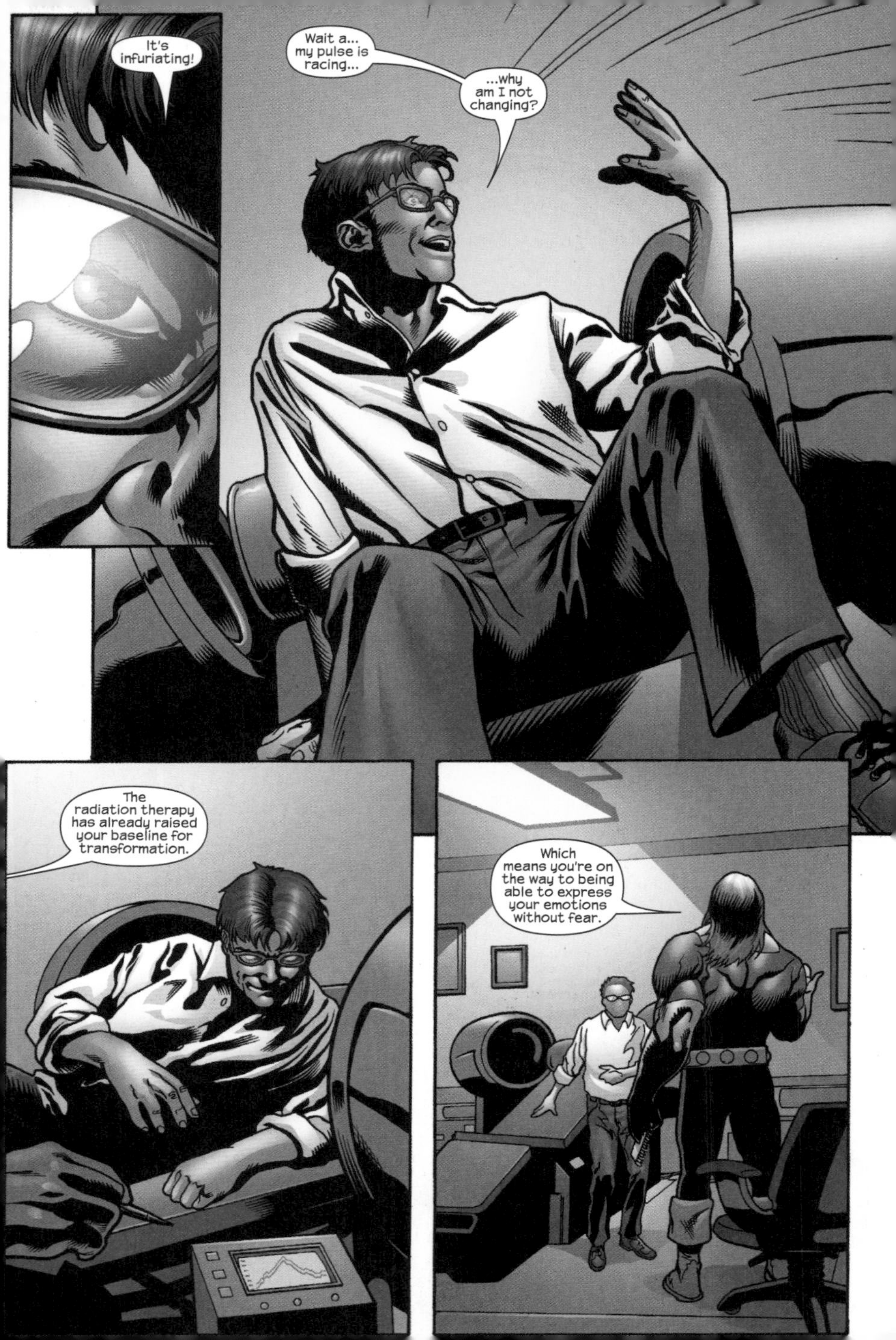
It's infuriating!
Wait a... my pulse is racing...
...why am I not changing?
The radiation therapy has already raised your baseline for transformation.
Which means you're on the way to being able to express your emotions without fear.

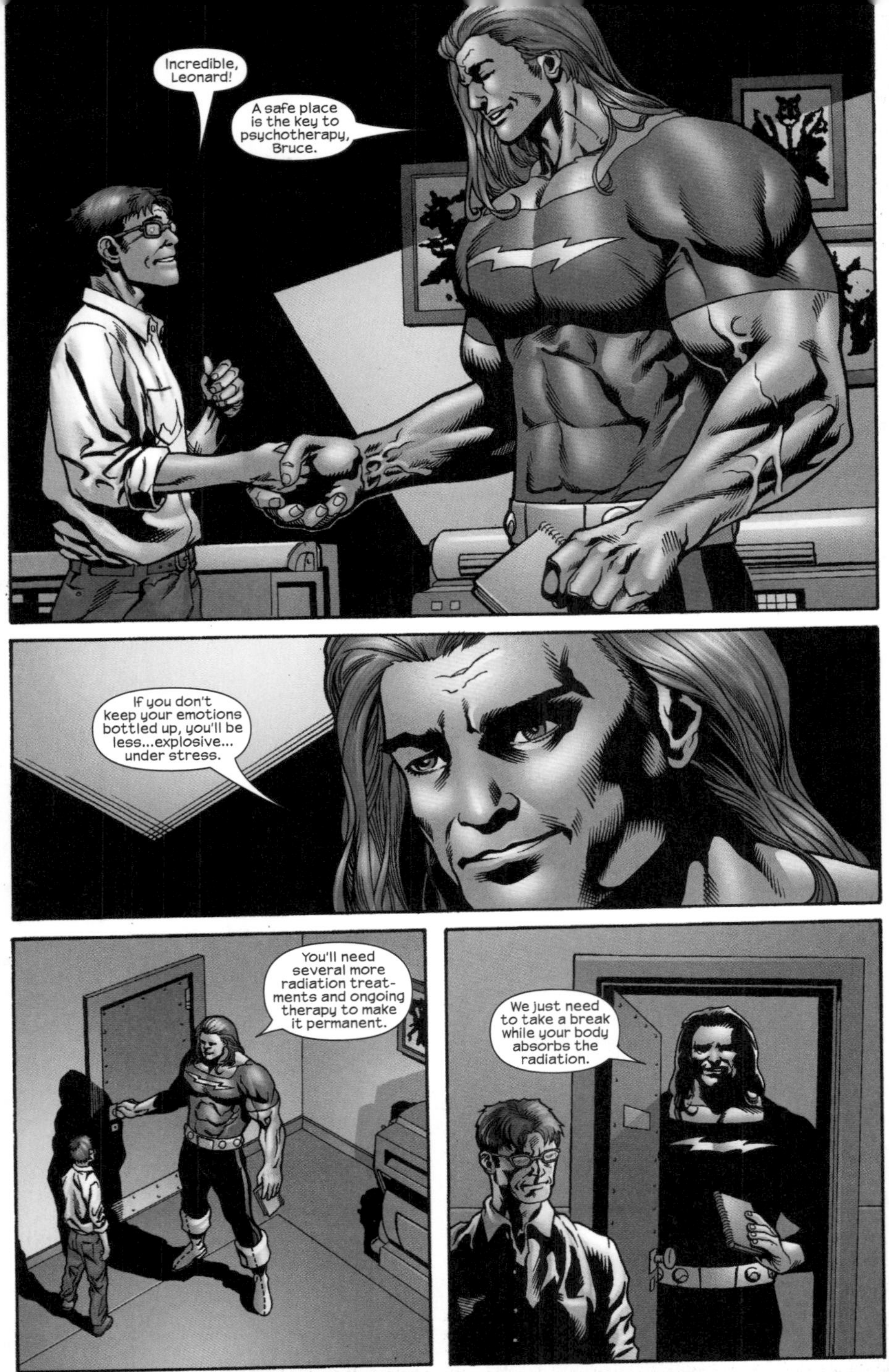
Incredible, Leonard!
A safe place is the key to psychotherapy, Bruce.
If you don't keep your emotions bottled up, you'll be less...explosive... under stress.
You'll need several more radiation treat-ments and ongoing therapy to make it permanent.
We just need to take a break while your body absorbs the radiation.

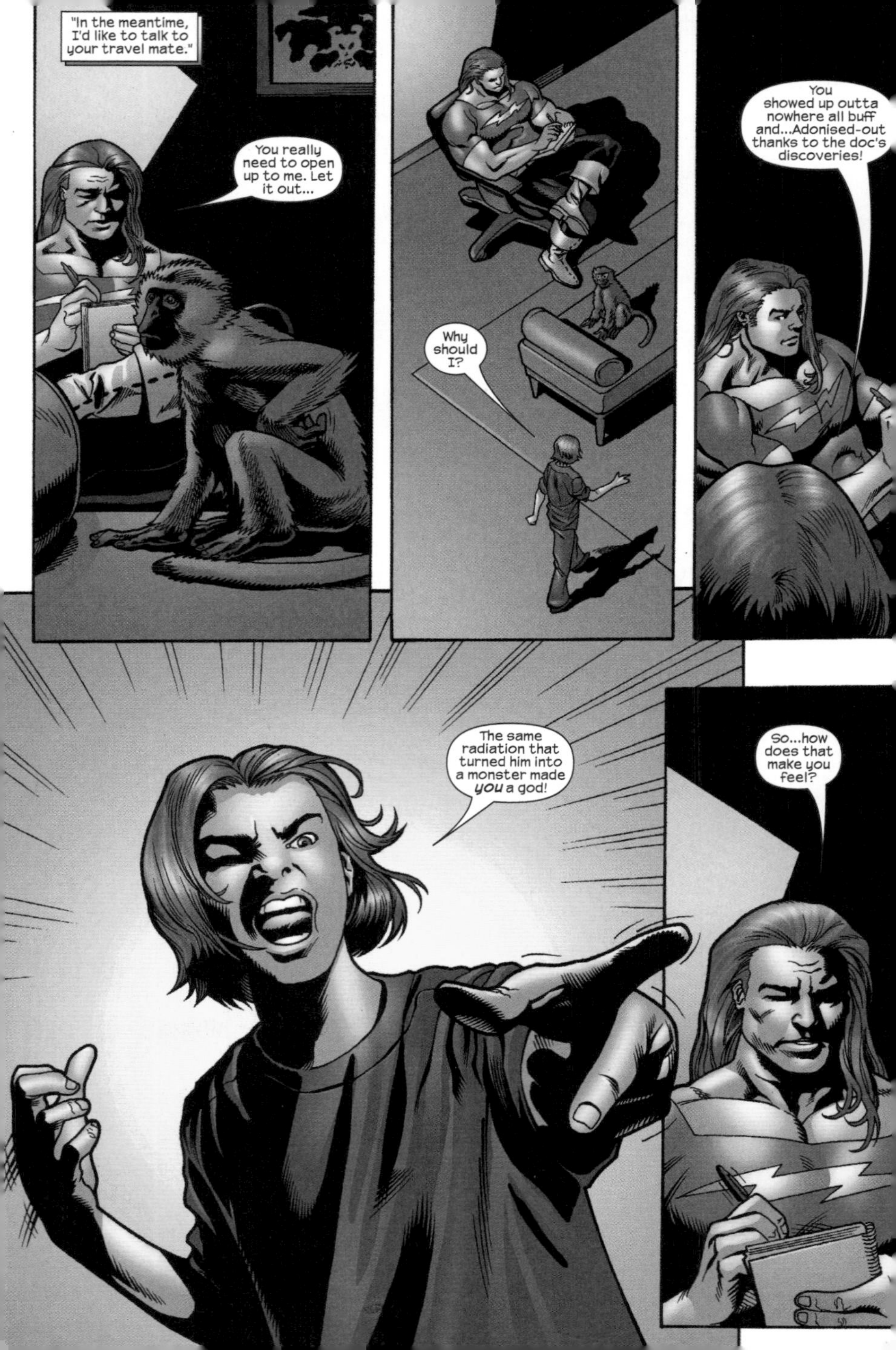
"In the meantime, I'd like to talk to your travel mate."
You really need to open up to me. Let it out...
Why should I?
You showed up outta nowhere all buff and...Adonised-out thanks to the doc's discoveries!
The same radiation that turned him into a monster made *YOU* a god!
So...how does that make you feel?

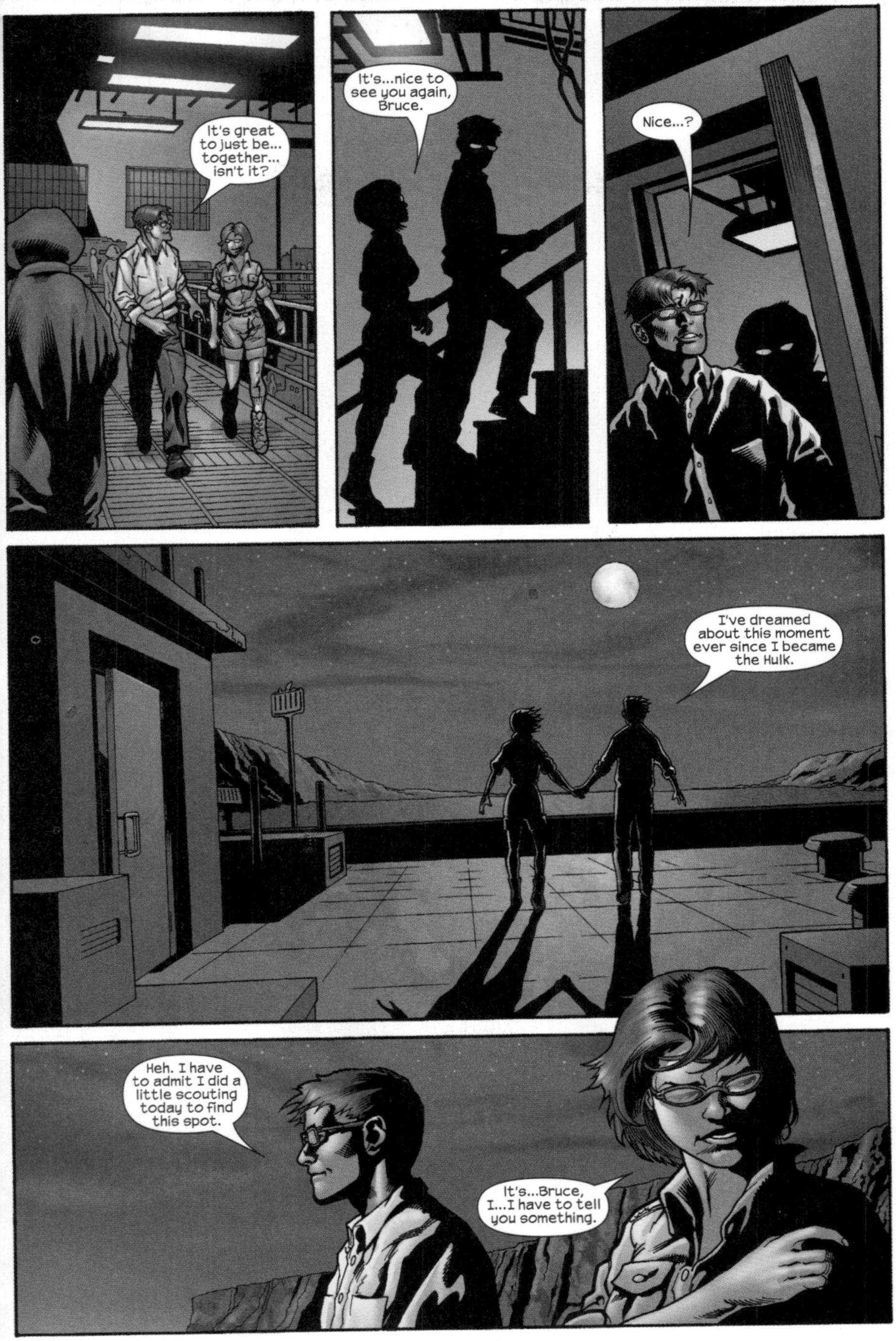

It's great to just be... together... isn't it?
It's...nice to see you again, Bruce.
Nice...?
I've dreamed about this moment ever since I became the Hulk.
Heh. I have to admit I did a little scouting today to find this spot.
It's...Bruce, I...I have to tell you something.

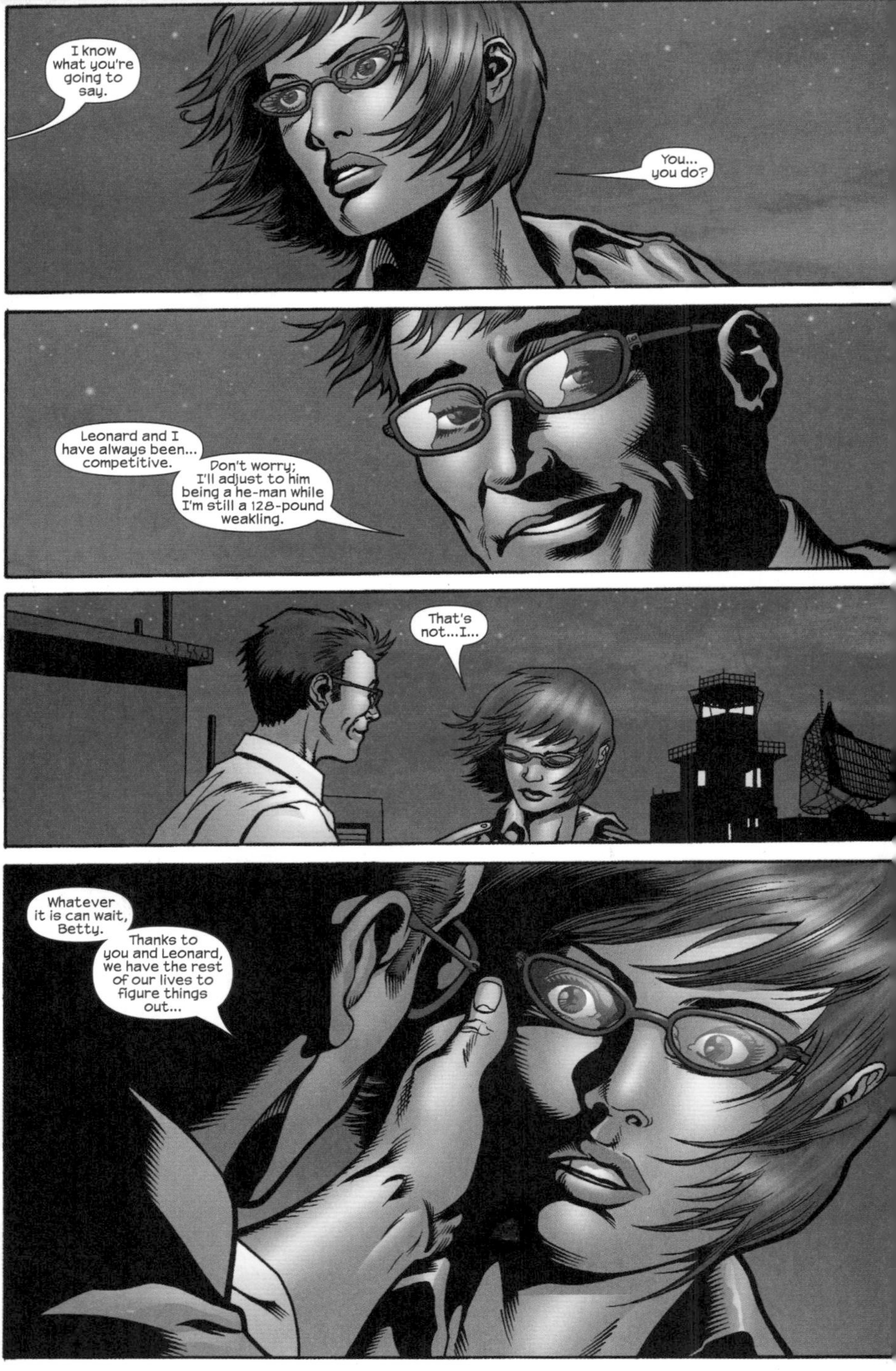
I know what you're going to say.
You... you do?
Leonard and I have always been... competitive.
Don't worry; I'll adjust to him being a he-man while I'm still a 128-pound weakling.
That's not...I...
Whatever it is can wait, Betty.
Thanks to you and Leonard, we have the rest of our lives to figure things out...

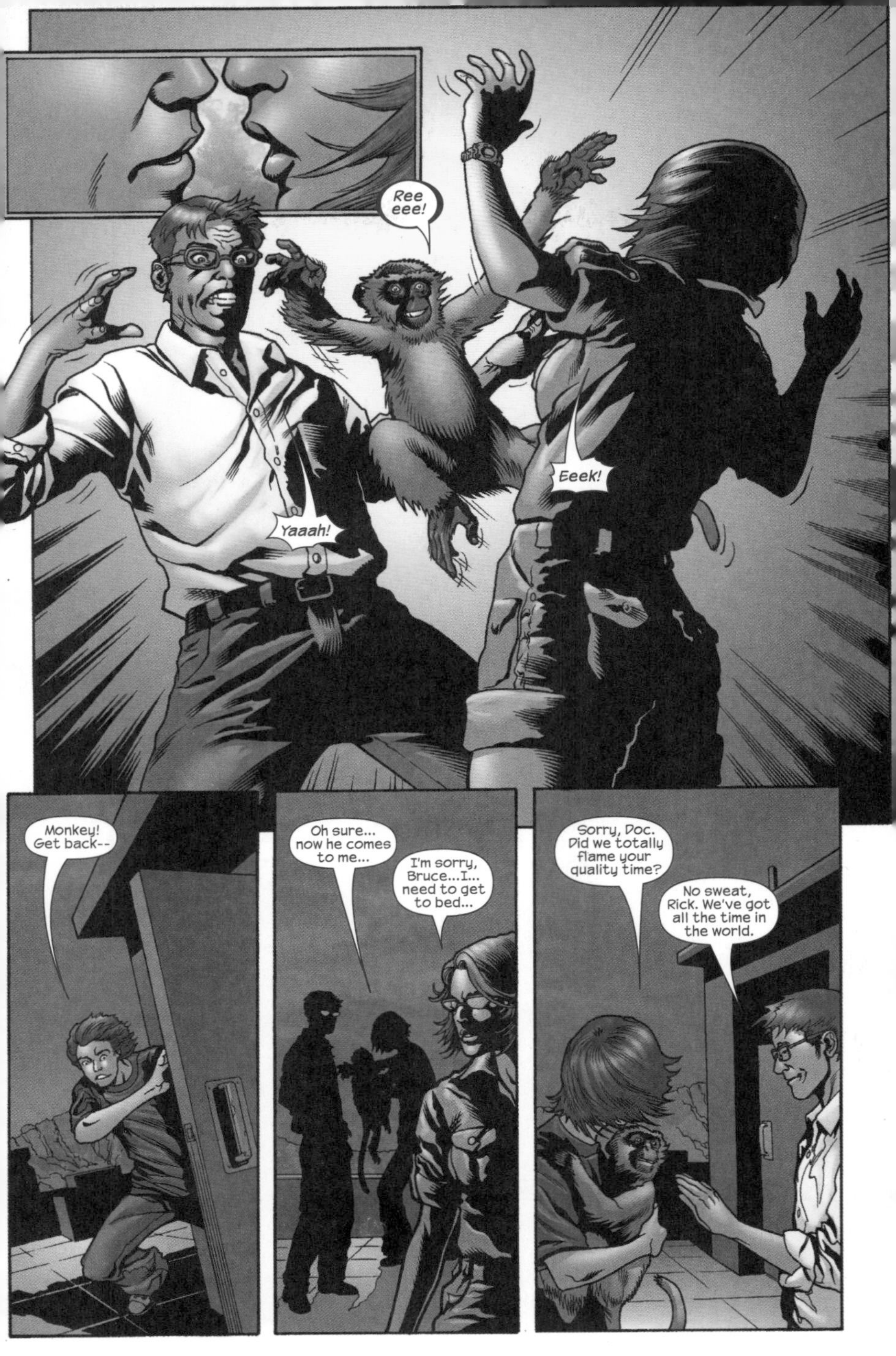
Ree eee!
Yaaah!
Eeek!
Monkey! Get back--
Oh sure... now he comes to me...
I'm sorry, Bruce...I... need to get to bed...
Sorry, Doc. Did we totally flame your quality time?
No sweat, Rick. We've got all the time in the world.

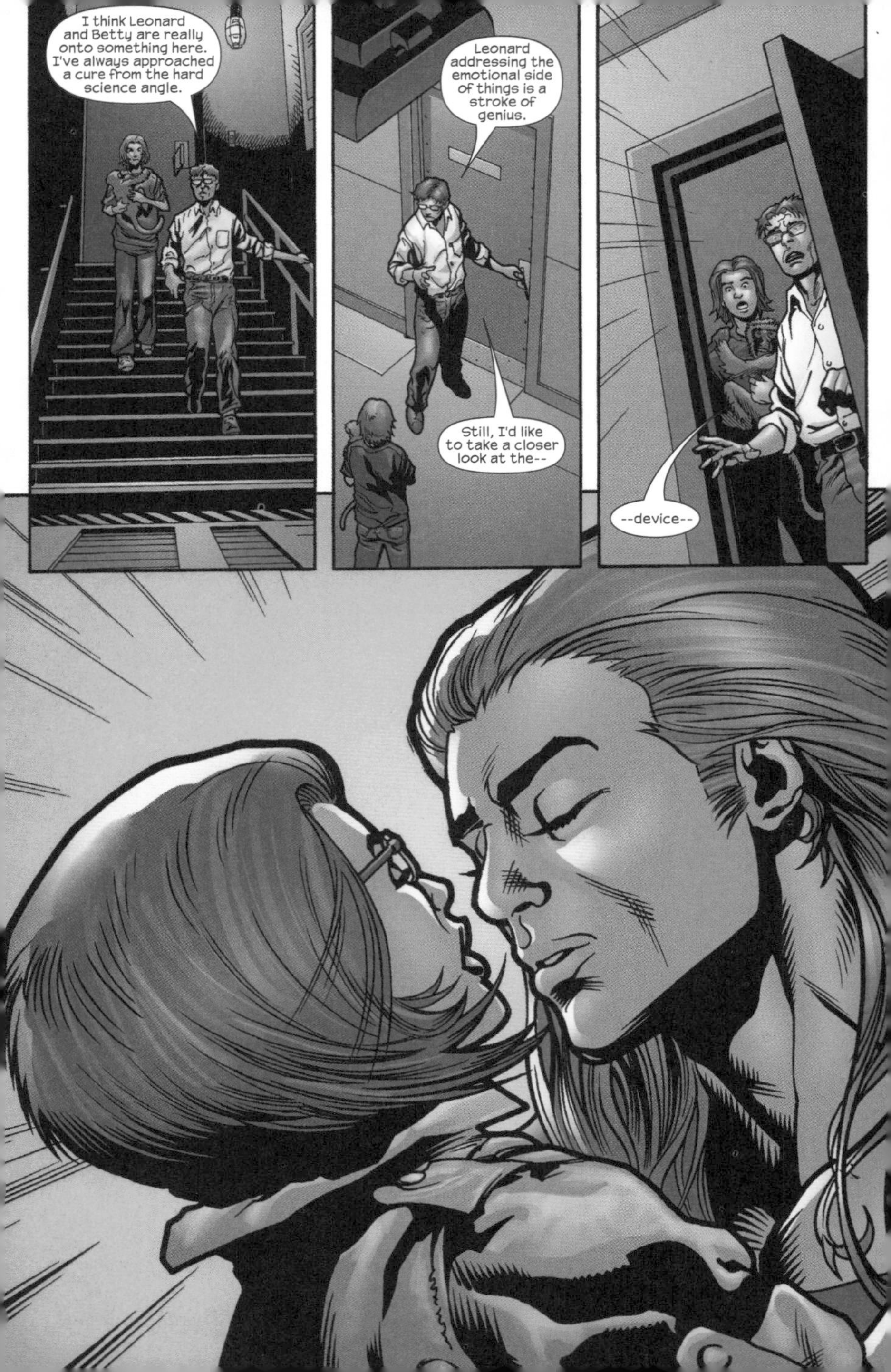
I think Leonard and Betty are really onto something here. I've always approached a cure from the hard science angle.
Leonard addressing the emotional side of things is a stroke of genius.
Still, I'd like to take a closer look at the--
--device--

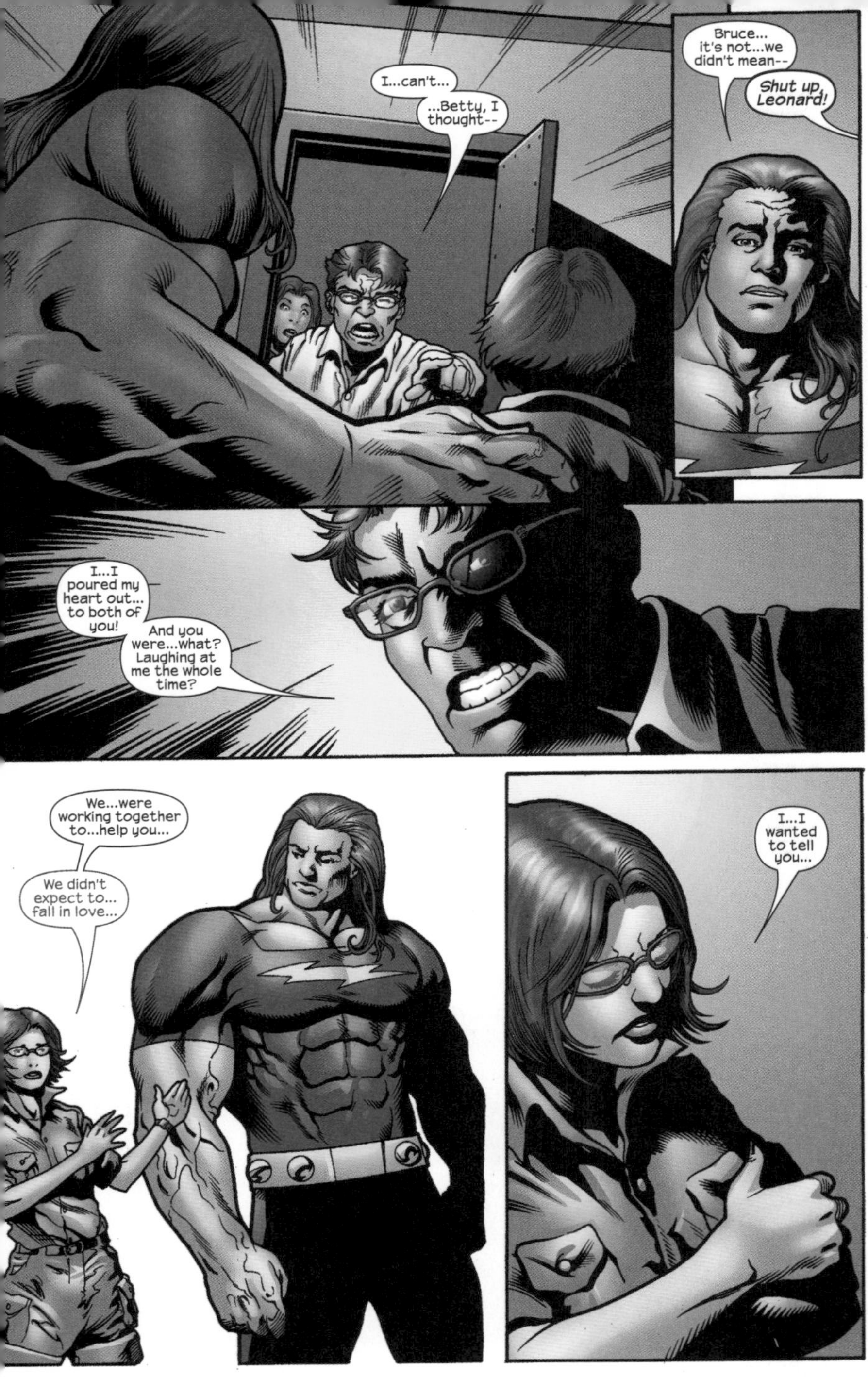
I...can't...
...Betty, I thought--
Bruce... it's not...we didn't mean--
Shut up, Leonard!
I...I poured my heart out... to both of you!
And you were...what? Laughing at me the whole time?
We...were working together to...help you...
We didn't expect to... fall in love...
I...I wanted to tell you...

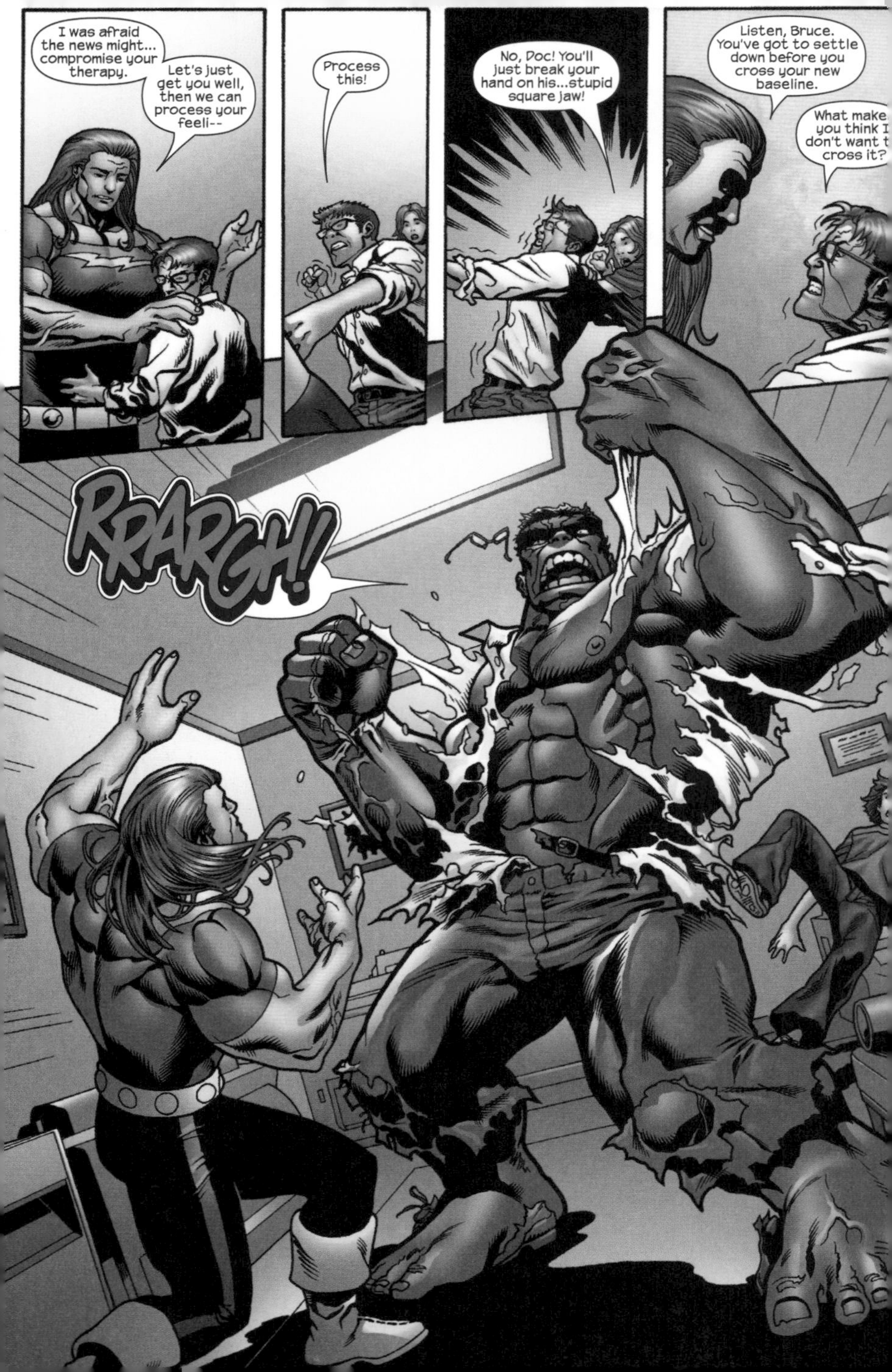

I was afraid the news might... compromise your therapy.
Let's just get you well, then we can process your feeli--
Process this!
No, Doc! You'll just break your hand on his...stupid square jaw!
Listen, Bruce. You've got to settle down before you cross your new baseline.
What make you think I don't want t cross it?
RRARGH!

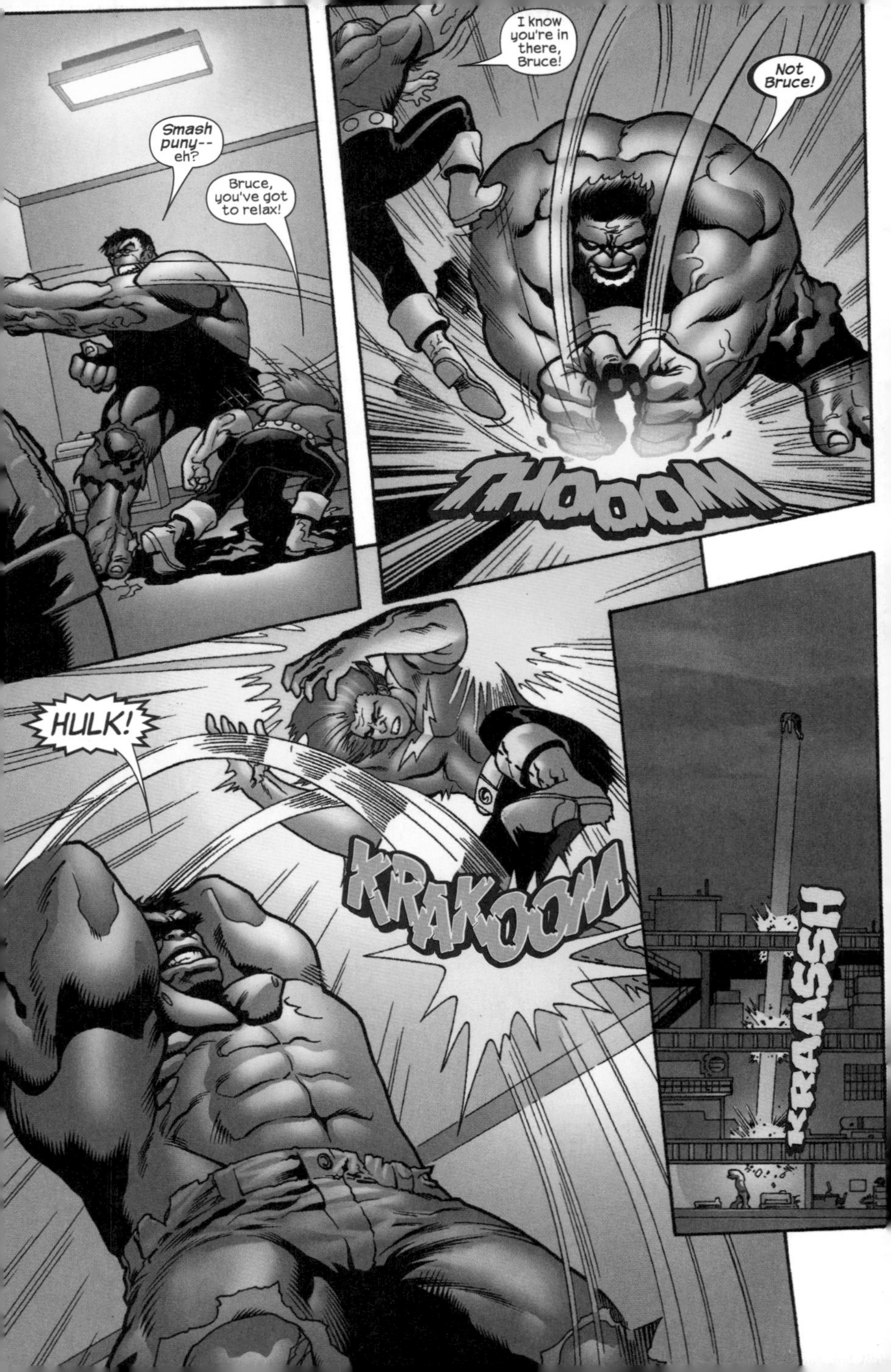
Smash puny-- eh?
Bruce, you've got to relax!
I know you're in there, Bruce!
Not Bruce!
THOOOM
HULK!
KRAKOOM
KRAASSH

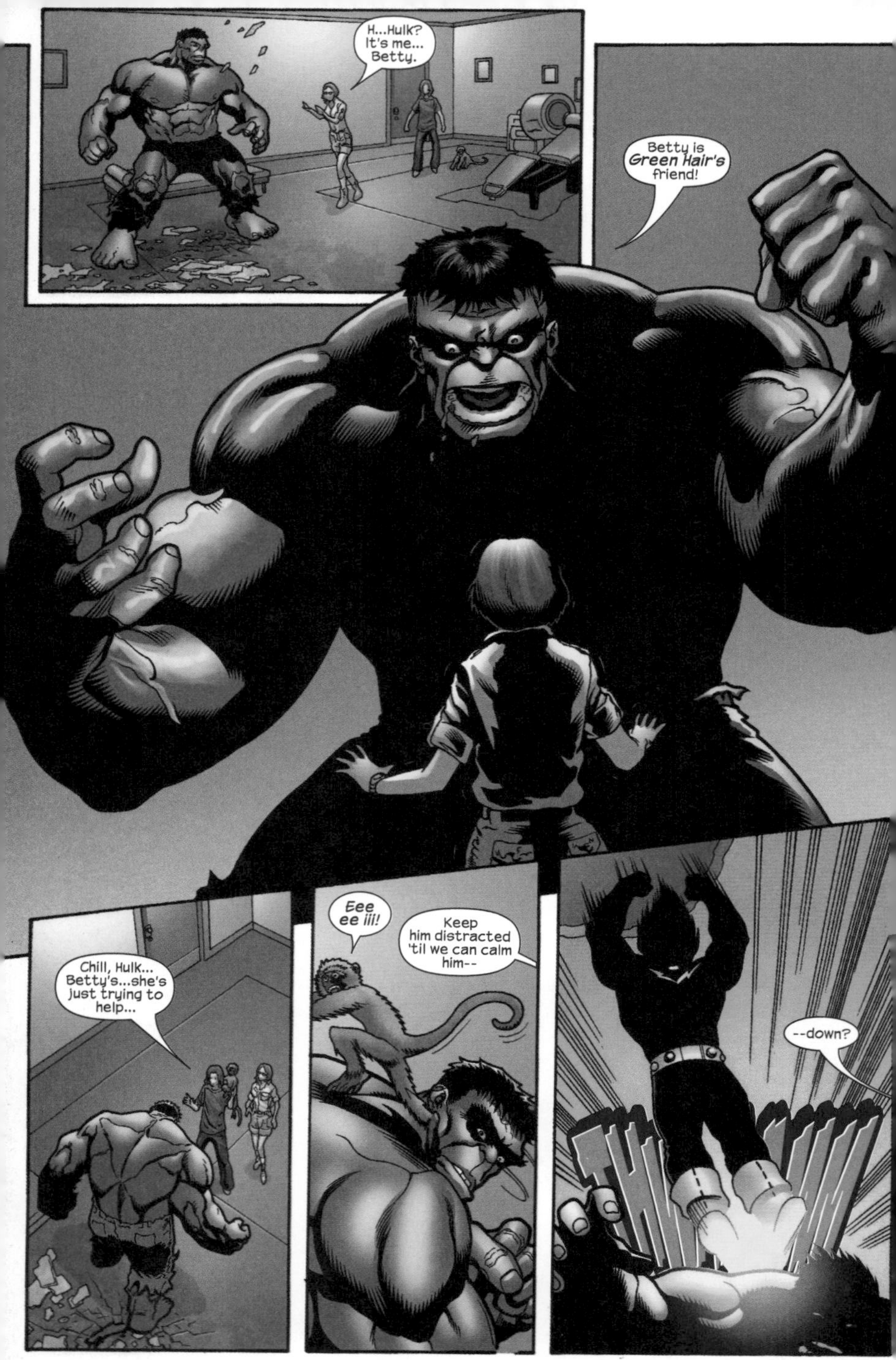

H...Hulk? It's me... Betty.
Betty is Green Hair's friend!
Chill, Hulk... Betty's...she's just trying to help...
Eee ee iii!
Keep him distracted 'til we can calm him--
--down?
THWUMP

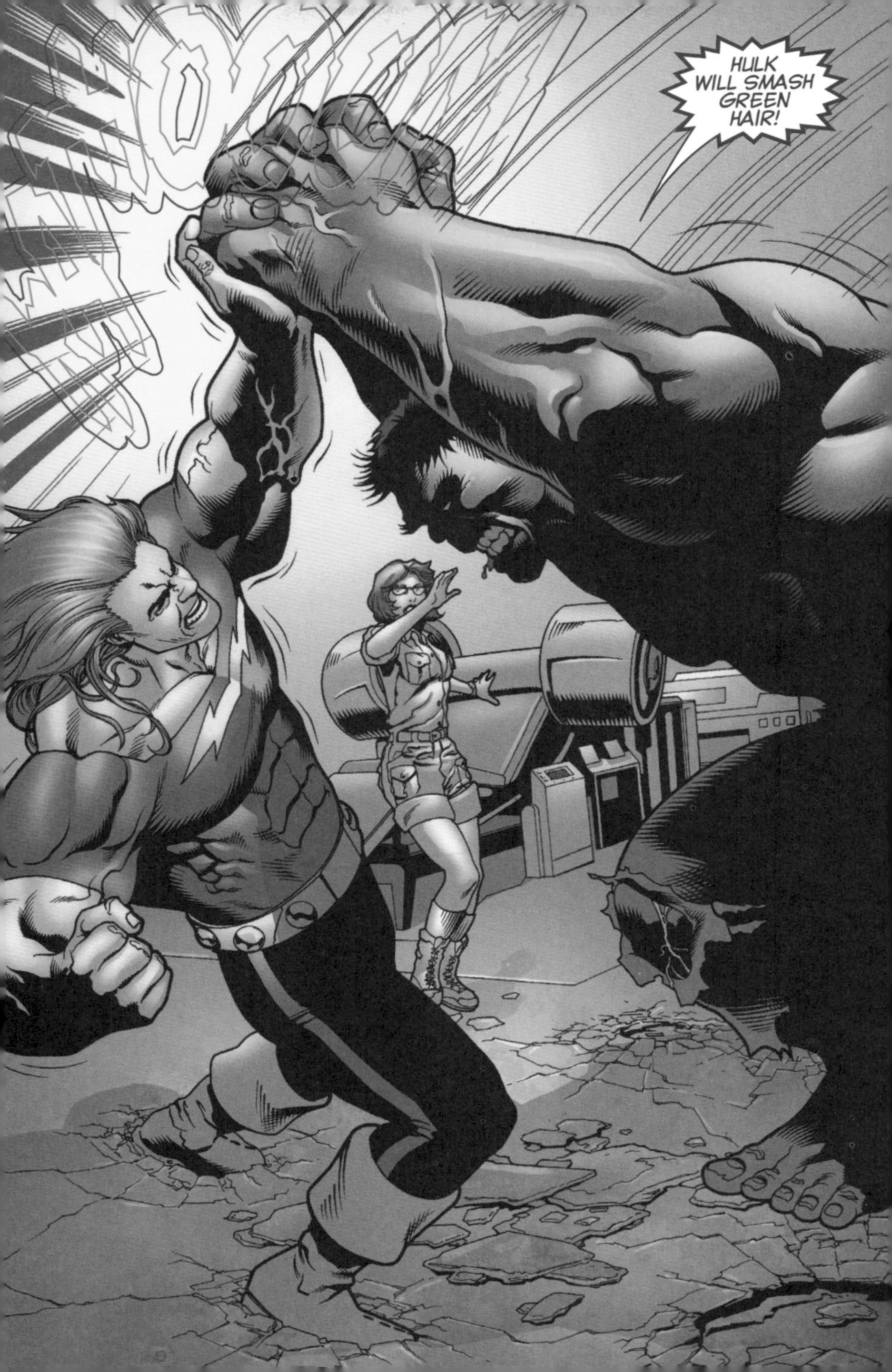
HULK WILL SMASH GREEN HAIR!

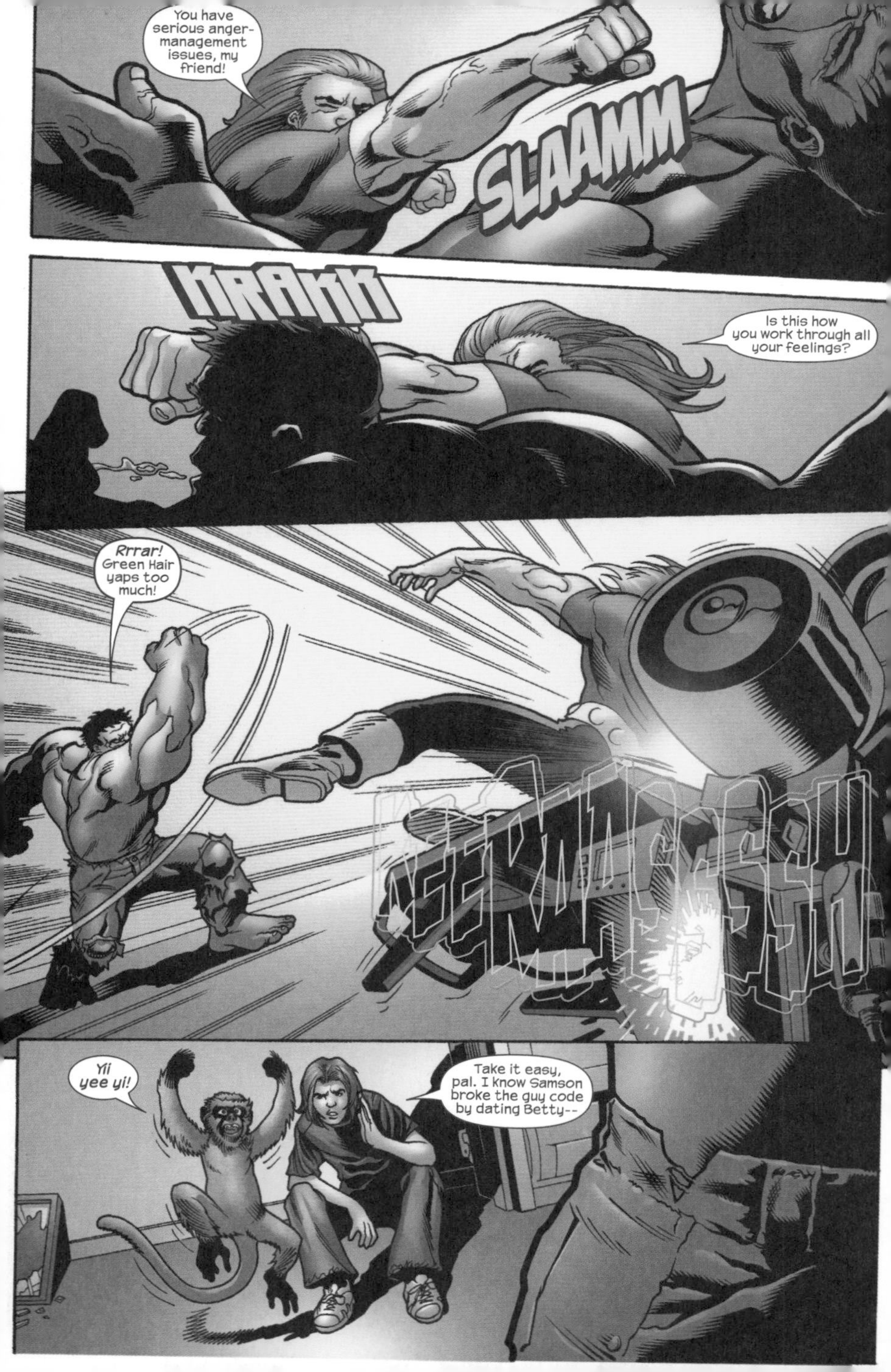

You have serious anger-management issues, my friend!
SLAAMM
KRAKK
Is this how you work through all your feelings?
Rrrar! Green Hair yaps too much!
Yii yee yi!
Take it easy, pal. I know Samson broke the guy code by dating Betty--

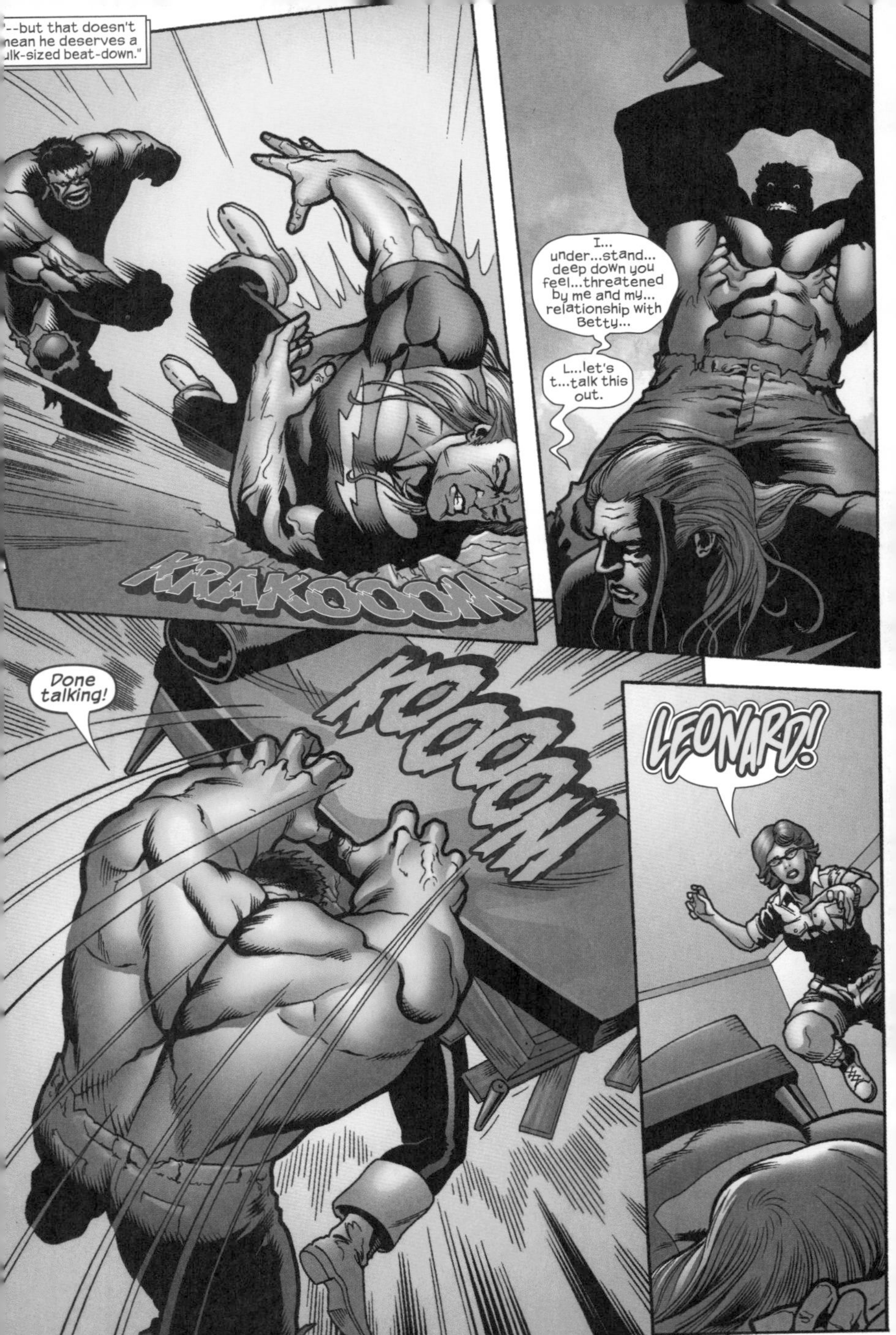
"--but that doesn't
mean he deserves a
ulk-sized beat-down."
KRAKOOOM
I... under...stand... deep down you feel...threatened by me and my... relationship with Betty...
L...let's t...talk this out.
Done talking!
KOOOOM
LEONARD!

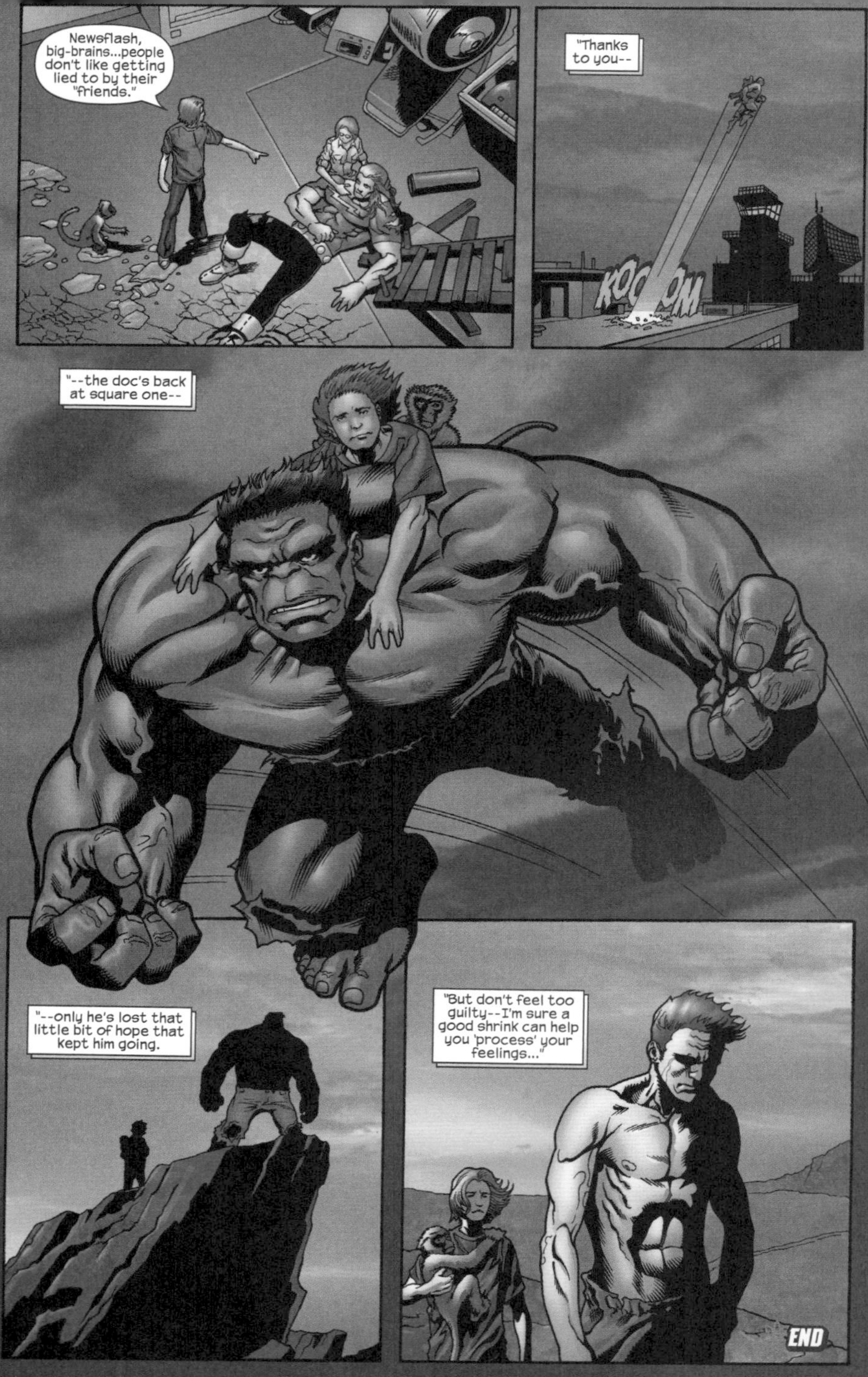
Newsflash, big-brains...people don't like getting lied to by their "friends."
"Thanks to you--
KOOOM
"--the doc's back at square one--
"--only he's lost that little bit of hope that kept him going.
"But don't feel too guilty--I'm sure a good shrink can help you 'process' your feelings..."
END

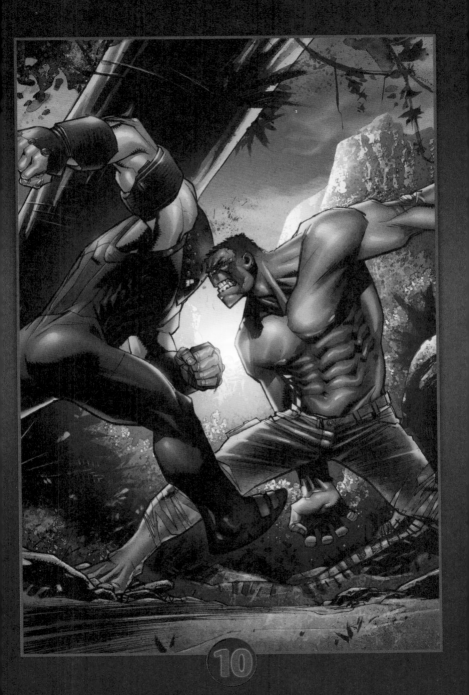

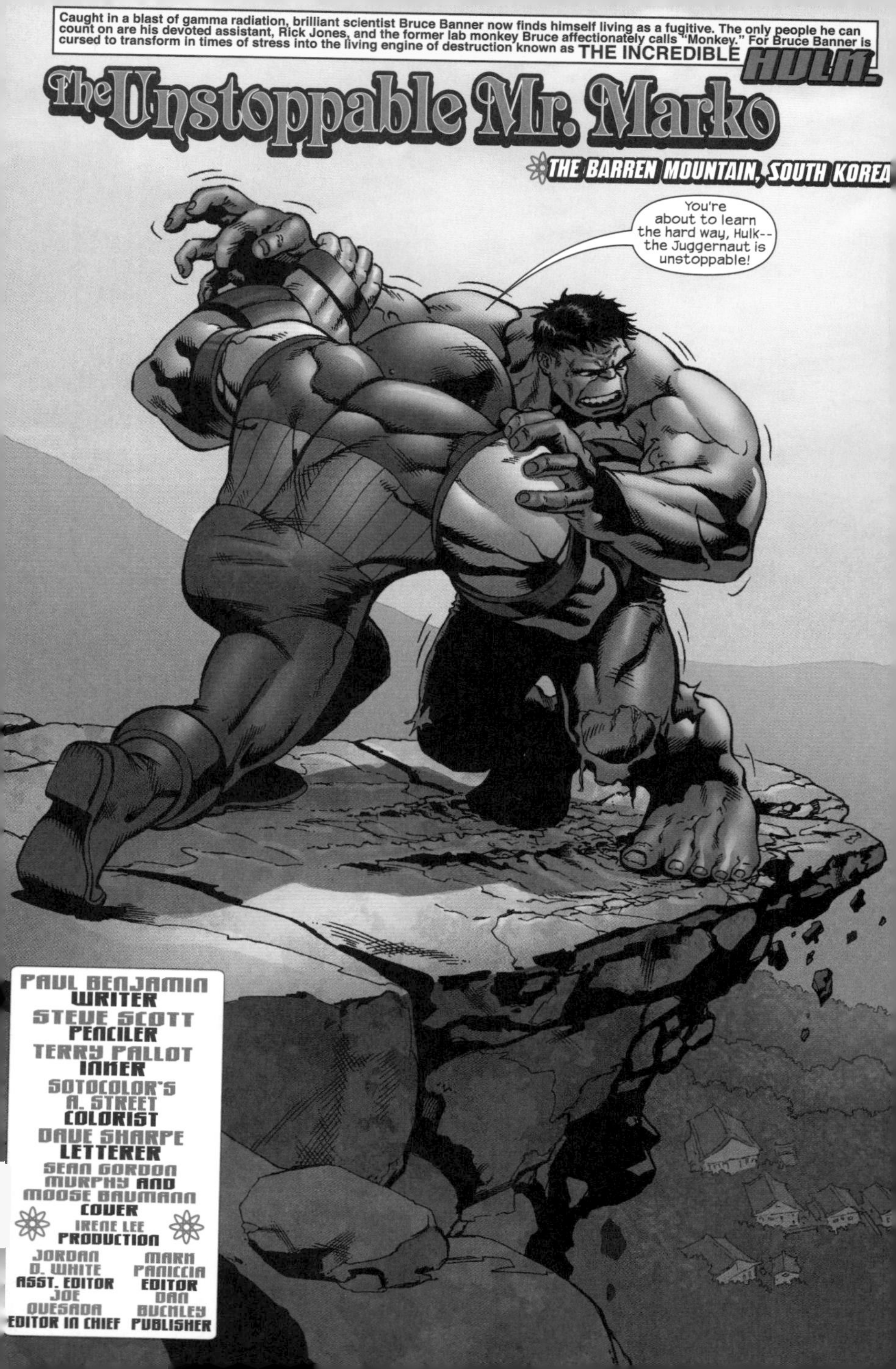

Caught in a blast of gamma radiation, brilliant scientist Bruce Banner now finds himself living as a fugitive. The only people he can count on are his devoted assistant, Rick Jones, and the former lab monkey Bruce affectionately calls "Monkey." For Bruce Banner is cursed to transform in times of stress into the living engine of destruction known as THE INCREDIBLE HULK.
The Unstoppable Mr. Marko
THE BARREN MOUNTAIN, SOUTH KOREA
You're about to learn the hard way, Hulk-- the Juggernaut is unstoppable!
PAUL BENJAMIN WRITER
STEVE SCOTT PENCILER
TERRY PALLOT INKER
SOTOCOLOR'S A. STREET COLORIST
DAVE SHARPE LETTERER
SEAN GORDON MURPHY AND MOOSE BAUMANN COVER
IRENE LEE PRODUCTION
JORDAN D. WHITE ASST. EDITOR
MARK PANICCIA EDITOR
JOE QUESADA EDITOR IN CHIEF
DAN BUCKLEY PUBLISHER

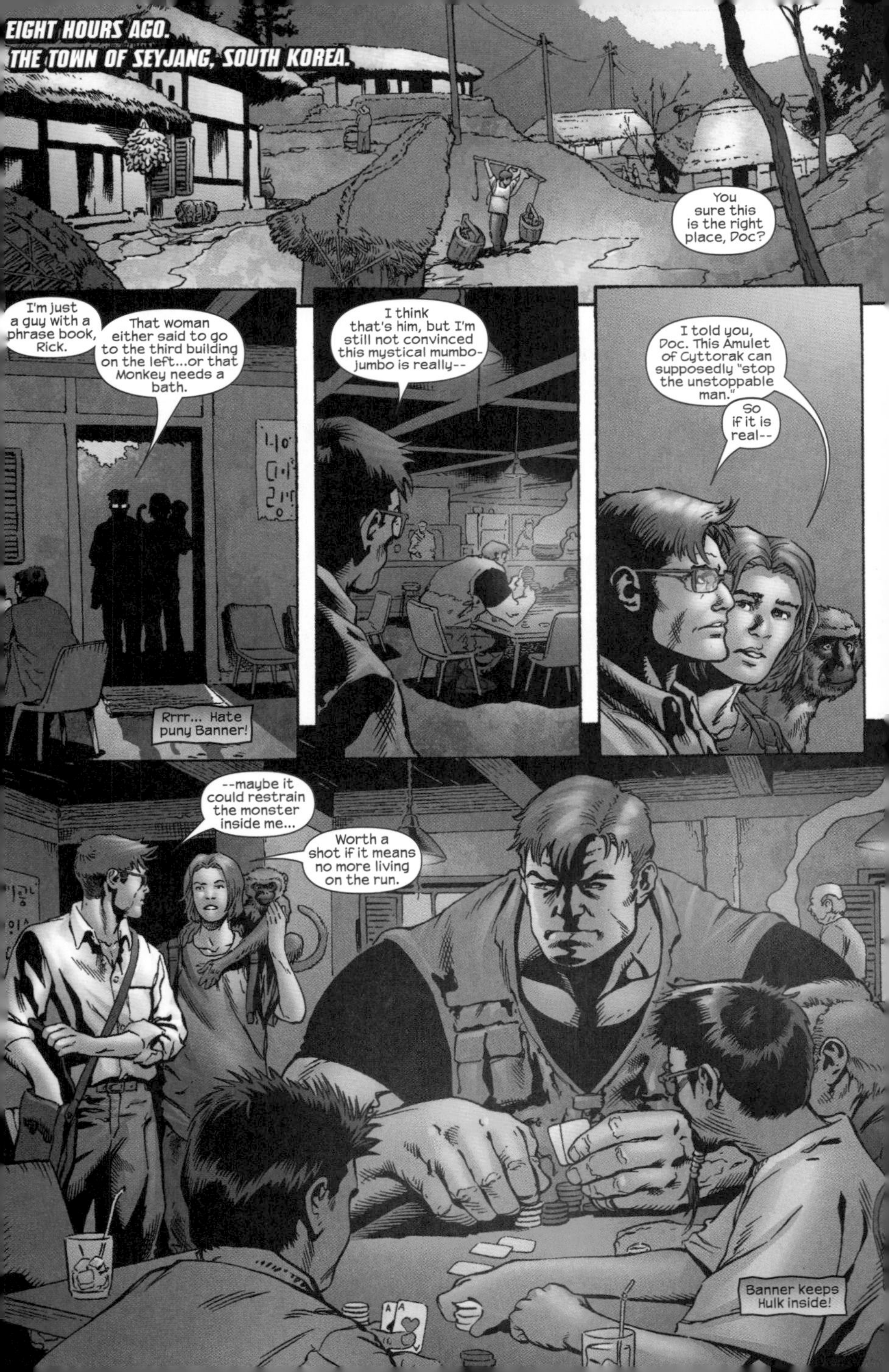
EIGHT HOURS AGO.
THE TOWN OF SEYJANG, SOUTH KOREA.
You sure this is the right place, Doc?
I'm just a guy with a phrase book, Rick.
That woman either said to go to the third building on the left...or that Monkey needs a bath.
Rrrr... Hate puny Banner!
I think that's him, but I'm still not convinced this mystical mumbo-jumbo is really--
I told you, Doc. This Amulet of Cyttorak can supposedly "stop the unstoppable man."
So if it is real--
--maybe it could restrain the monster inside me...
Worth a shot if it means no more living on the run.
Banner keeps Hulk inside!

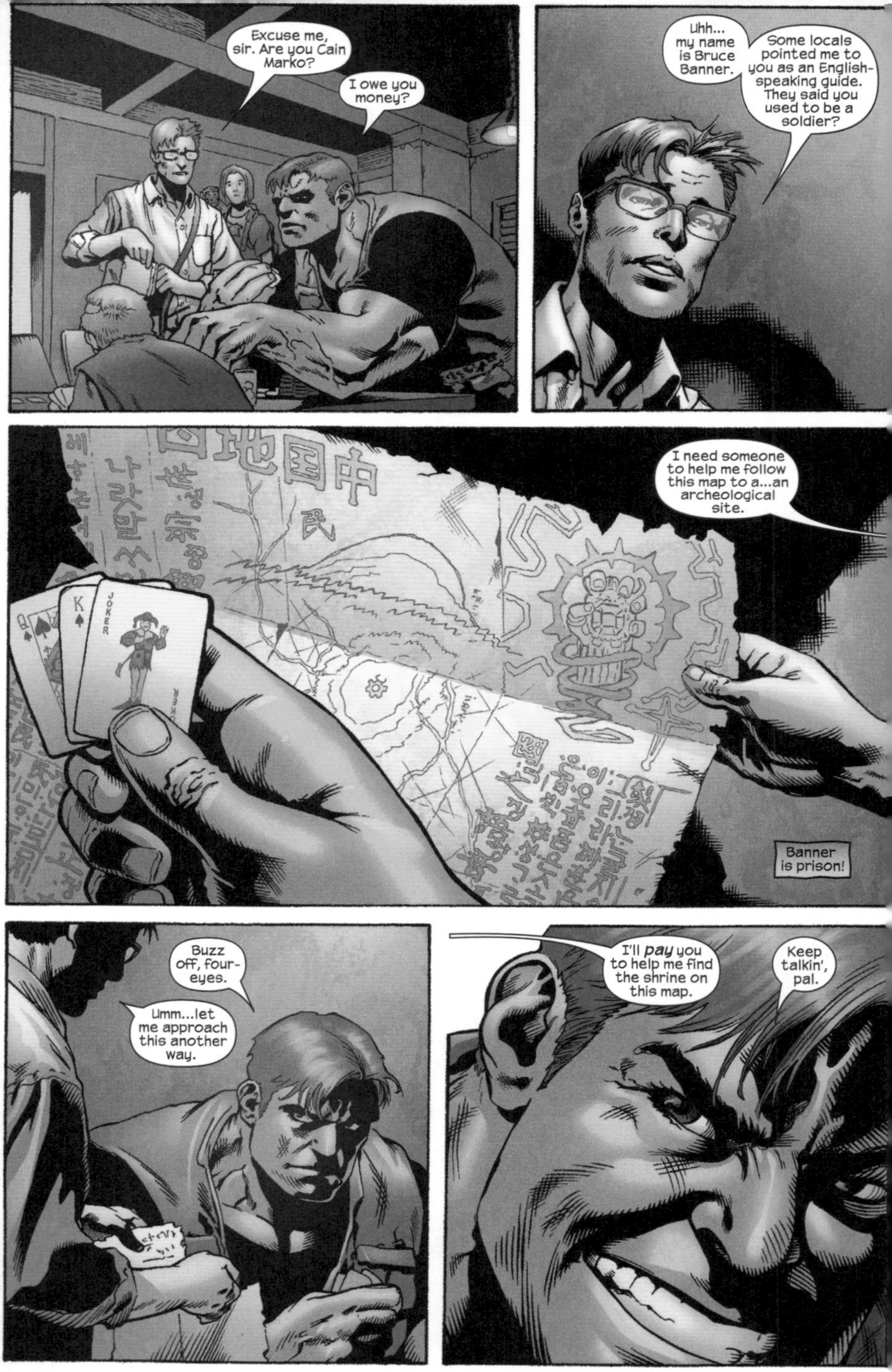
Excuse me, sir. Are you Cain Marko?
I owe you money?
Uhh... my name is Bruce Banner.
Some locals pointed me to you as an English-speaking guide. They said you used to be a soldier?
I need someone to help me follow this map to a...an archeological site.
Banner is prison!
Buzz off, four-eyes.
Umm...let me approach this another way.
I'll *pay* you to help me find the shrine on this map.
Keep talkin', pal.

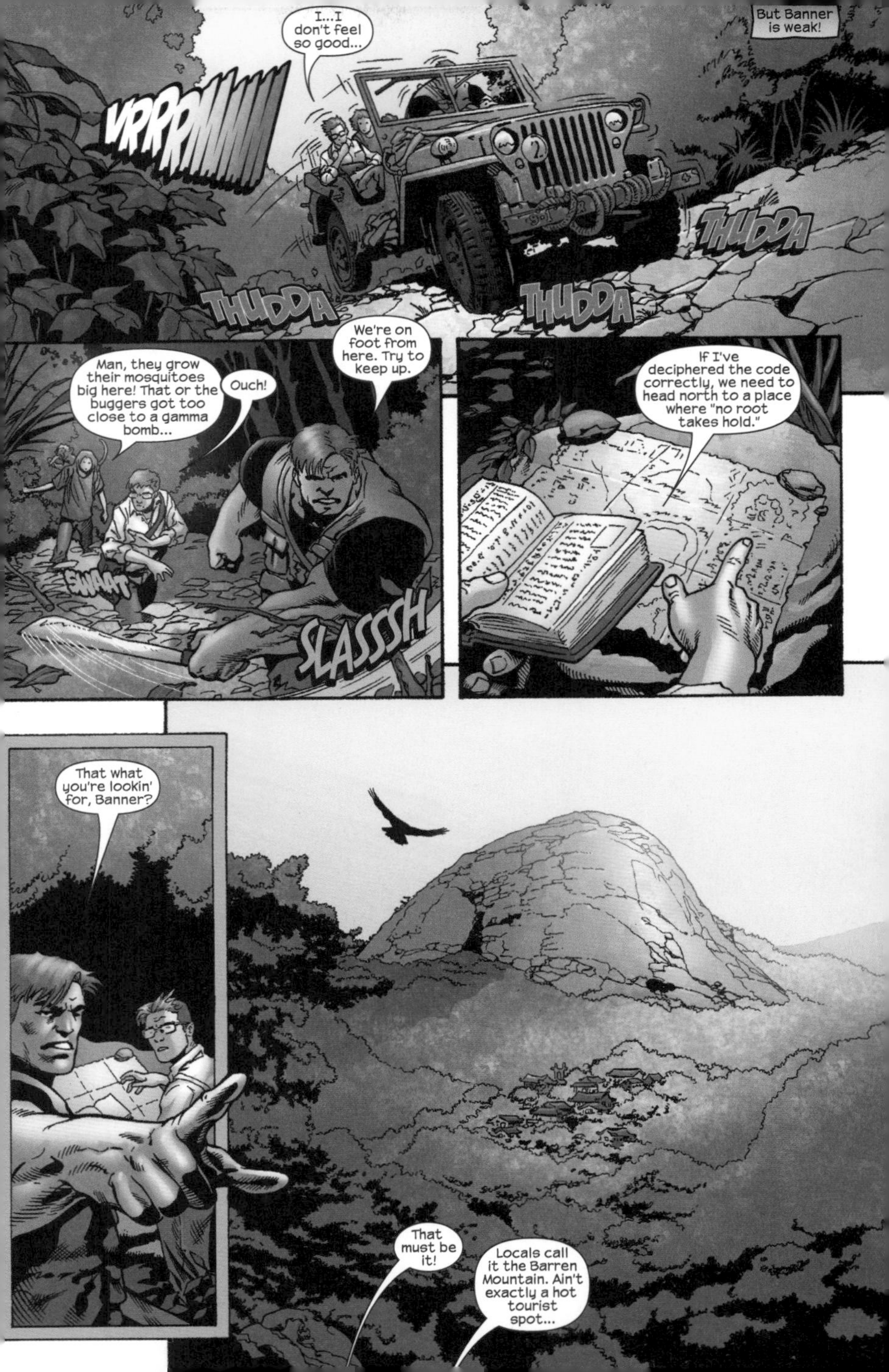
But Banner is weak!
I...I don't feel so good...
VRRRMMMM
THUDDA
THUDDA
THUDDA
Man, they grow their mosquitoes big here! That or the buggers got too close to a gamma bomb...
Ouch!
SWAAT
We're on foot from here. Try to keep up.
SLASSSH
If I've deciphered the code correctly, we need to head north to a place where "no root takes hold."
That what you're lookin' for, Banner?
That must be it!
Locals call it the Barren Mountain. Ain't exactly a hot tourist spot...

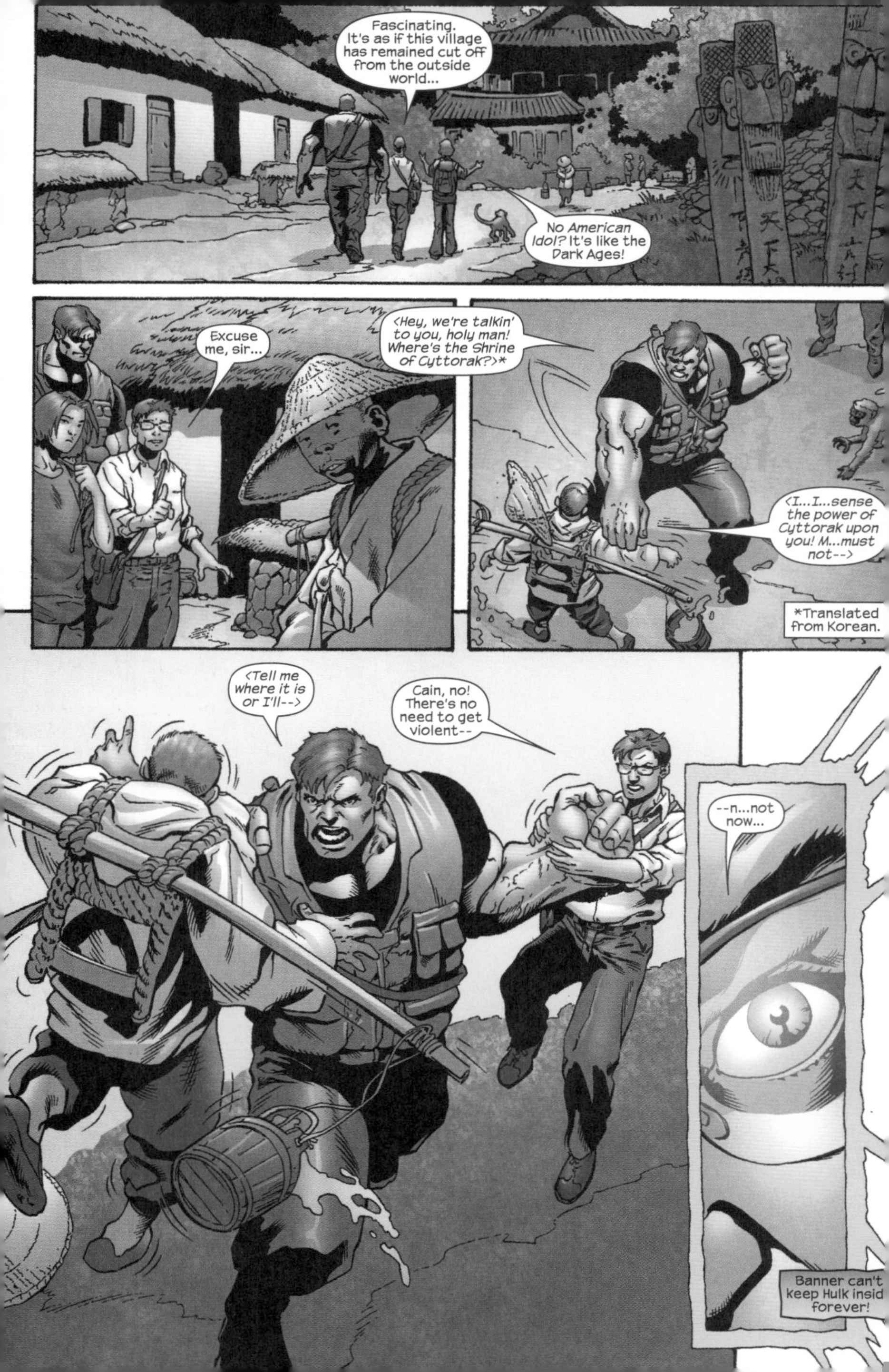
Fascinating. It's as if this village has remained cut off from the outside world...
No *American Idol*? It's like the Dark Ages!
Excuse me, sir...
<Hey, we're talkin' to you, holy man! Where's the Shrine of Cyttorak?>*
<I...I...sense the power of Cyttorak upon you! M...must not-->
*Translated from Korean.
<Tell me where it is or I'll-->
Cain, no! There's no need to get violent--
--n...not now...
Banner can't keep Hulk insid forever!

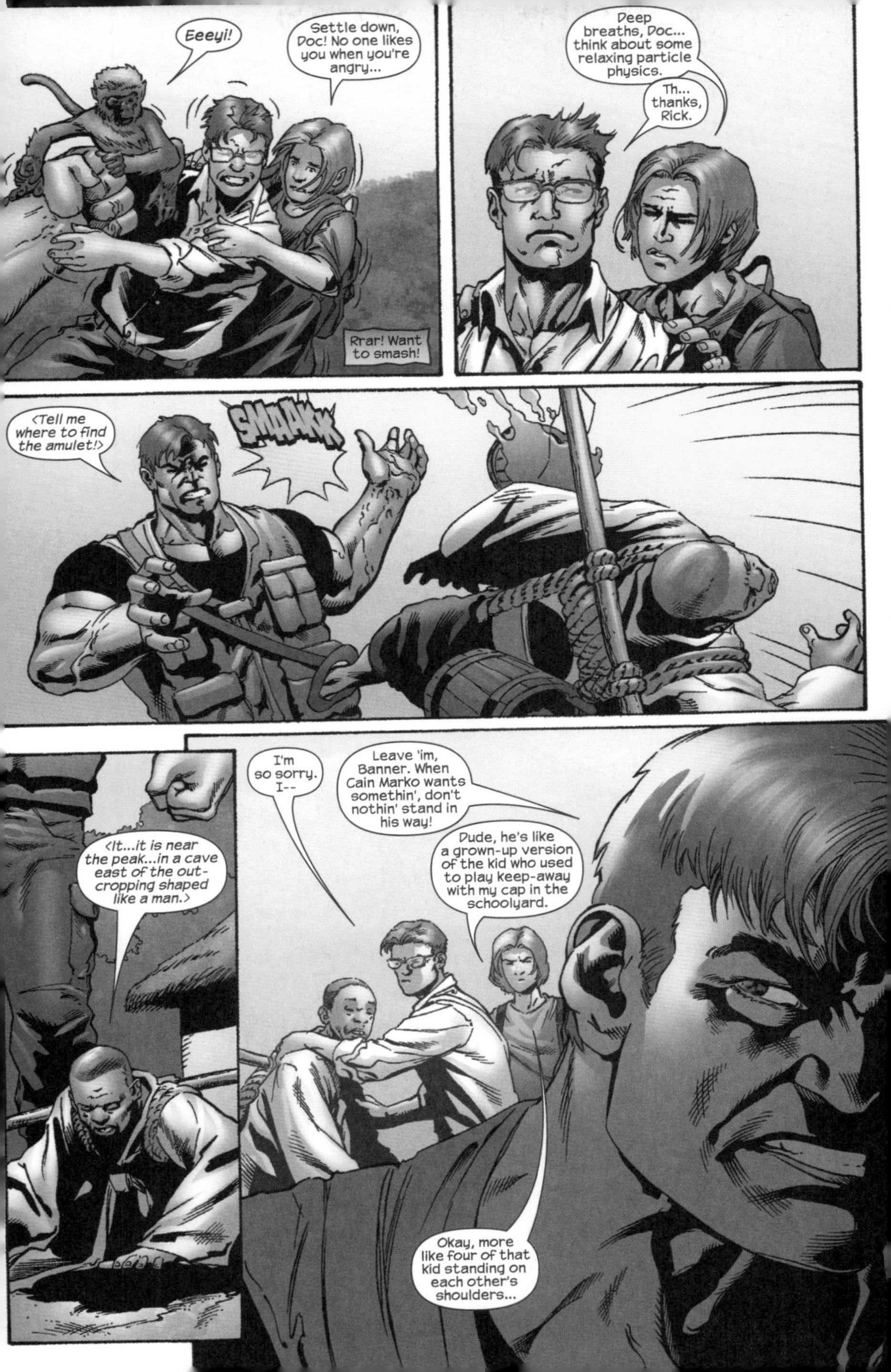
Eeeyi!
Settle down, Doc! No one likes you when you're angry...
Rrar! Want to smash!
Deep breaths, Doc... think about some relaxing particle physics.
Th... thanks, Rick.
<Tell me where to find the amulet!>
SMAKK
<It...it is near the peak...in a cave east of the out-cropping shaped like a man.>
I'm so sorry. I--
Leave 'im, Banner. When Cain Marko wants somethin', don't nothin' stand in his way!
Dude, he's like a grown-up version of the kid who used to play keep-away with my cap in the schoolyard.
Okay, more like four of that kid standing on each other's shoulders...

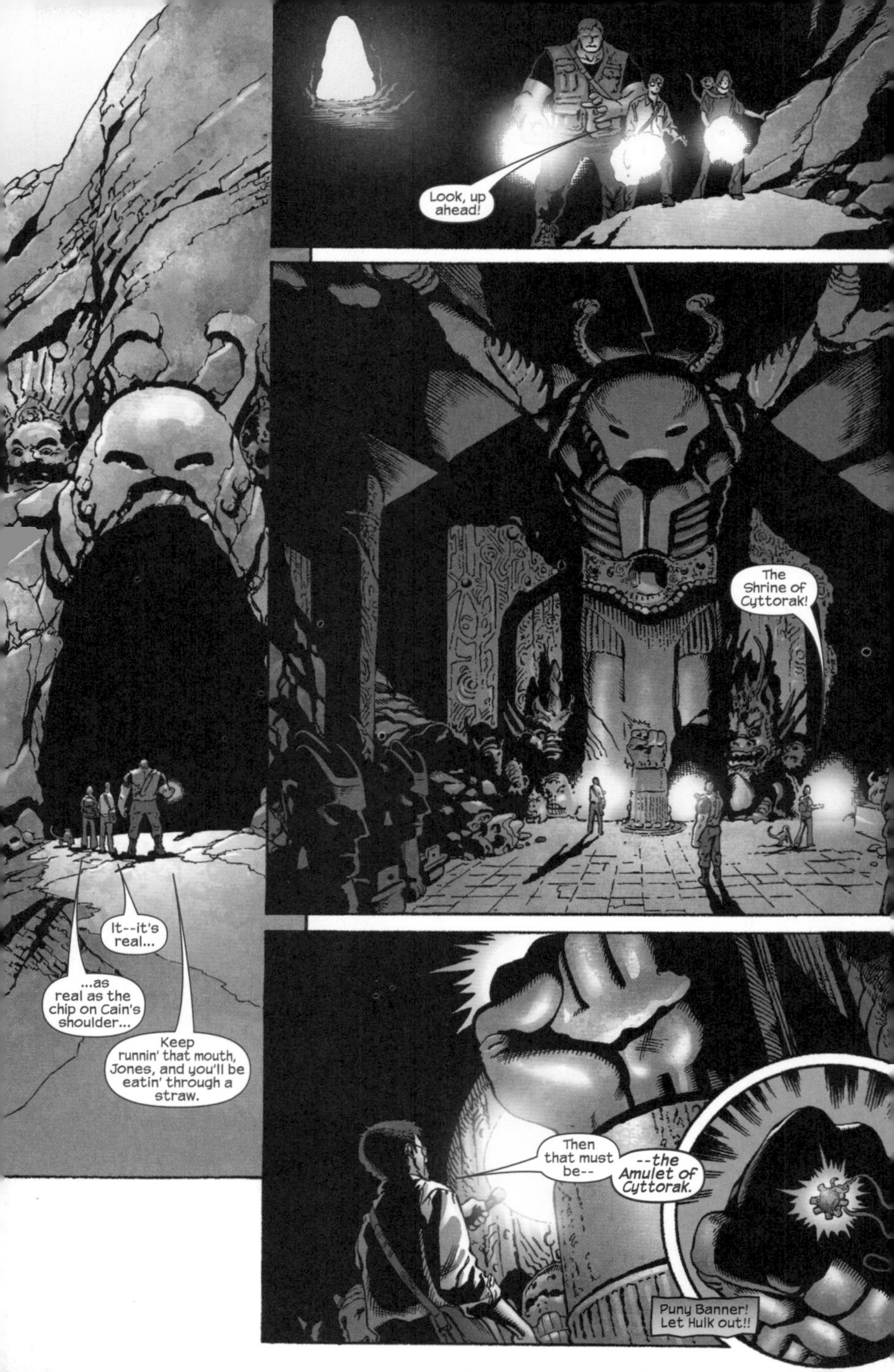
Look, up ahead!
It--it's real...
...as real as the chip on Cain's shoulder...
Keep runnin' that mouth, Jones, and you'll be eatin' through a straw.
The Shrine of Cyttorak!
Then that must be--
--the Amulet of Cyttorak.
Puny Banner! Let Hulk out!!

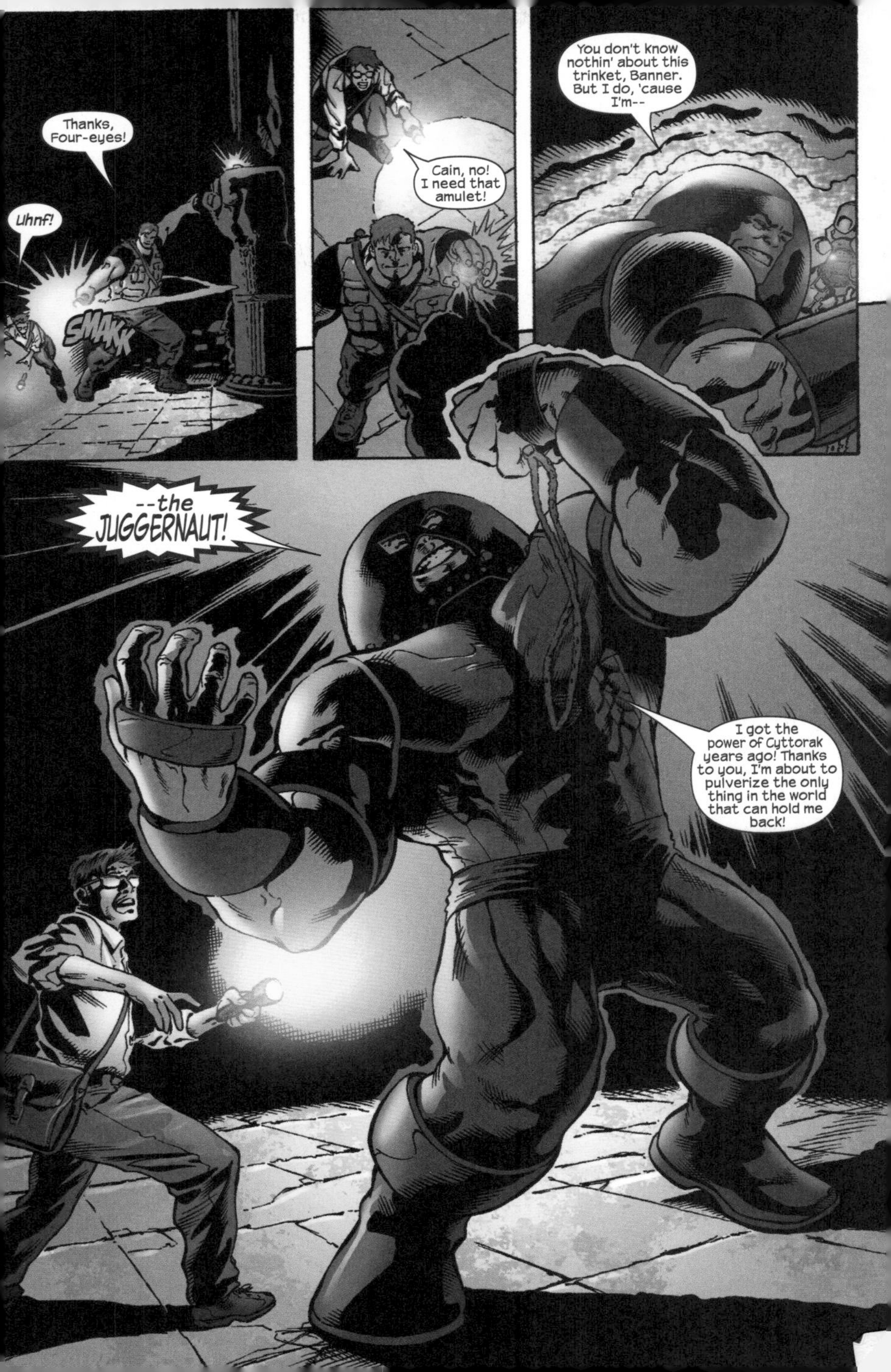
Thanks, Four-eyes!
Uhnf!
SMAKK
Cain, no! I need that amulet!
You don't know nothin' about this trinket, Banner. But I do, 'cause I'm--
--the JUGGERNAUT!
I got the power of Cyttorak years ago! Thanks to you, I'm about to pulverize the only thing in the world that can hold me back!

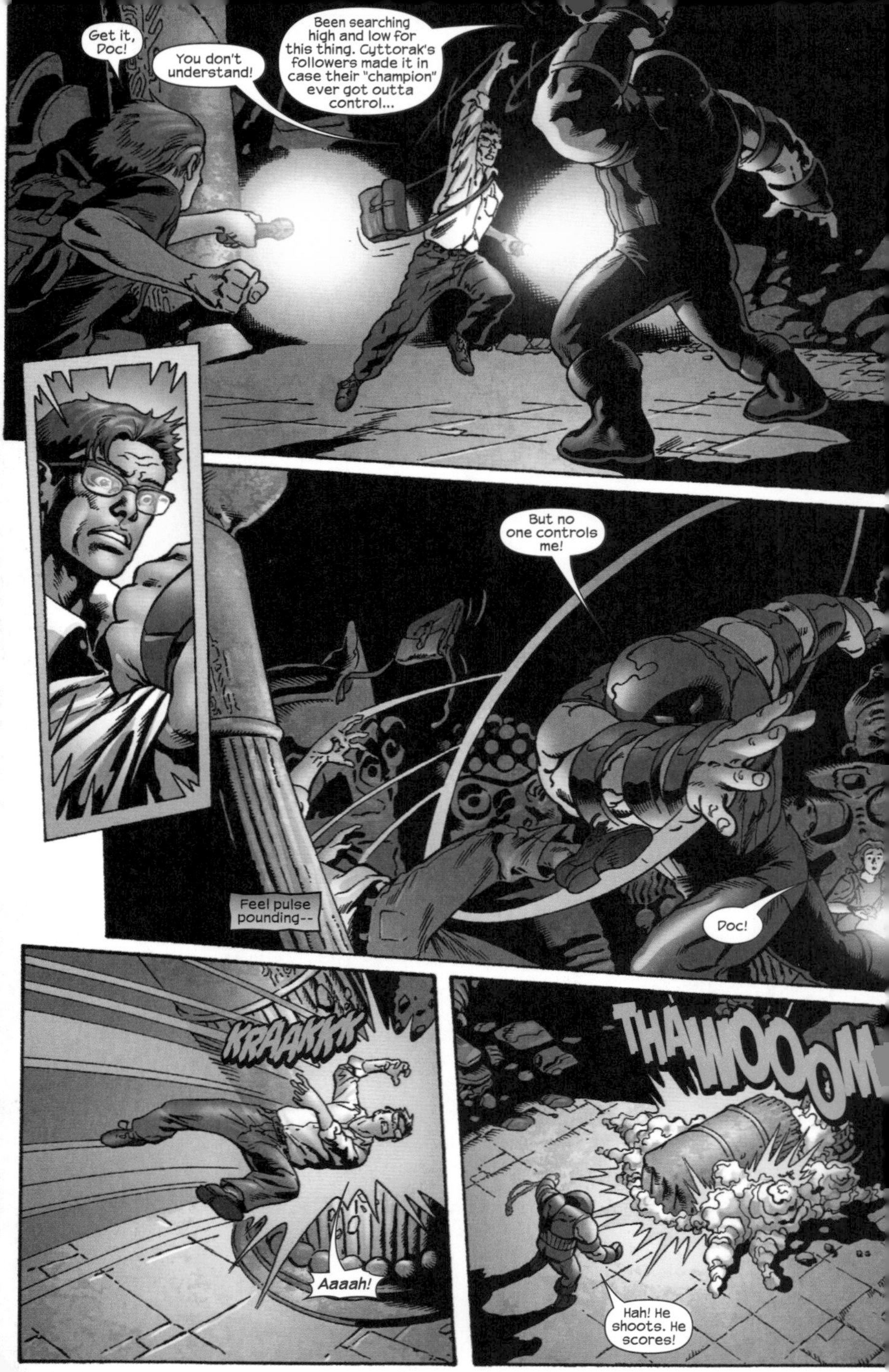
Get it, Doc!
You don't understand!
Been searching high and low for this thing. Cyttorak's followers made it in case their "champion" ever got outta control...
But no one controls me!
Feel pulse pounding--
Doc!
KRAAKKK
Aaaah!
THAWOOOM
Hah! He shoots. He scores!

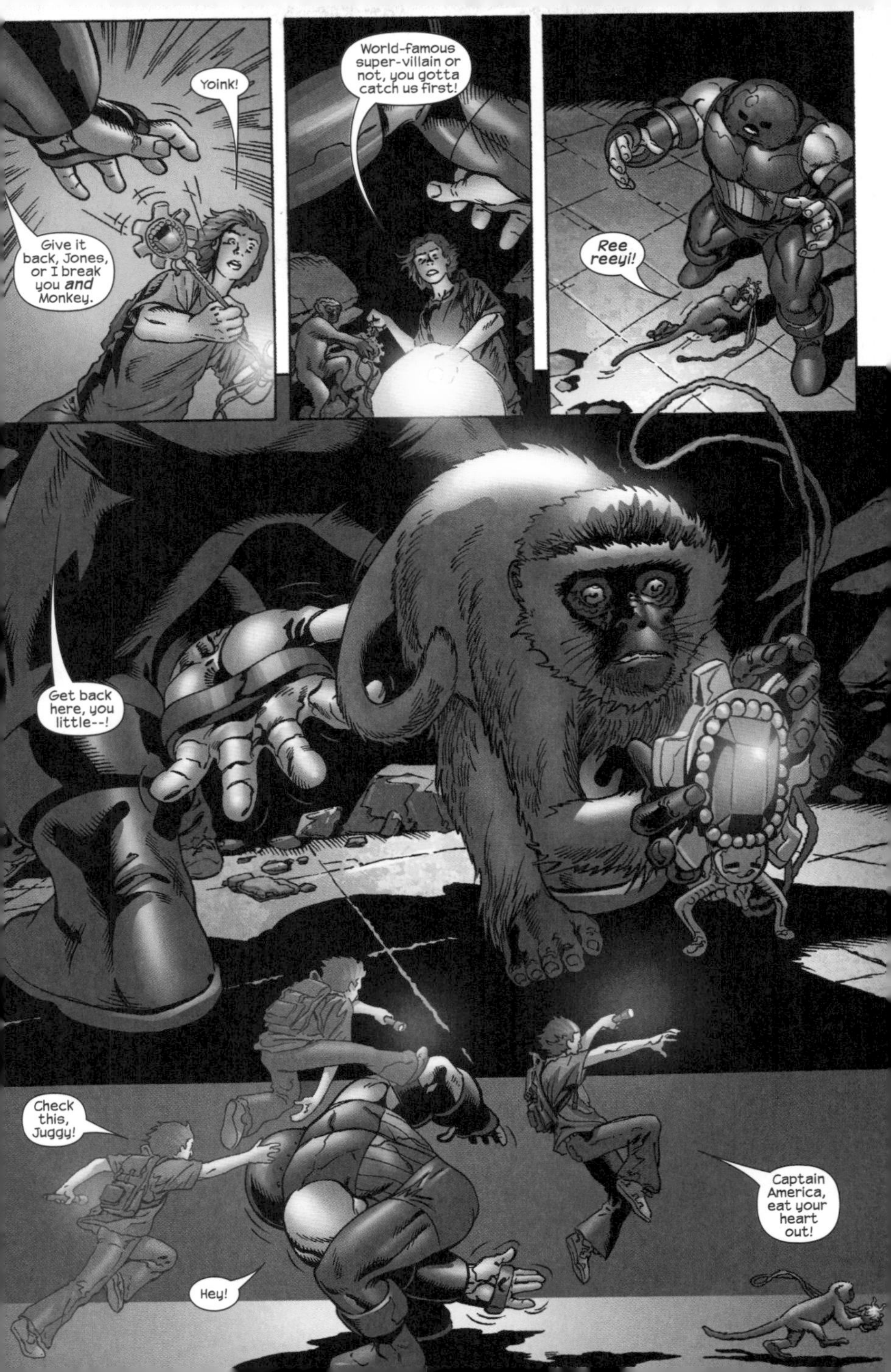
Yoink!
Give it back, Jones, or I break you *and* Monkey.
World-famous super-villain or not, you gotta catch us first!
Ree reeyi!
Get back here, you little--!
Check this, Juggy!
Captain America, eat your heart out!
Hey!

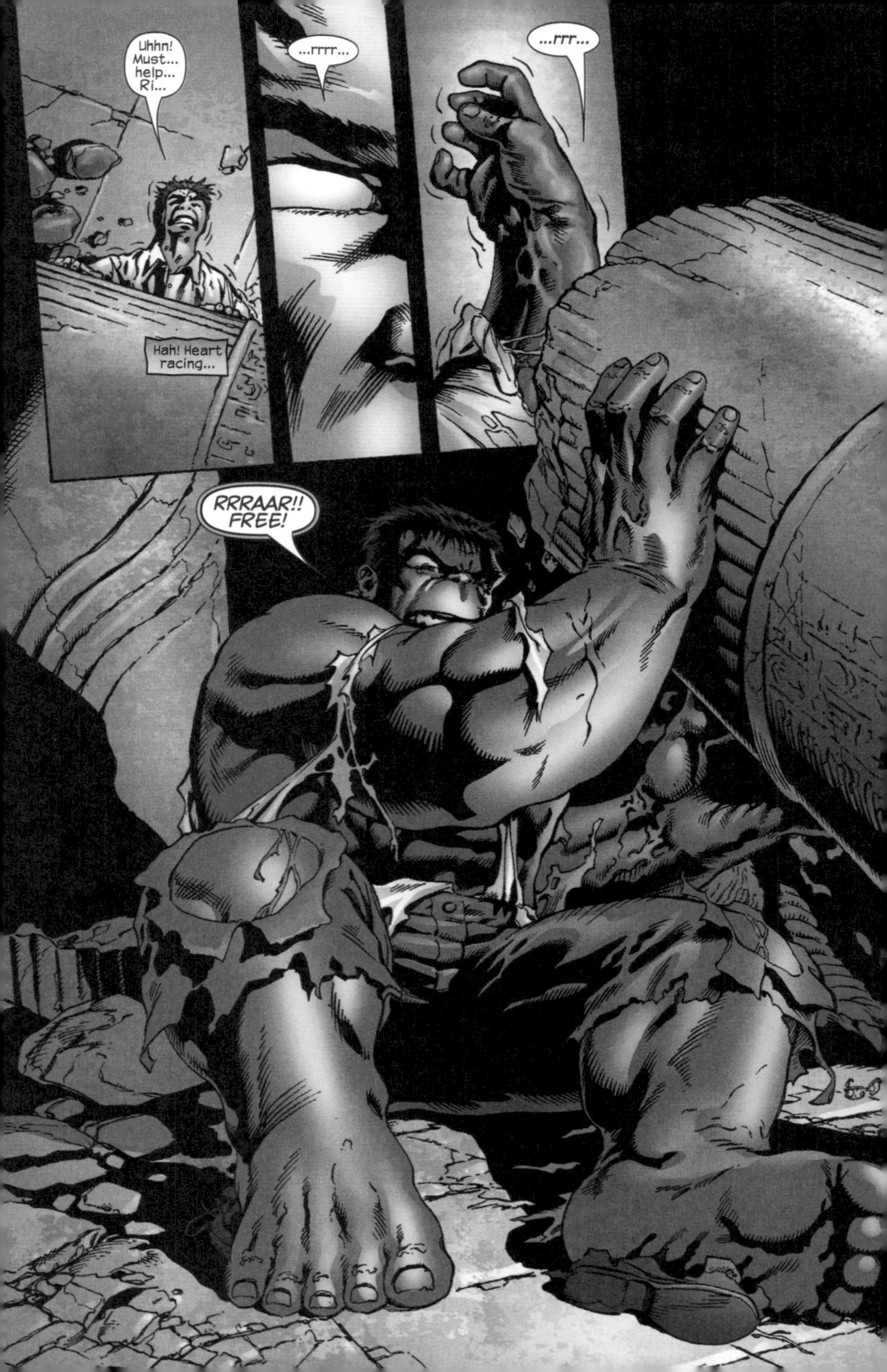

Uhhn! Must... help... Ri...
Hah! Heart racing...
...rrrr...
...rrr...
RRRAAR!! FREE!

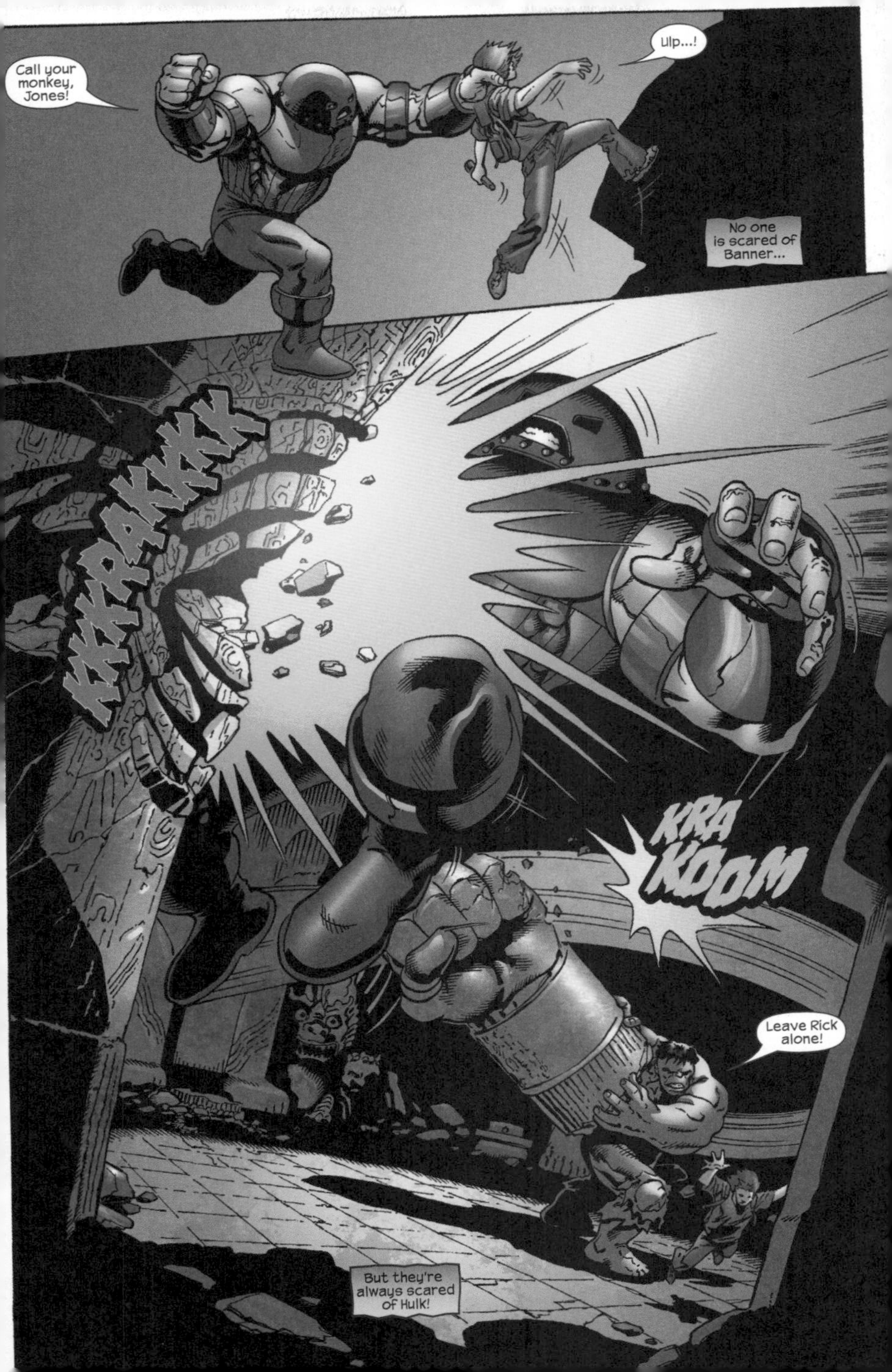
Call your monkey, Jones!
Ulp...!
No one is scared of Banner...
KKTRAKKKK
KRA KOOM
Leave Rick alone!
But they're always scared of Hulk!

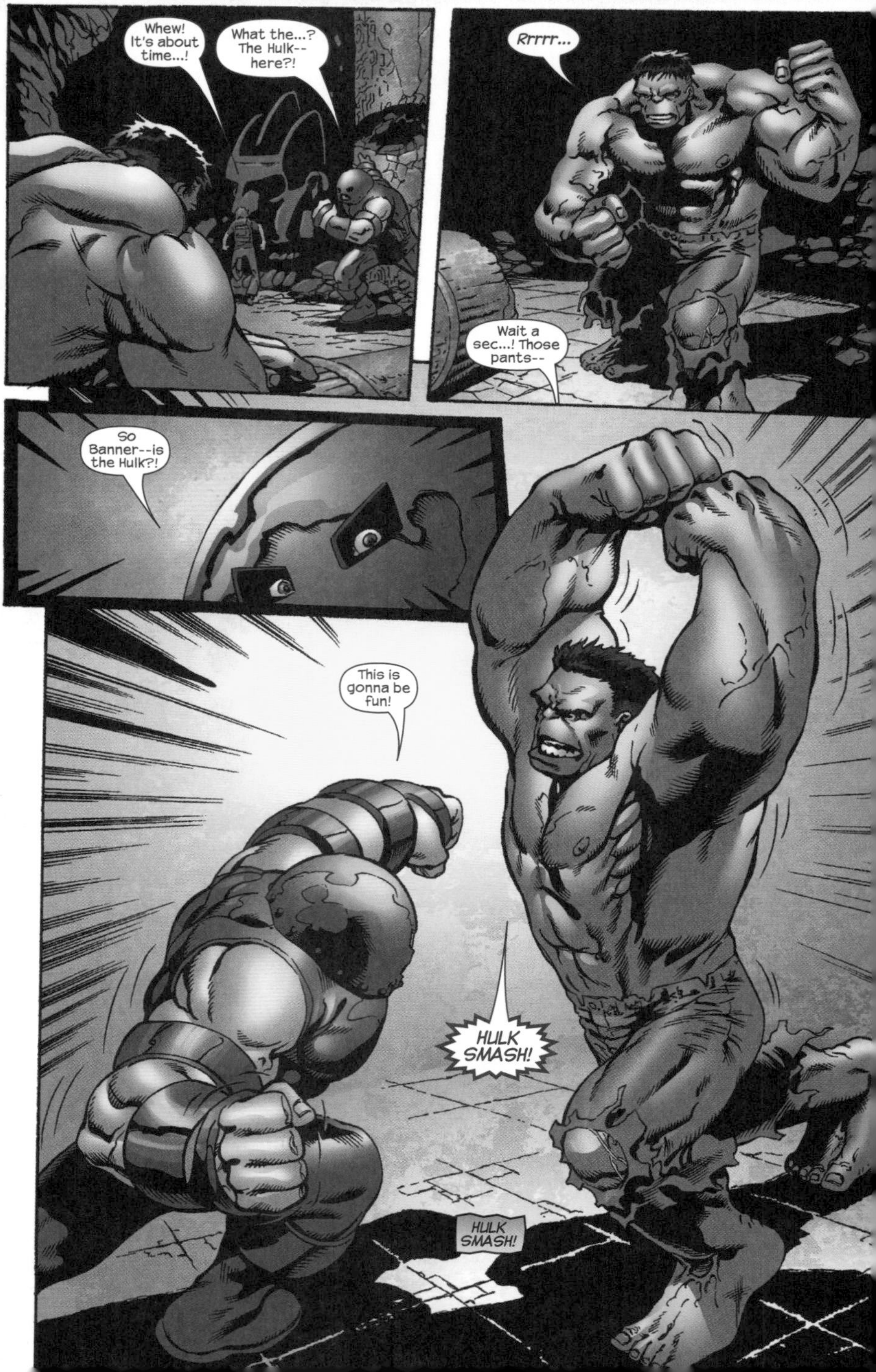
Whew! It's about time...!
What the...? The Hulk--here?!
Rrrrr...
Wait a sec...! Those pants--
So Banner--is the Hulk?!
This is gonna be fun!
HULK SMASH!
HULK SMASH!

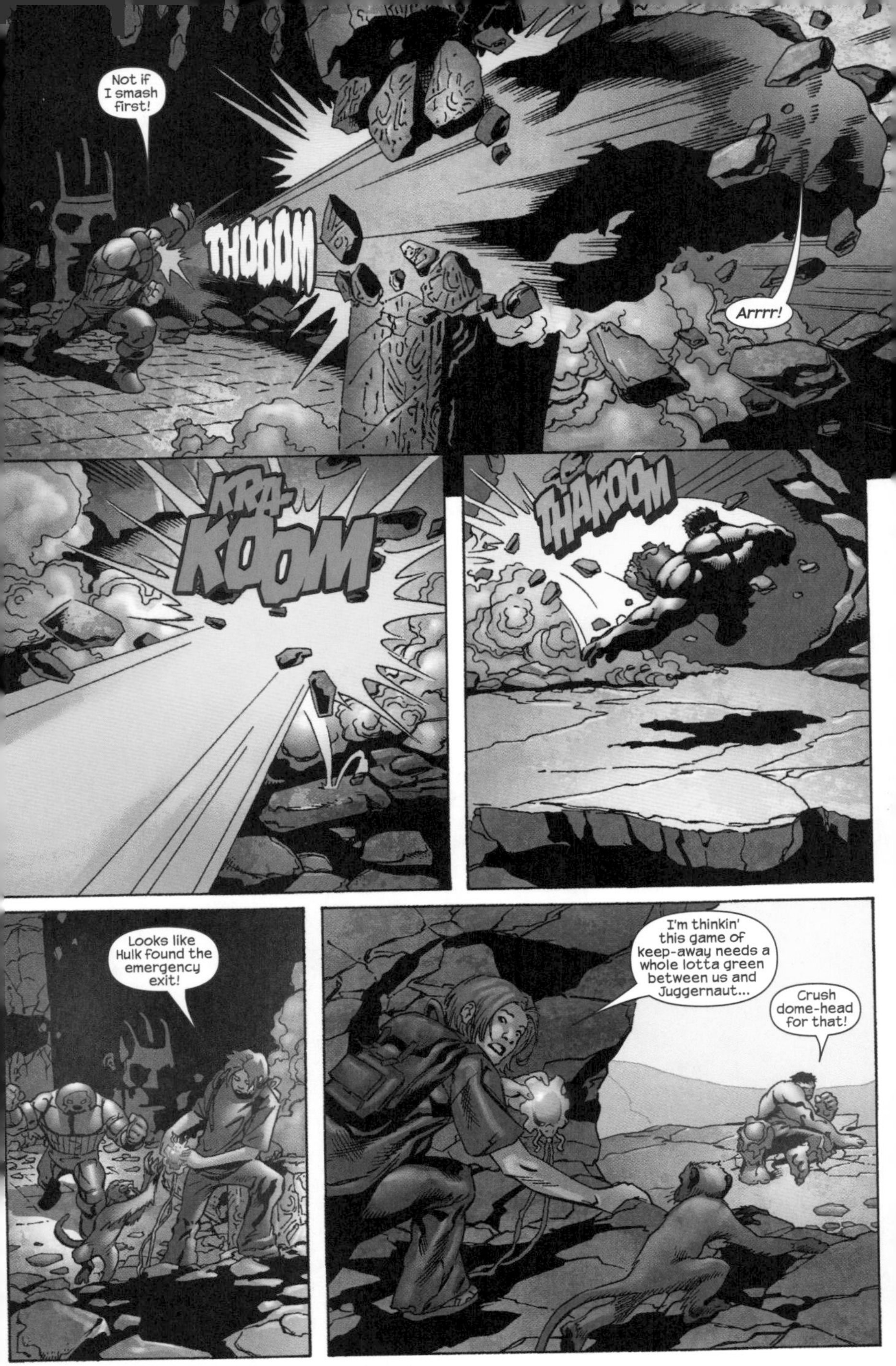

Not if I smash first!
THOOOM
Arrrr!
KRA-KOOOM
THAKOOOM
Looks like Hulk found the emergency exit!
I'm thinkin' this game of keep-away needs a whole lotta green between us and Juggernaut...
Crush dome-head for that!

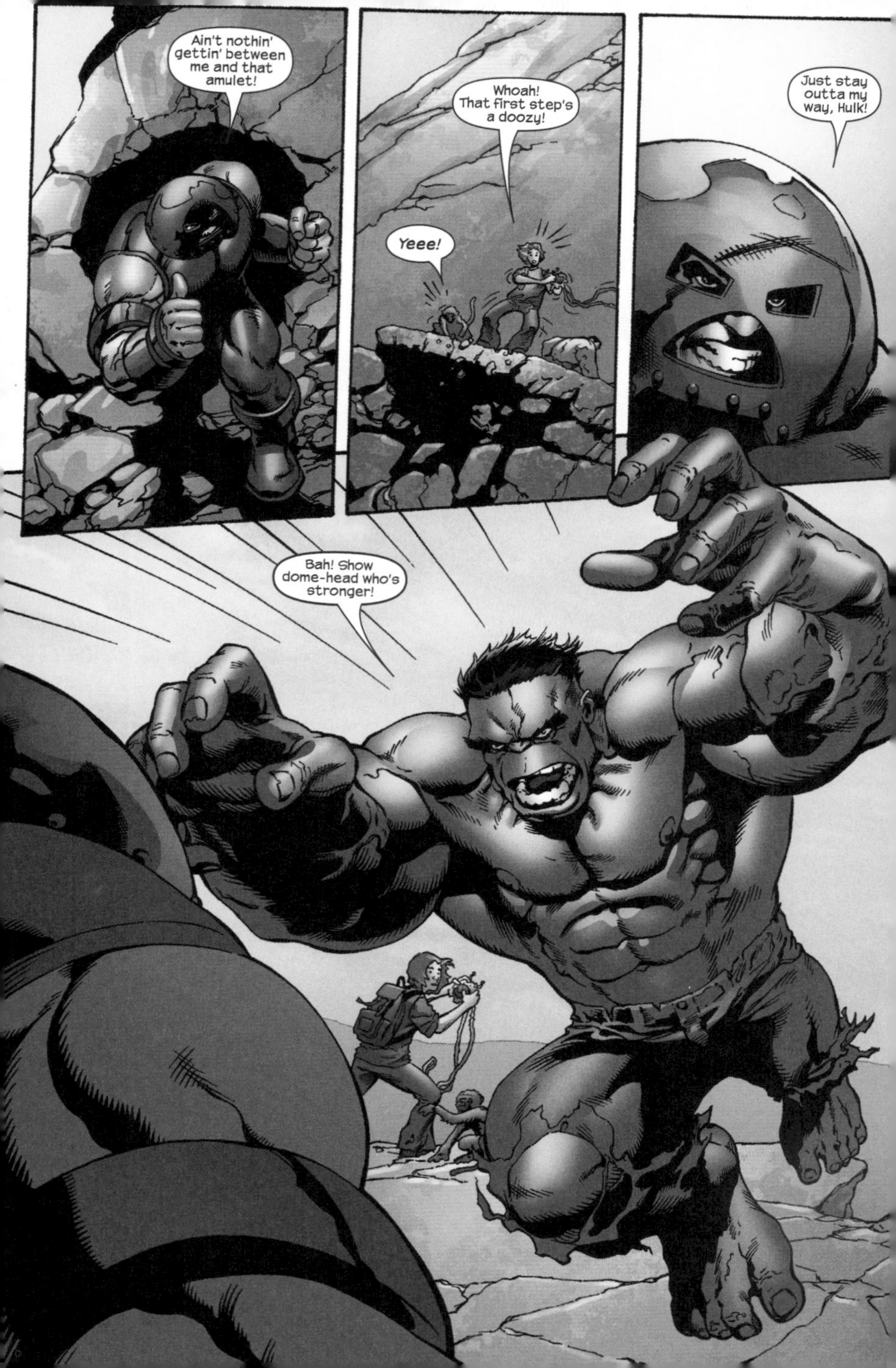
Ain't nothin' gettin' between me and that amulet!
Whoah! That first step's a doozy!
Yeee!
Just stay outta my way, Hulk!
Bah! Show dome-head who's stronger!

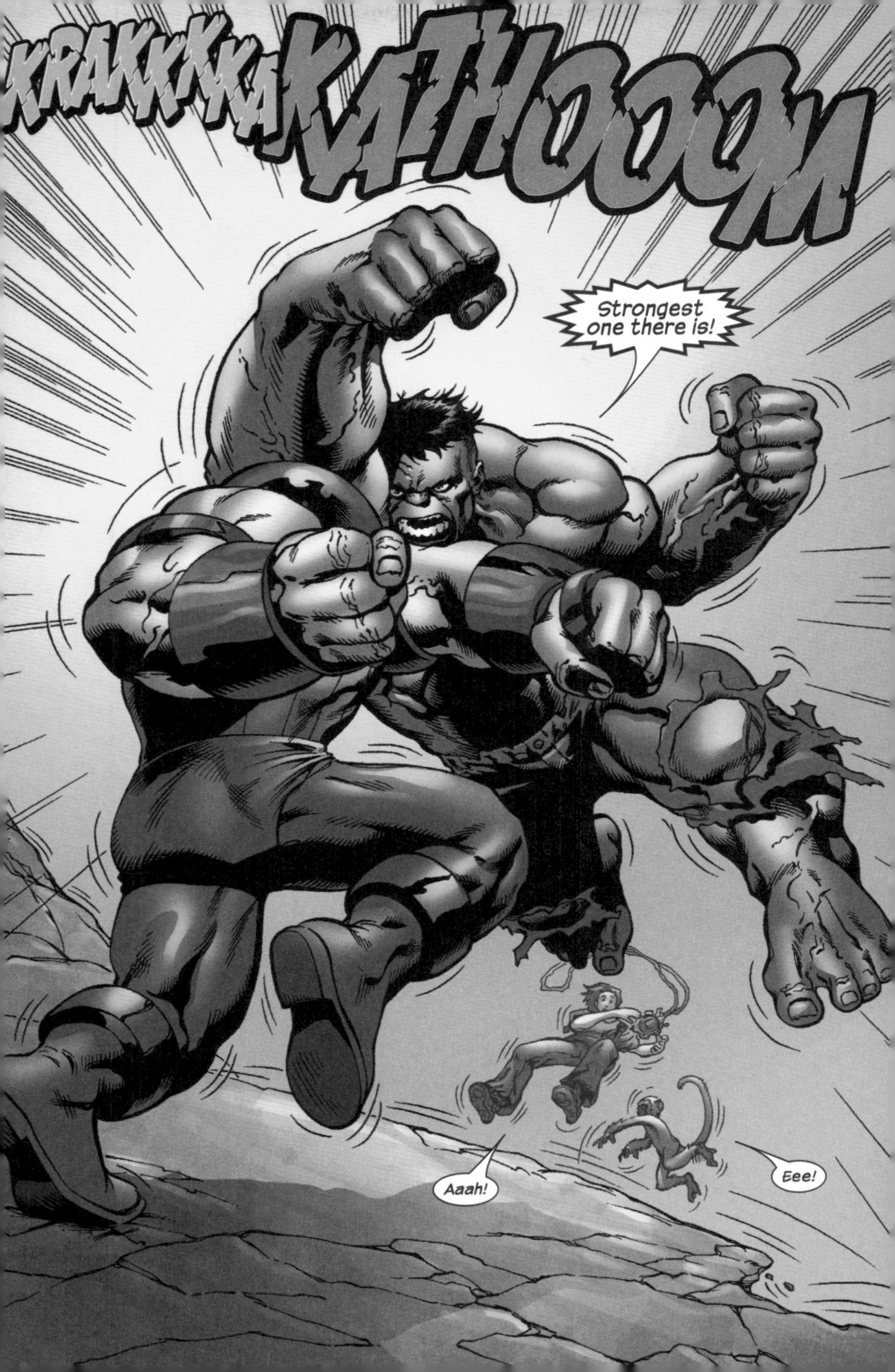
KRAKKKKAK KATHOOOM
Strongest one there is!
Aaah!
Eee!

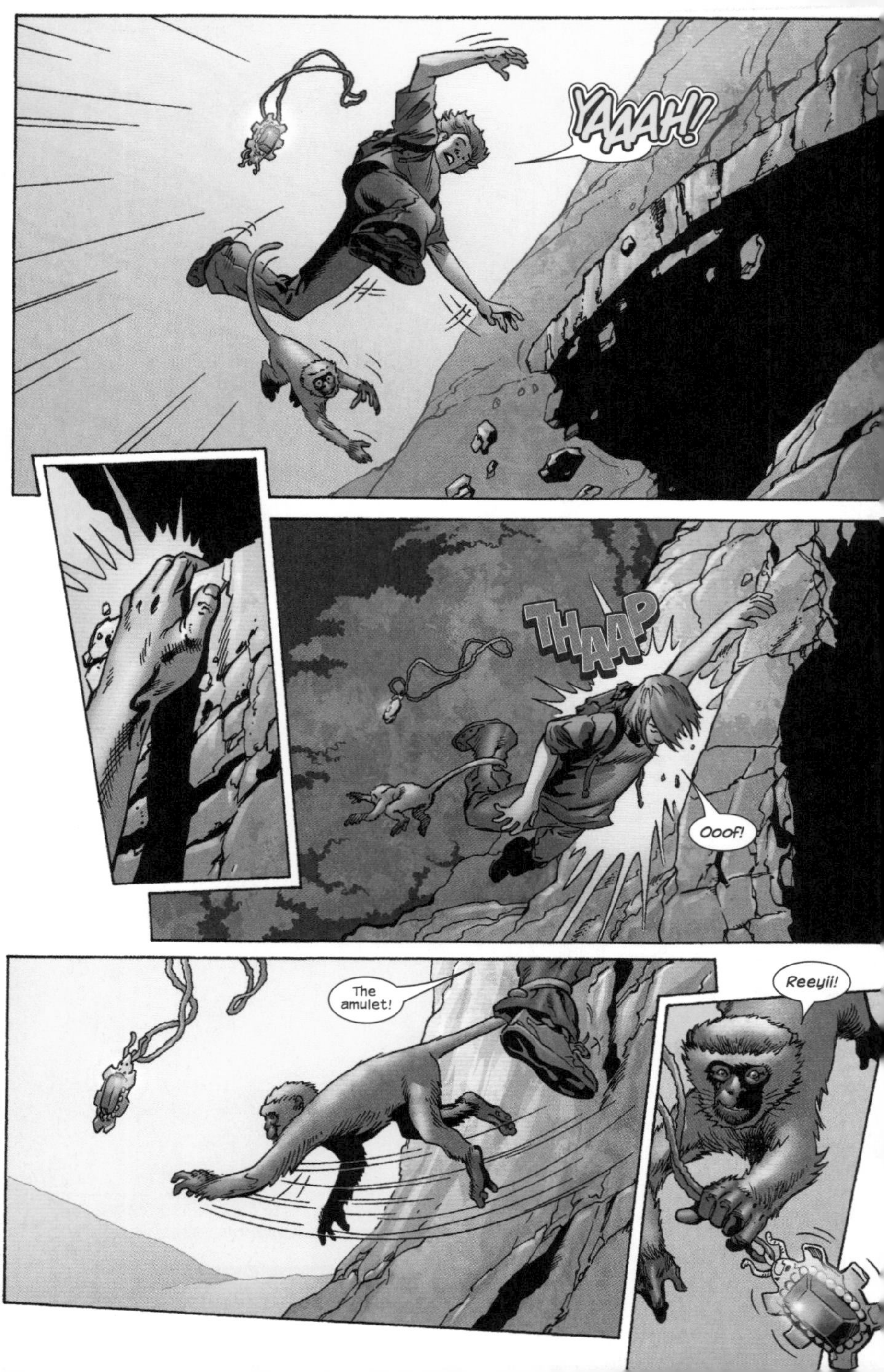
YAAAH!
THAAP
Ooof!
The amulet!
Reeyii!

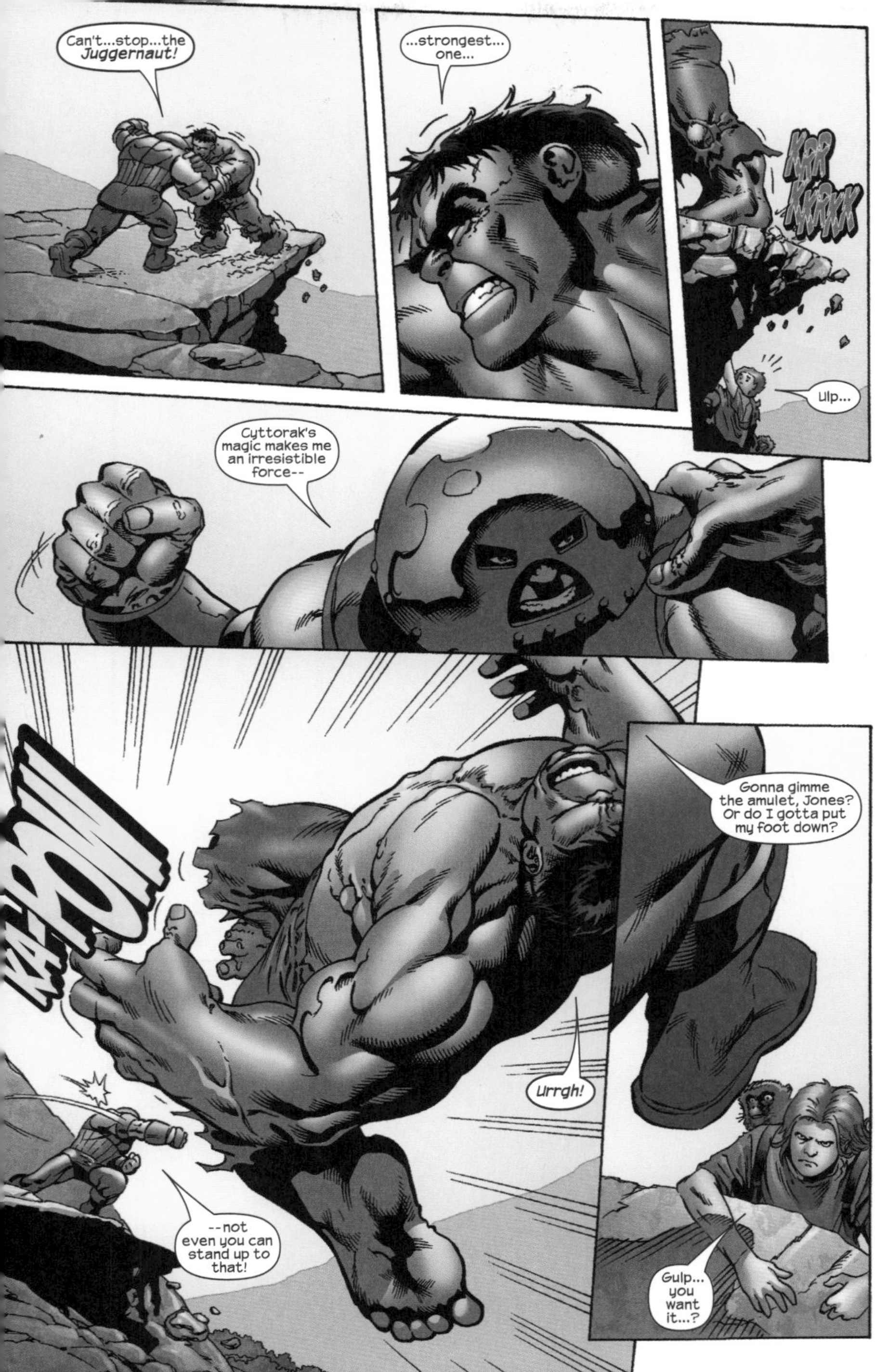
Can't...stop...the Juggernaut!
...strongest... one...
KRR KKRKK
Ulp...
Cyttorak's magic makes me an irresistible force--
KA-POW
Urrgh!
--not even you can stand up to that!
Gonna gimme the amulet, Jones? Or do I gotta put my foot down?
Gulp... you want it...?

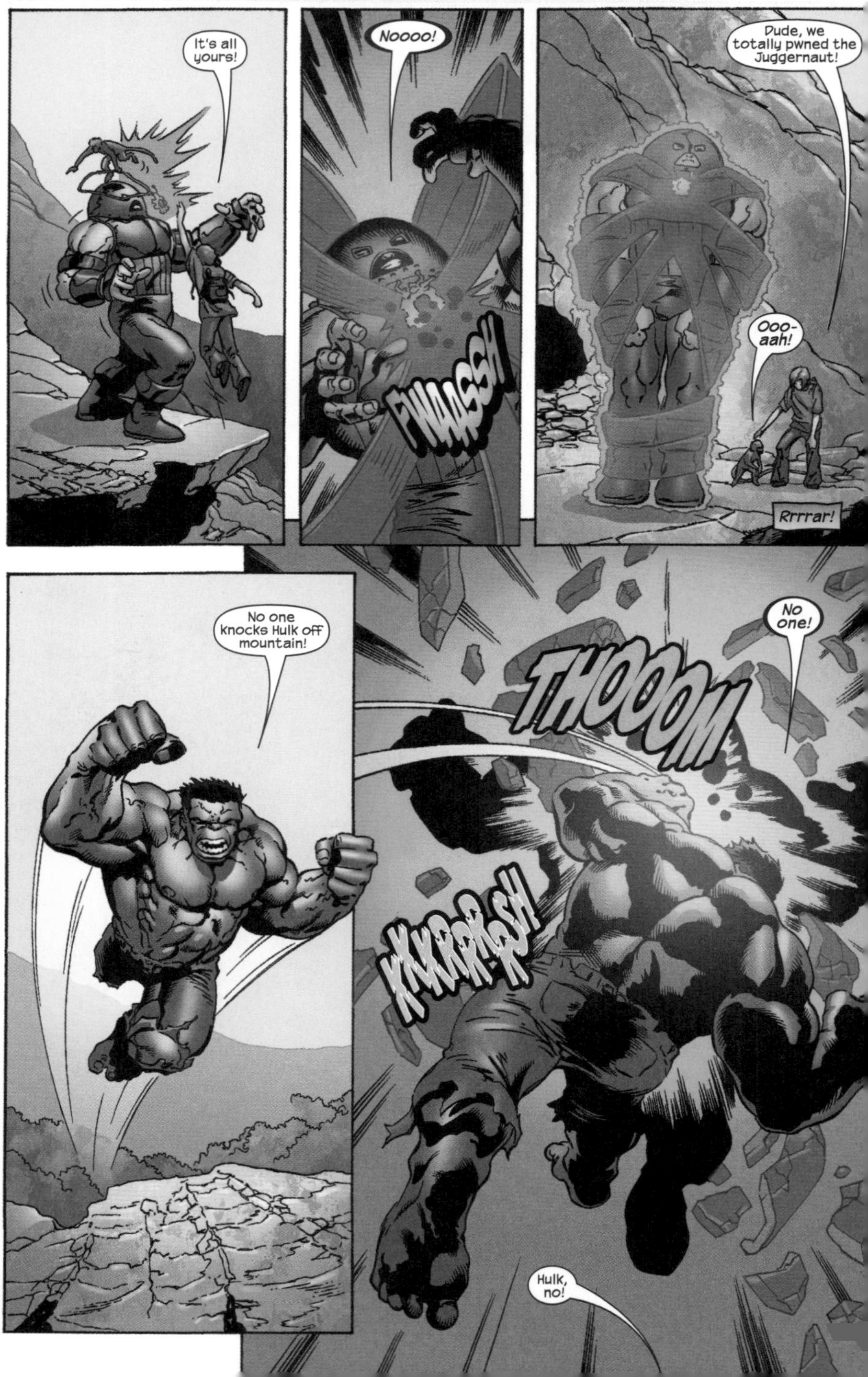

It's all yours!
Noooo!
FWOOSSH
Dude, we totally pwned the Juggernaut!
Ooo-aah!
Rrrrar!
No one knocks Hulk off mountain!
THOOOM
No one!
KKKRRRSH
Hulk, no!

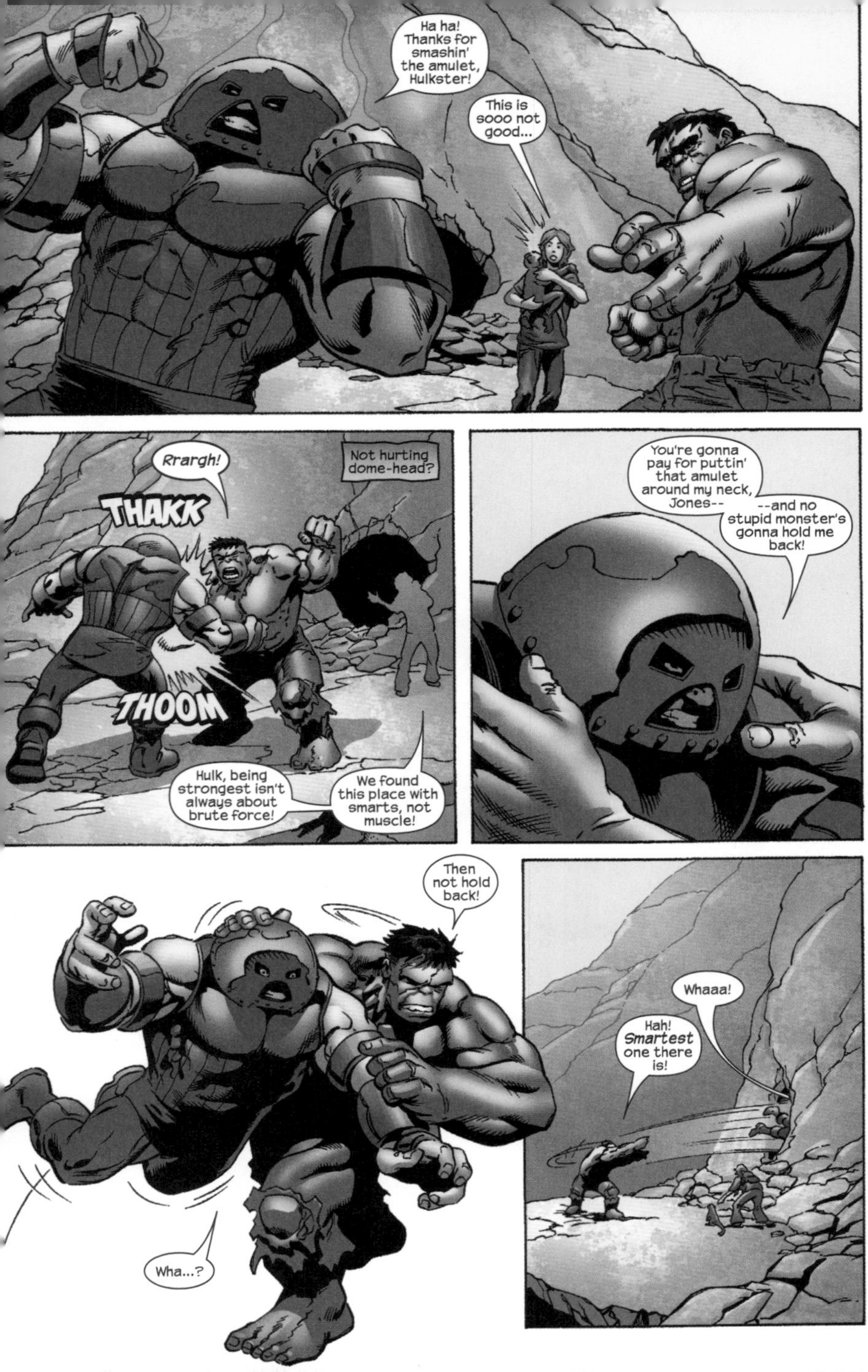

Ha ha! Thanks for smashin' the amulet, Hulkster!
This is sooo not good...
Rrargh!
THAKK
Not hurting dome-head?
THOOM
Hulk, being strongest isn't always about brute force!
We found this place with smarts, not muscle!
You're gonna pay for puttin' that amulet around my neck, Jones--
--and no stupid monster's gonna hold me back!
Then not hold back!
Wha...?
Whaaa!
Hah! *Smartest* one there is!

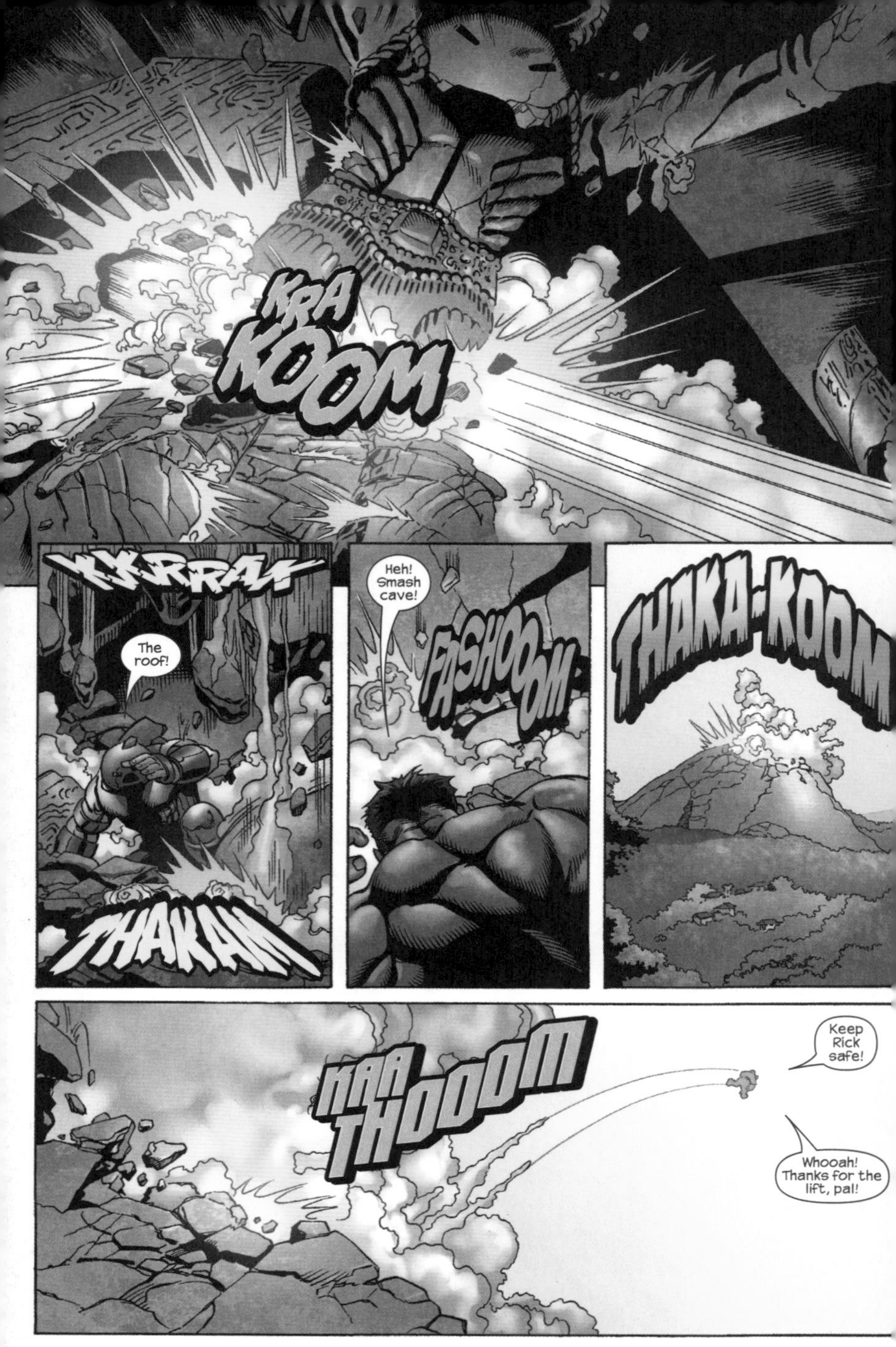

KRA
KOOM
KKRRAK
The roof!
THAKAM
Heh! Smash cave!
FASHOOOOM
THAKA-KOOM
KRA
THOOOM
Keep Rick safe!
Whooah! Thanks for the lift, pal!

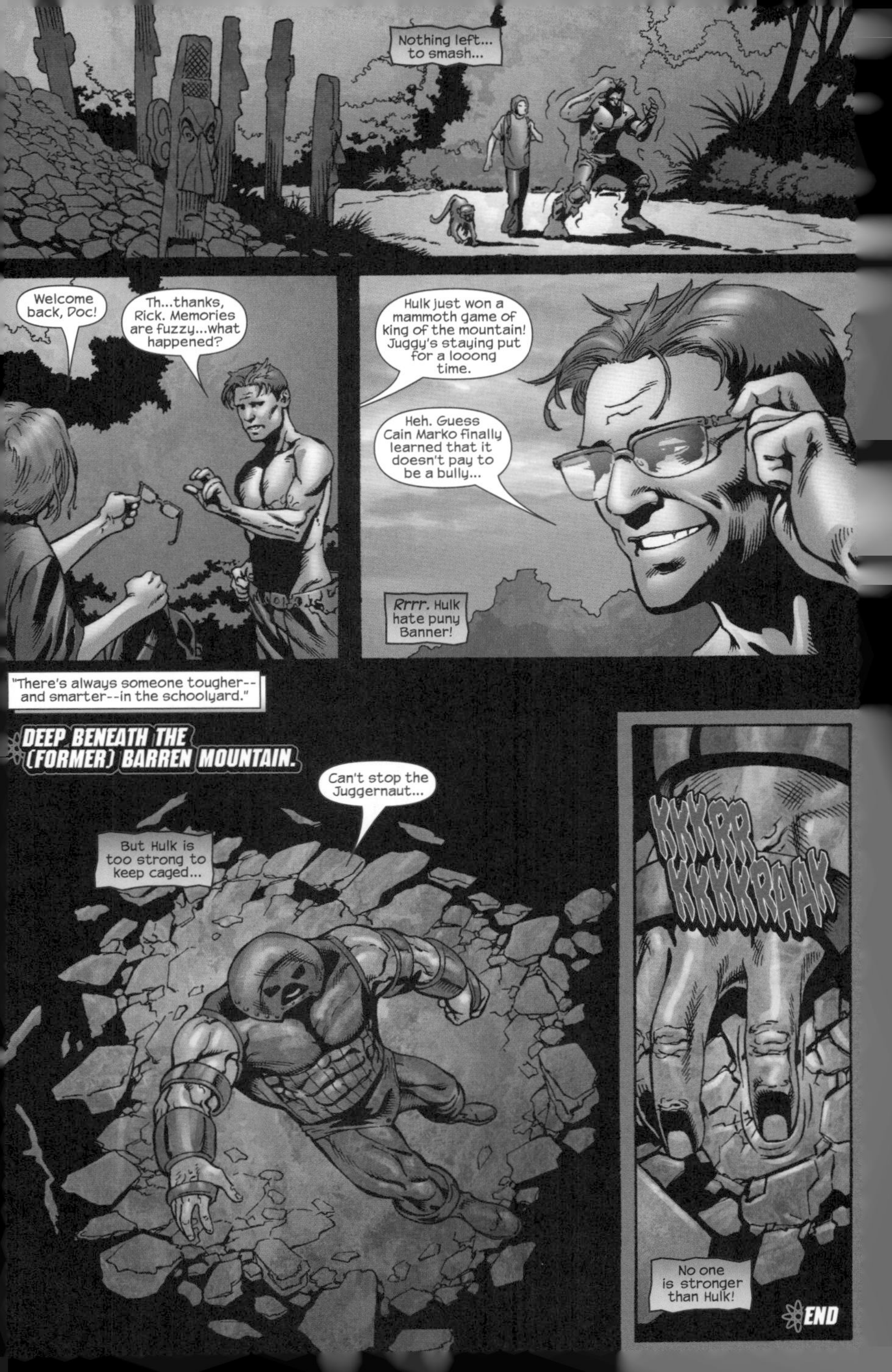

Nothing left... to smash...
Welcome back, Doc!
Th...thanks, Rick. Memories are fuzzy...what happened?
Hulk just won a mammoth game of king of the mountain! Juggy's staying put for a looong time.
Heh. Guess Cain Marko finally learned that it doesn't pay to be a bully...
Rrrr. Hulk hate puny Banner!
"There's always someone tougher--and smarter--in the schoolyard."
DEEP BENEATH THE (FORMER) BARREN MOUNTAIN.
Can't stop the Juggernaut...
But Hulk is too strong to keep caged...
KKKRR KKKKRAAK
No one is stronger than Hulk!
END

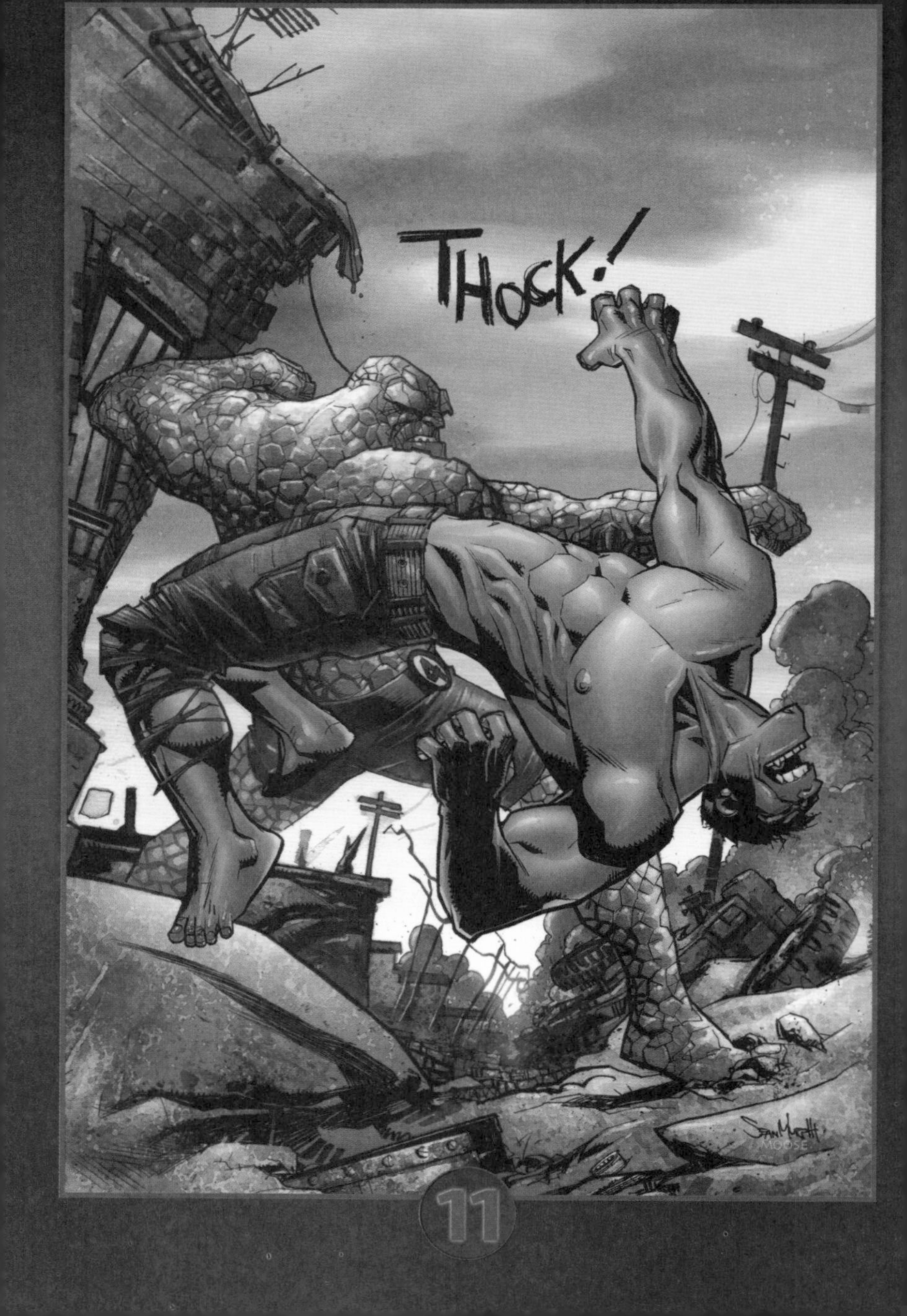
THOCK!

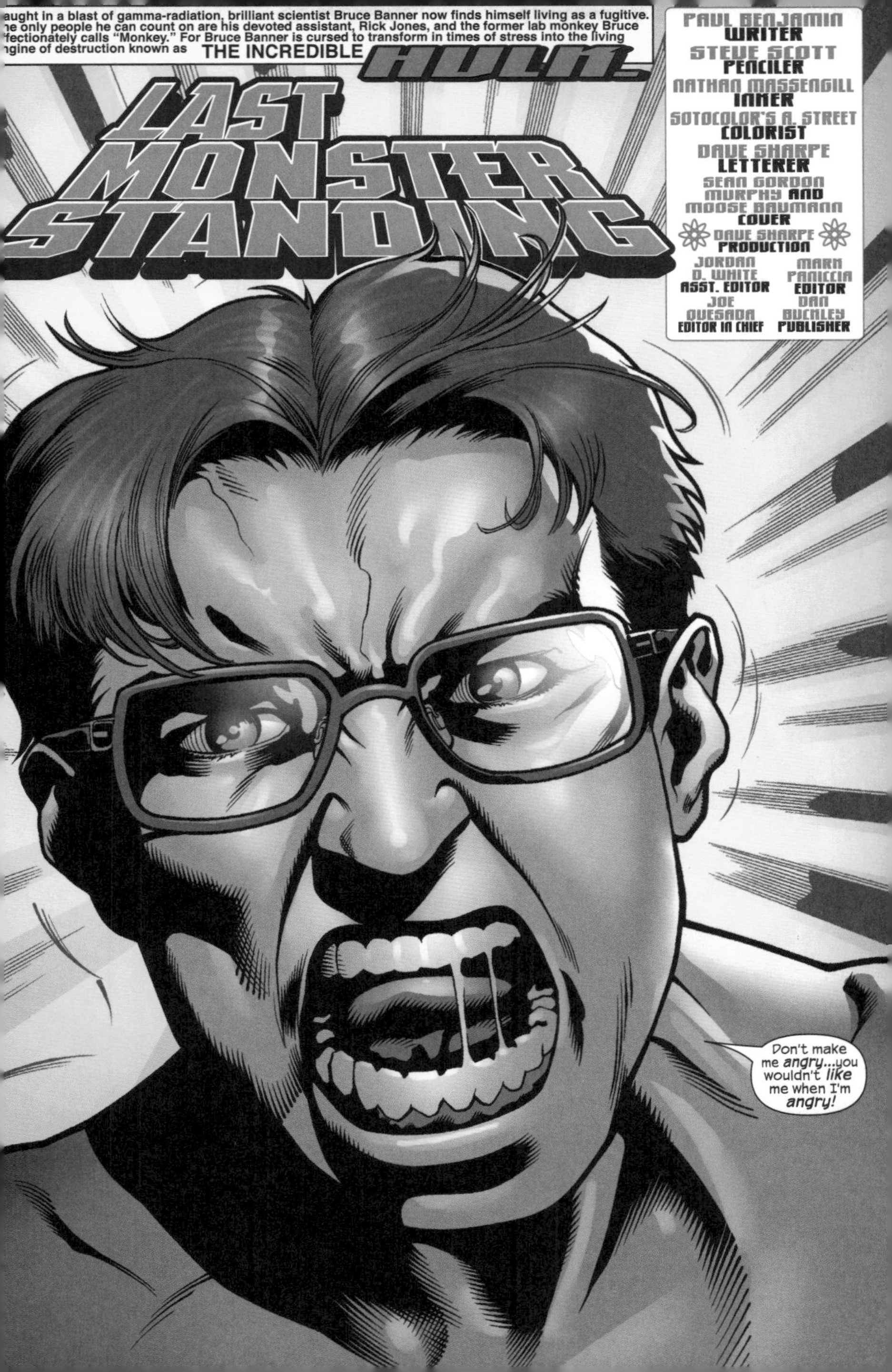

aught in a blast of gamma-radiation, brilliant scientist Bruce Banner now finds himself living as a fugitive. he only people he can count on are his devoted assistant, Rick Jones, and the former lab monkey Bruce ffectionately calls "Monkey." For Bruce Banner is cursed to transform in times of stress into the living ngine of destruction known as THE INCREDIBLE HULK.
LAST MONSTER STANDING
PAUL BENJAMIN WRITER
STEVE SCOTT PENCILER
NATHAN MASSENGILL INKER
SOTOCOLOR'S A. STREET COLORIST
DAVE SHARPE LETTERER
SEAN GORDON MURPHY AND MOOSE BAUMANN COVER
DAVE SHARPE PRODUCTION
JORDAN D. WHITE ASST. EDITOR
MARK PANICCIA EDITOR
JOE QUESADA EDITOR IN CHIEF
DAN BUCKLEY PUBLISHER
Don't make me *angry*...you wouldn't *like* me when I'm *angry!*

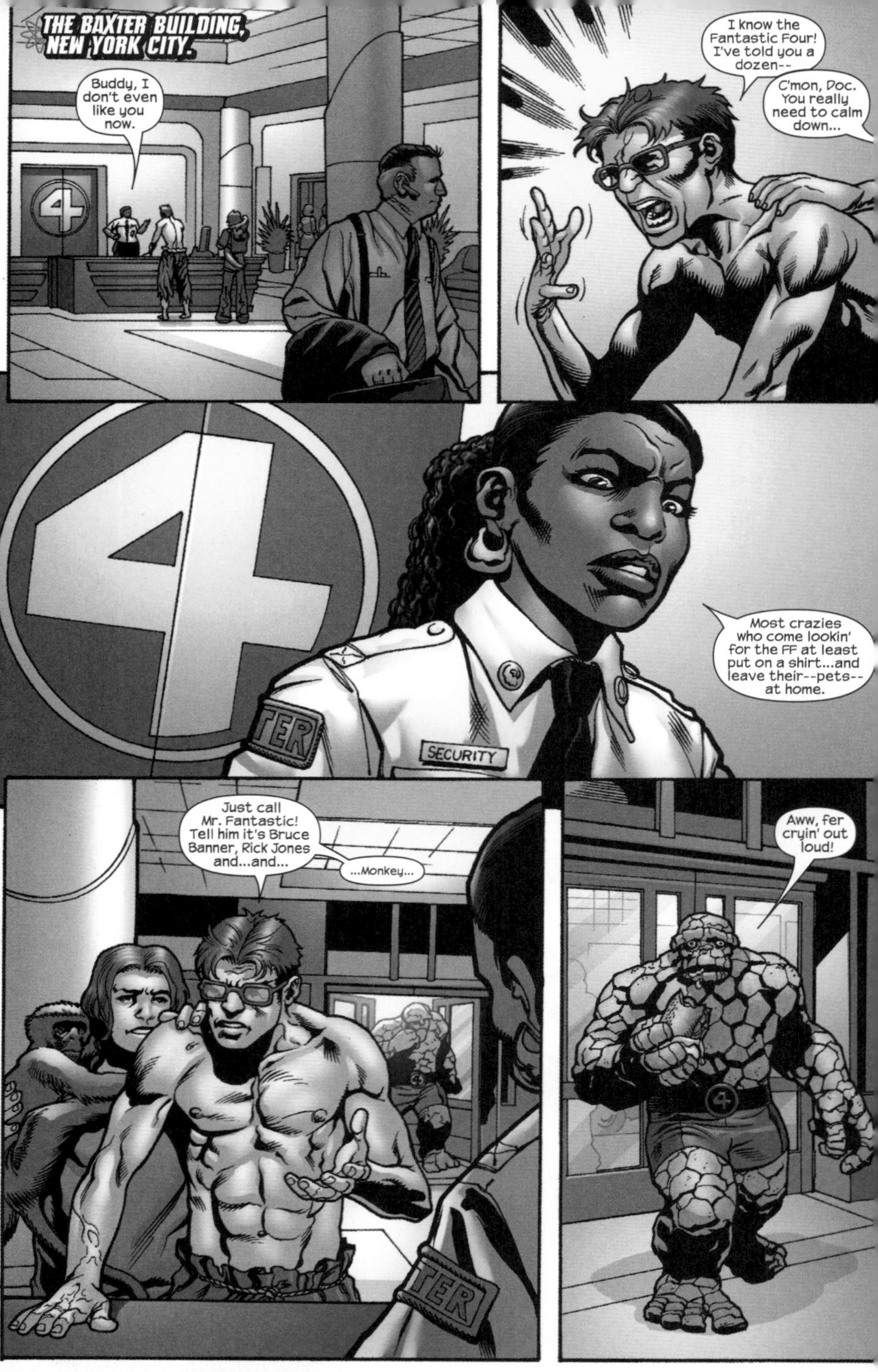
THE BAXTER BUILDING, NEW YORK CITY.
Buddy, I don't even like you now.
I know the Fantastic Four! I've told you a dozen--
C'mon, Doc. You really need to calm down...
Most crazies who come lookin' for the FF at least put on a shirt...and leave their--pets--at home.
SECURITY
Just call Mr. Fantastic! Tell him it's Bruce Banner, Rick Jones and...and...
...Monkey...
Aww, fer cryin' out loud!

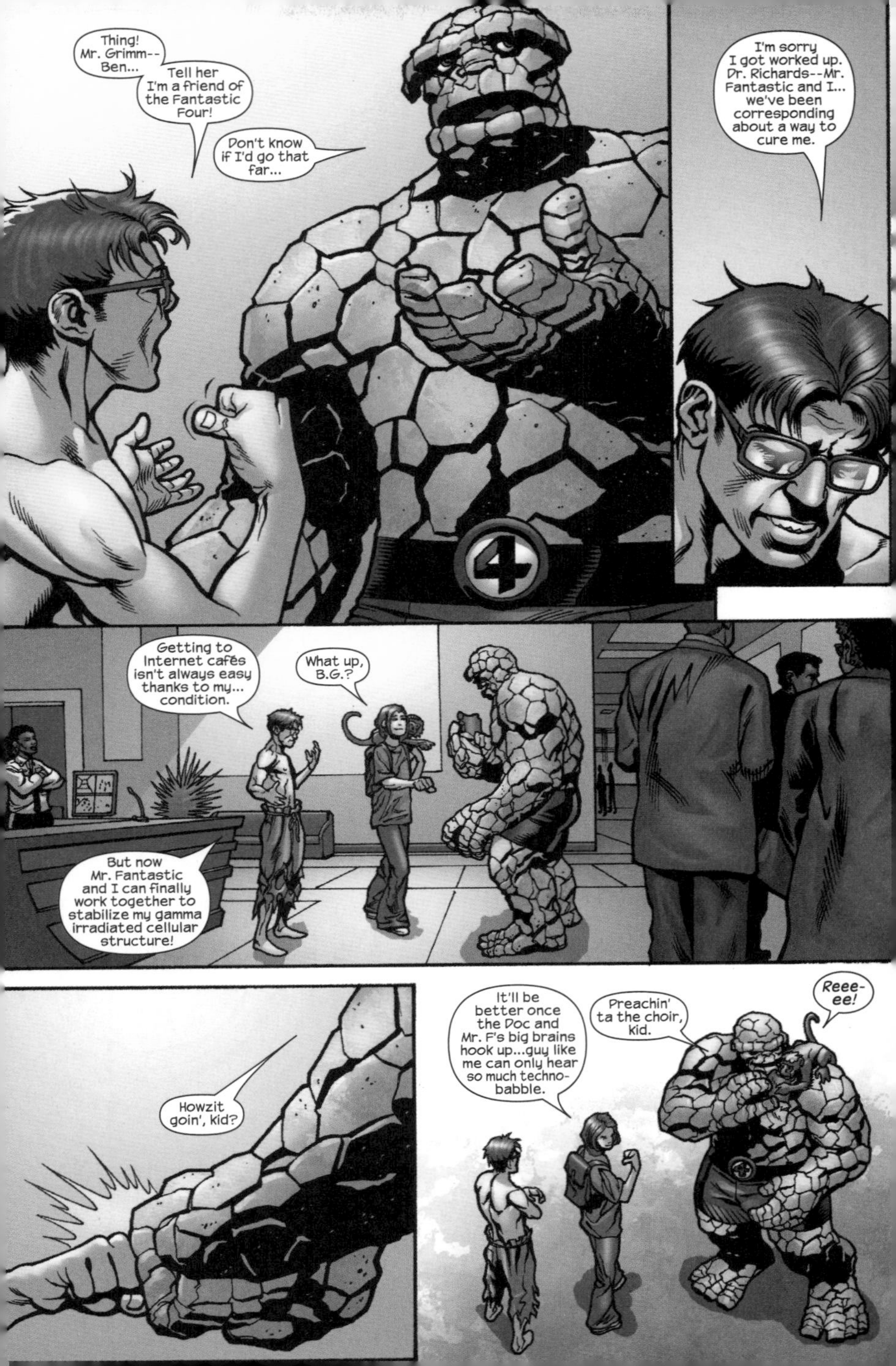
Thing! Mr. Grimm-- Ben...
Tell her I'm a friend of the Fantastic Four!
Don't know if I'd go that far...
I'm sorry I got worked up. Dr. Richards--Mr. Fantastic and I... we've been corresponding about a way to cure me.
Getting to Internet cafés isn't always easy thanks to my... condition.
What up, B.G.?
But now Mr. Fantastic and I can finally work together to stabilize my gamma irradiated cellular structure!
Howzit goin', kid?
It'll be better once the Doc and Mr. F's big brains hook up...guy like me can only hear so much techno-babble.
Preachin' ta the choir, kid.
Reee-ee!

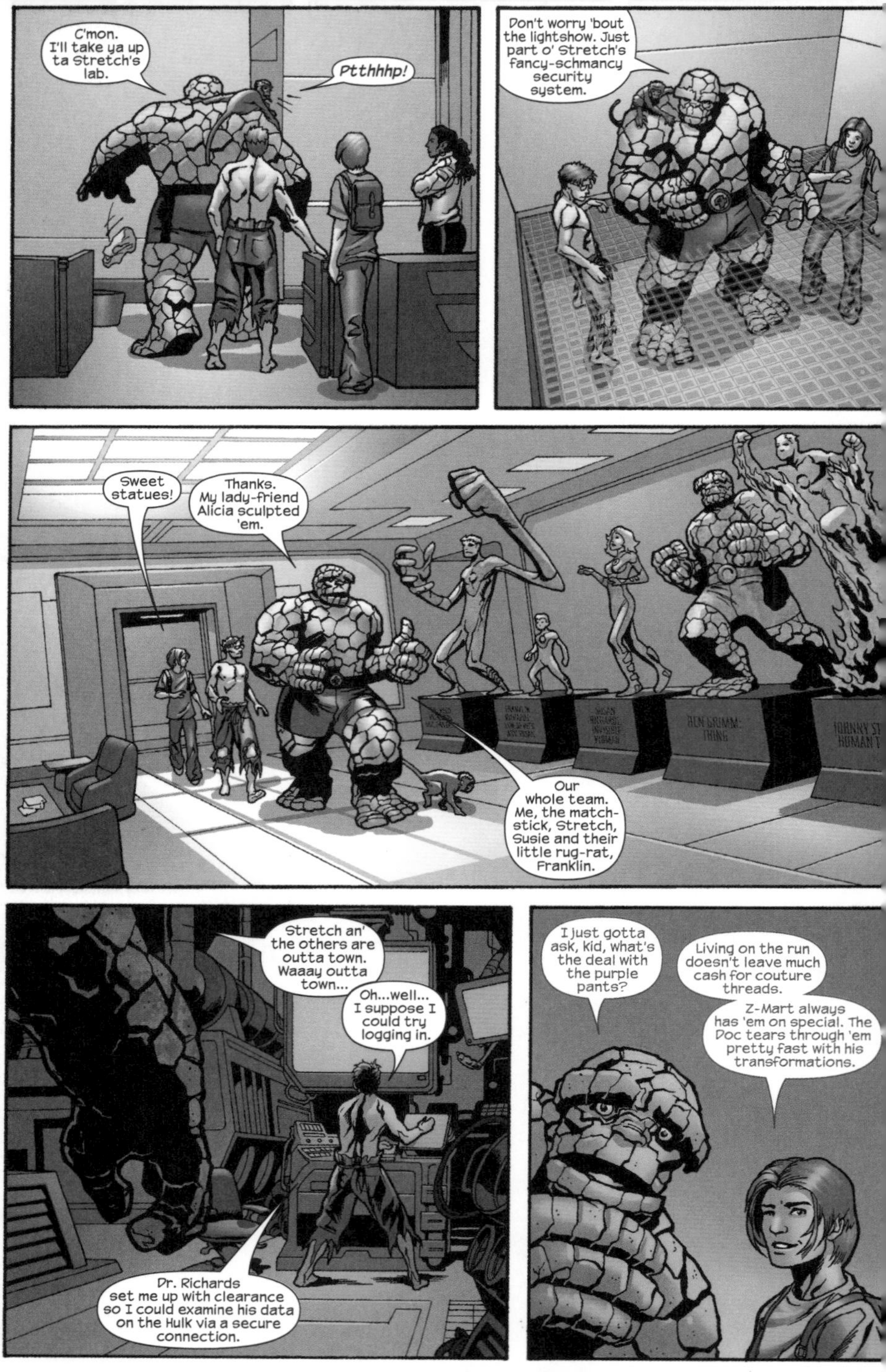

C'mon. I'll take ya up ta Stretch's lab.
Ptthhhp!
Don't worry 'bout the lightshow. Just part o' Stretch's fancy-schmancy security system.
Sweet statues!
Thanks. My lady-friend Alicia sculpted 'em.
BEN GRIMM: THING
Our whole team. Me, the match-stick, Stretch, Susie and their little rug-rat, Franklin.
Stretch an' the others are outta town. Waaay outta town...
Oh...well... I suppose I could try logging in.
Dr. Richards set me up with clearance so I could examine his data on the Hulk via a secure connection.
I just gotta ask, kid, what's the deal with the purple pants?
Living on the run doesn't leave much cash for couture threads.
Z-Mart always has 'em on special. The Doc tears through 'em pretty fast with his transformations.

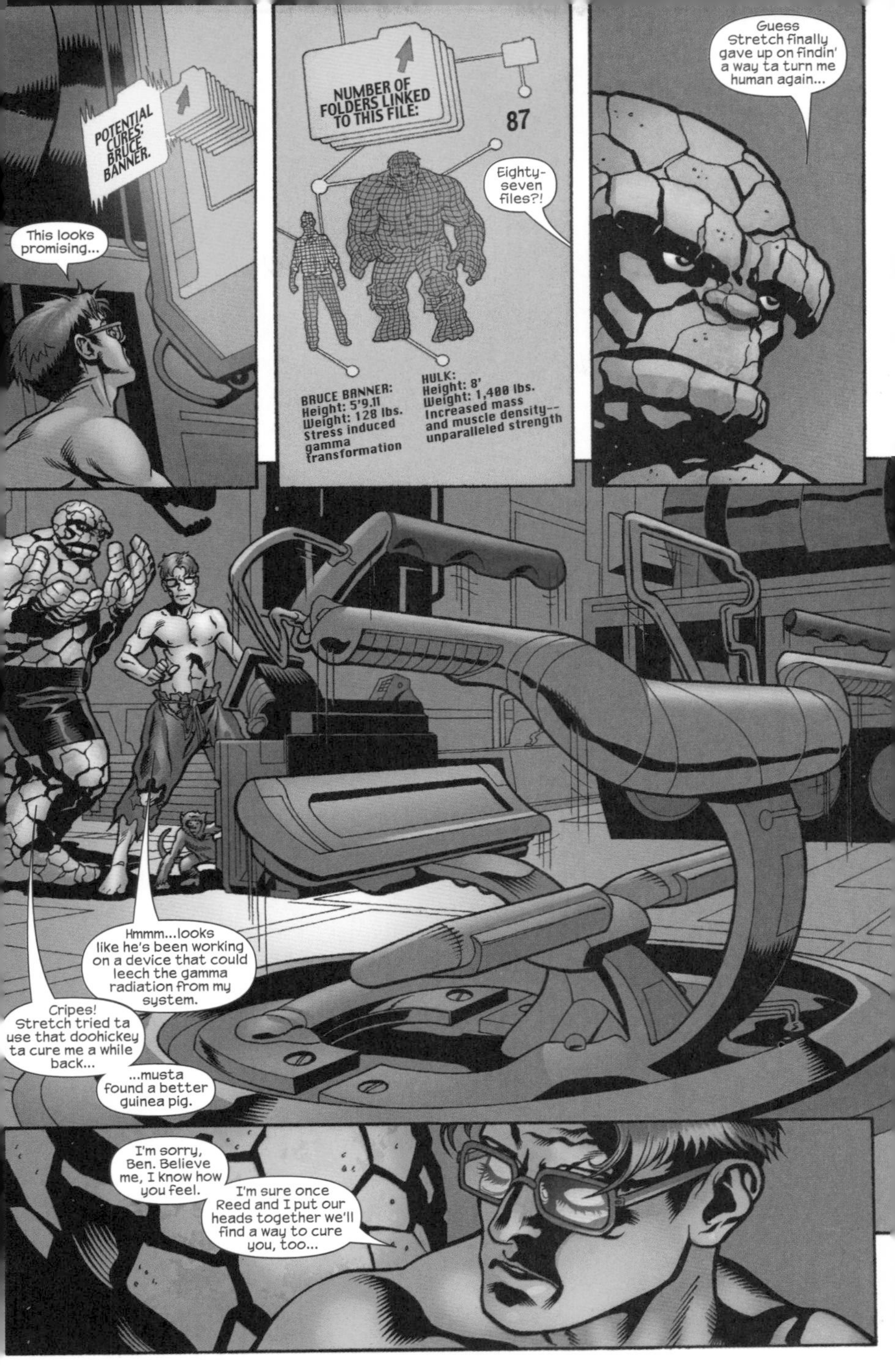
POTENTIAL CURES: BRUCE BANNER.
This looks promising...
NUMBER OF FOLDERS LINKED TO THIS FILE:
87
BRUCE BANNER: Height: 5'9.11 Weight: 128 lbs. Stress induced gamma transformation
HULK: Height: 8' Weight: 1,400 lbs. Increased mass and muscle density-- unparalleled strength
Eighty-seven files?!
Guess Stretch finally gave up on findin' a way ta turn me human again...
Hmmm...looks like he's been working on a device that could leech the gamma radiation from my system.
Cripes! Stretch tried ta use that doohickey ta cure me a while back...
...musta found a better guinea pig.
I'm sorry, Ben. Believe me, I know how you feel.
I'm sure once Reed and I put our heads together we'll find a way to cure you, too...

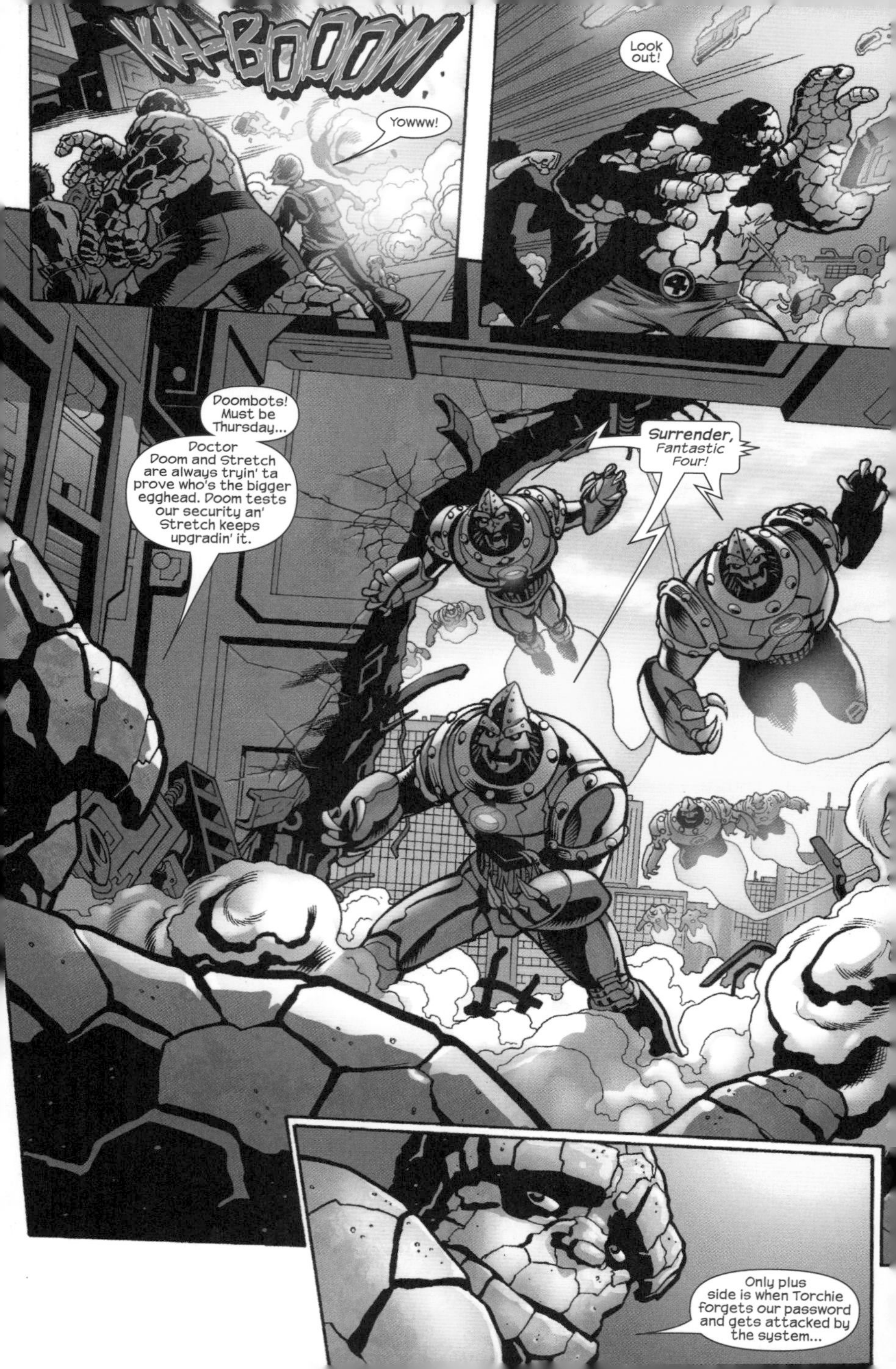
KA-BOOOM
YOWWW!
Look out!
Doombots! Must be Thursday...
Doctor Doom and Stretch are always tryin' ta prove who's the bigger egghead. Doom tests our security an' Stretch keeps upgradin' it.
Surrender, Fantastic Four!
Only plus side is when Torchie forgets our password and gets attacked by the system...

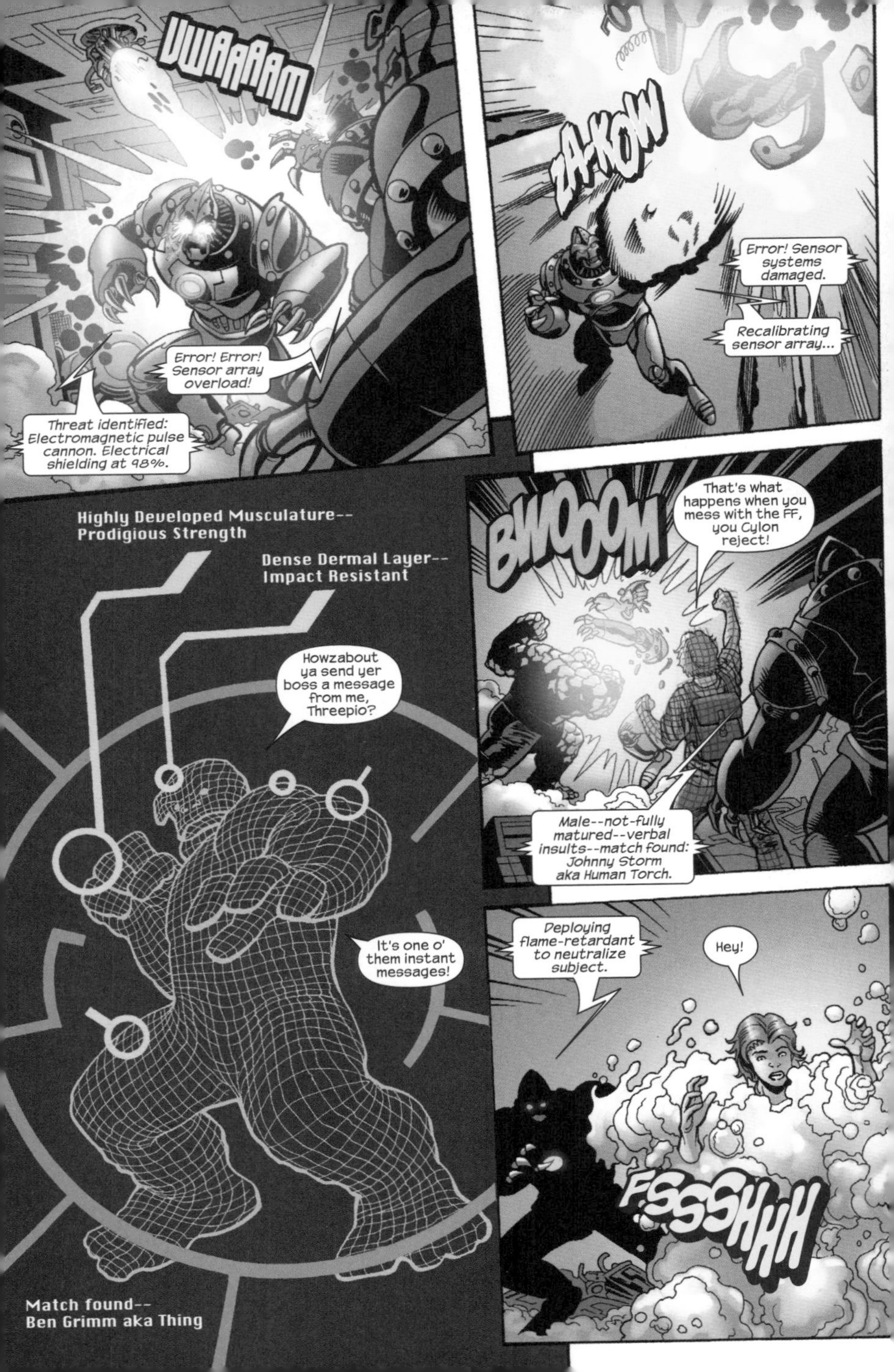
VWAAAAM
Threat identified: Electromagnetic pulse cannon. Electrical shielding at 98%.
Error! Error! Sensor array overload!
ZA-KOW
Error! Sensor systems damaged.
Recalibrating sensor array...
Highly Developed Musculature-- Prodigious Strength
Dense Dermal Layer-- Impact Resistant
Howzabout ya send yer boss a message from me, Threepio?
It's one o' them instant messages!
Match found-- Ben Grimm aka Thing
BWOOOM
That's what happens when you mess with the FF, you Cylon reject!
Male--not-fully matured--verbal insults--match found: Johnny Storm aka Human Torch.
Deploying flame-retardant to neutralize subject.
Hey!
FSSSHHH

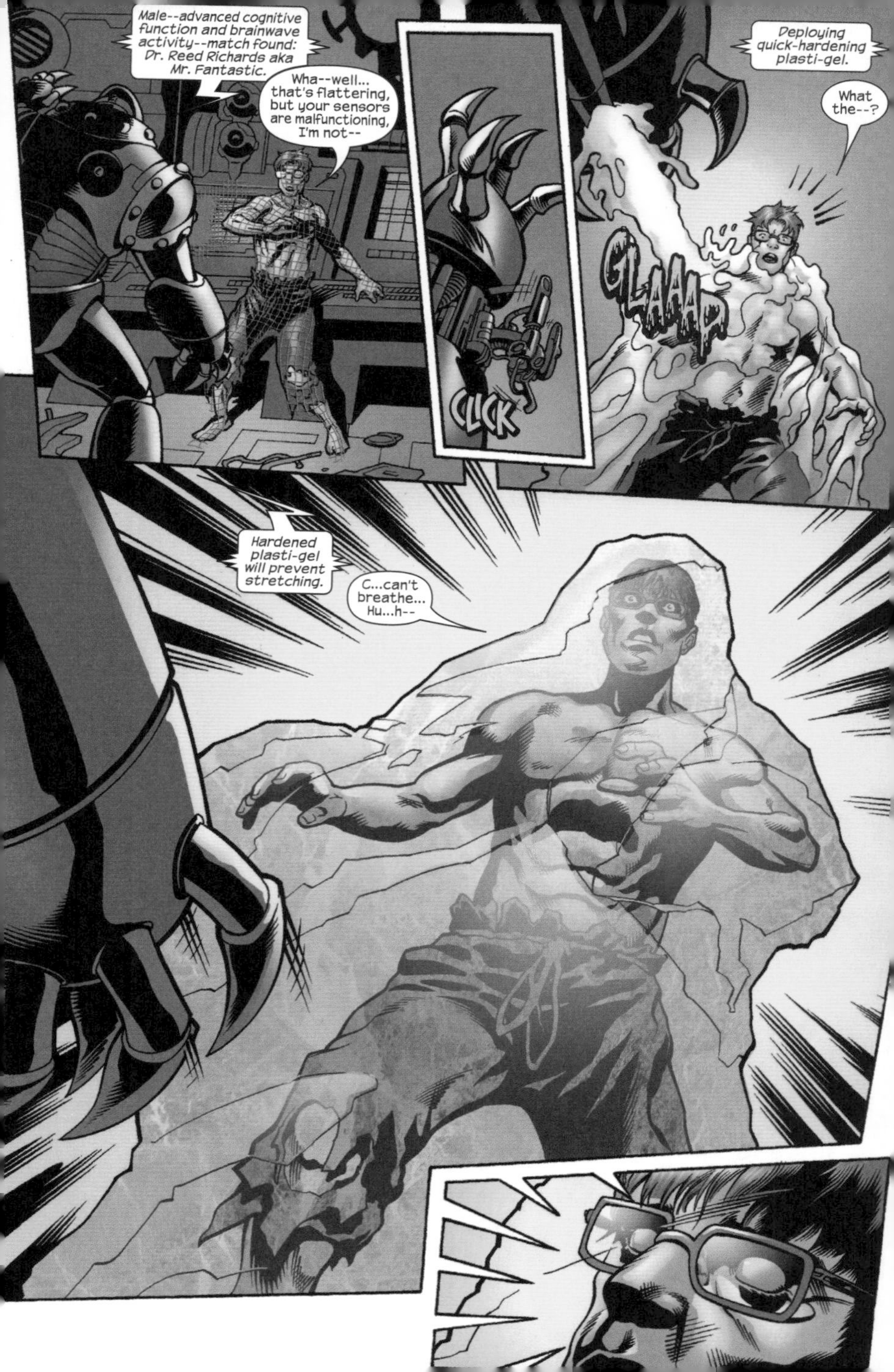
Male--advanced cognitive function and brainwave activity--match found: Dr. Reed Richards aka Mr. Fantastic.
Wha--well... that's flattering, but your sensors are malfunctioning, I'm not--
CLICK
Deploying quick-hardening plasti-gel.
What the--?
GLAAAP
Hardened plasti-gel will prevent stretching.
C...can't breathe... Hu...h--

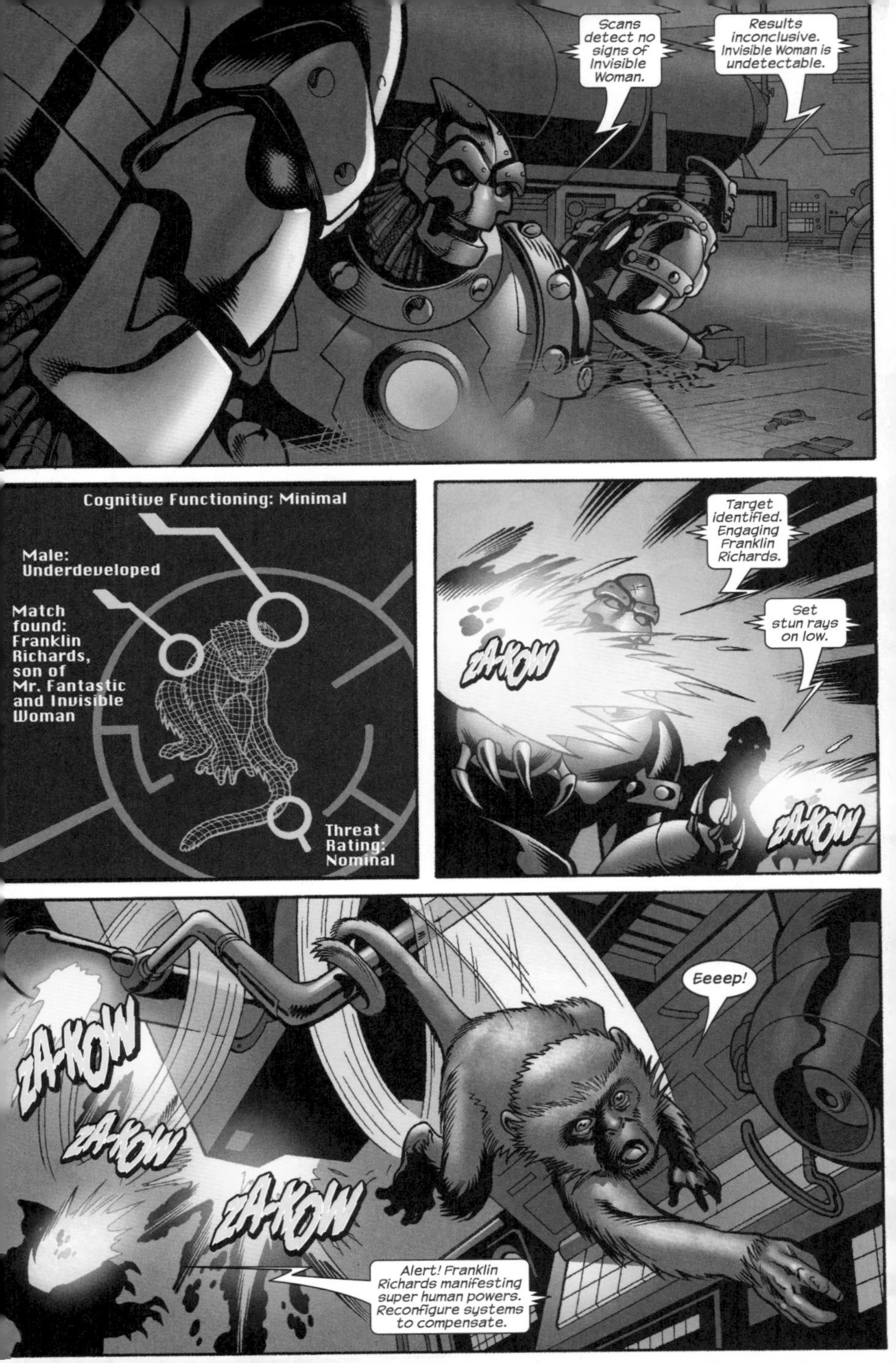
Scans detect no signs of Invisible Woman.
Results inconclusive. Invisible Woman is undetectable.
Cognitive Functioning: Minimal
Male: Underdeveloped
Match found: Franklin Richards, son of Mr. Fantastic and Invisible Woman
Threat Rating: Nominal
Target identified. Engaging Franklin Richards.
Set stun rays on low.
ZA-KOW
ZA-KOW
Eeeep!
ZA-KOW
ZA-KOW
ZA-KOW
Alert! Franklin Richards manifesting super human powers. Reconfigure systems to compensate.

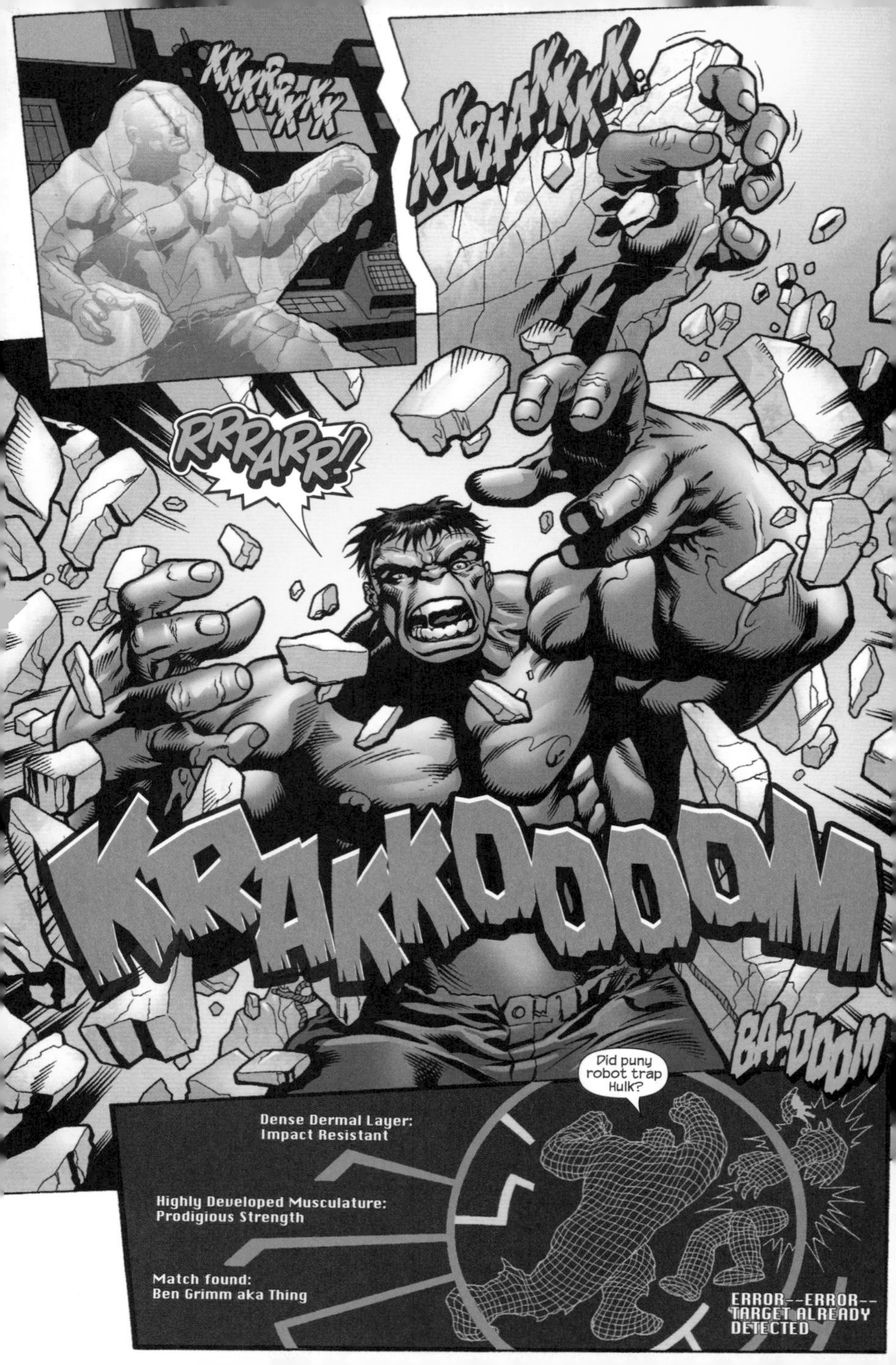

KKKKRRKKKK
KKKRRAAKKKK
RRRARR!
KRAKKOOOOM
BA-DOOM
Did puny robot trap Hulk?
Dense Dermal Layer:
Impact Resistant
Highly Developed Musculature:
Prodigious Strength
Match found:
Ben Grimm aka Thing
ERROR--ERROR--
TARGET ALREADY
DETECTED

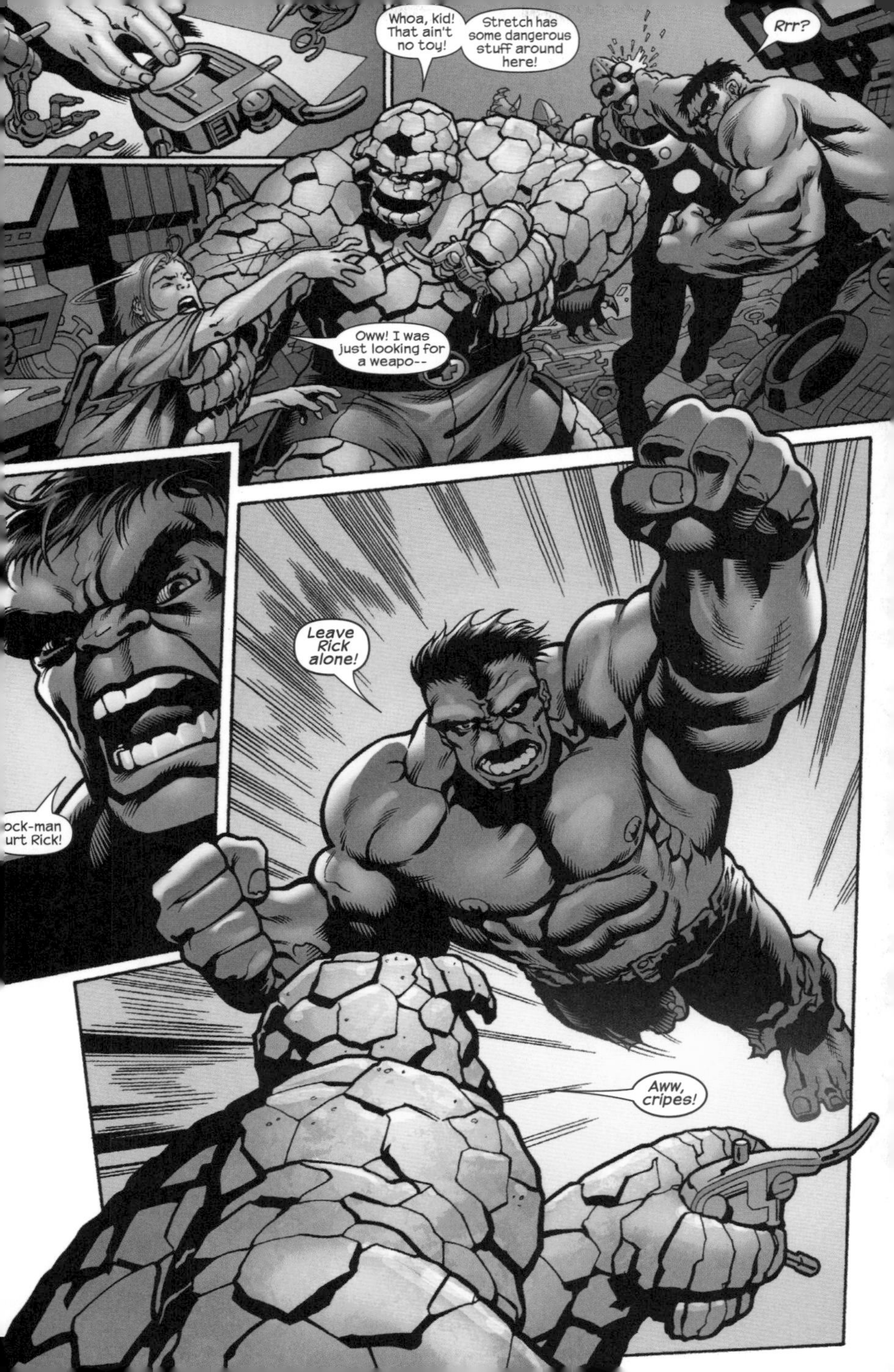
Whoa, kid! That ain't no toy!
Stretch has some dangerous stuff around here!
Rrr?
Oww! I was just looking for a weapo--
ock-man urt Rick!
Leave Rick alone!
Aww, cripes!

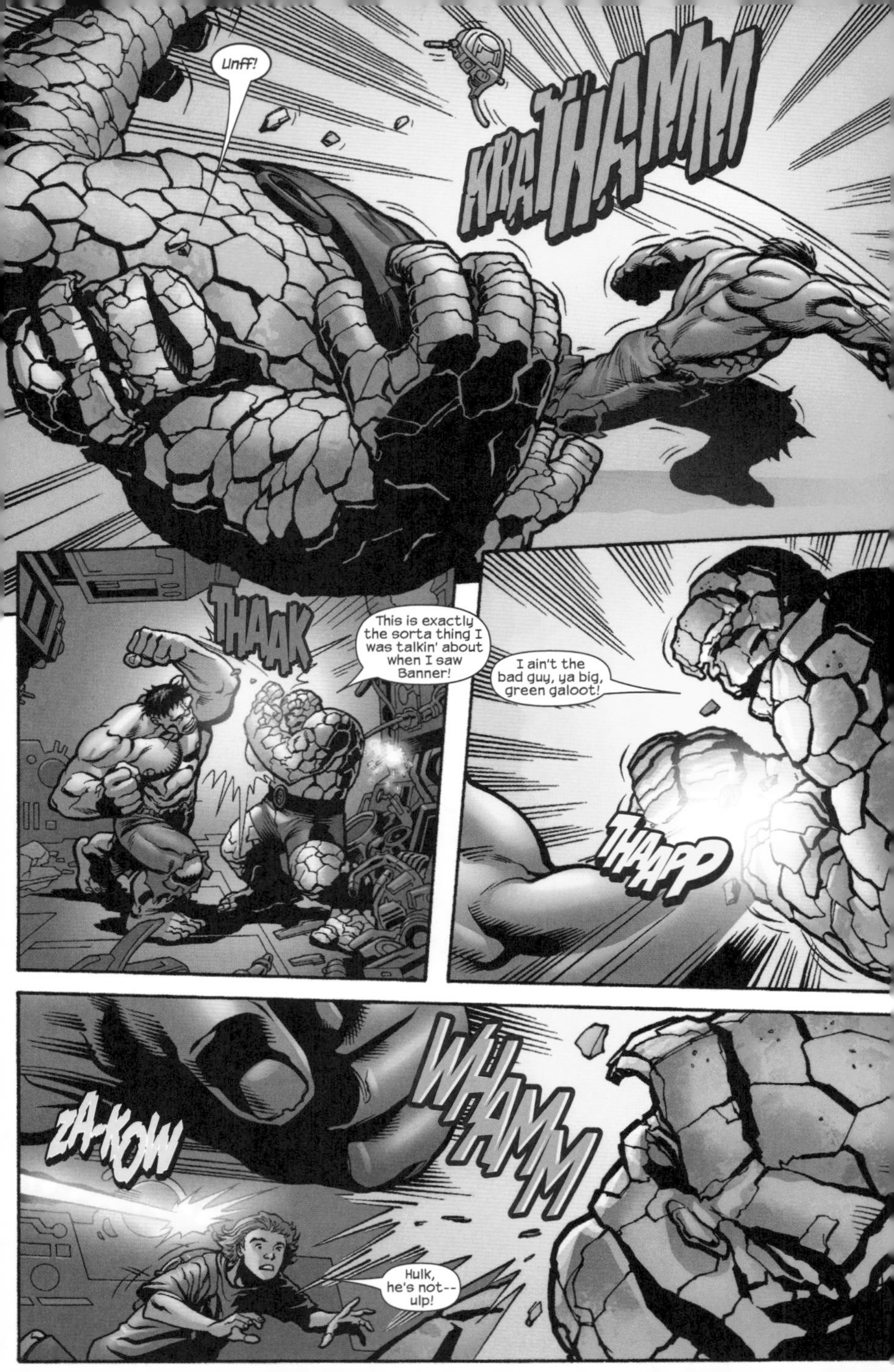
Unff!
KRATHAMM
THAAK
This is exactly the sorta thing I was talkin' about when I saw Banner!
I ain't the bad guy, ya big, green galoot!
THAAPP
ZA-KOW
WHAMM
Hulk, he's not-- ulp!

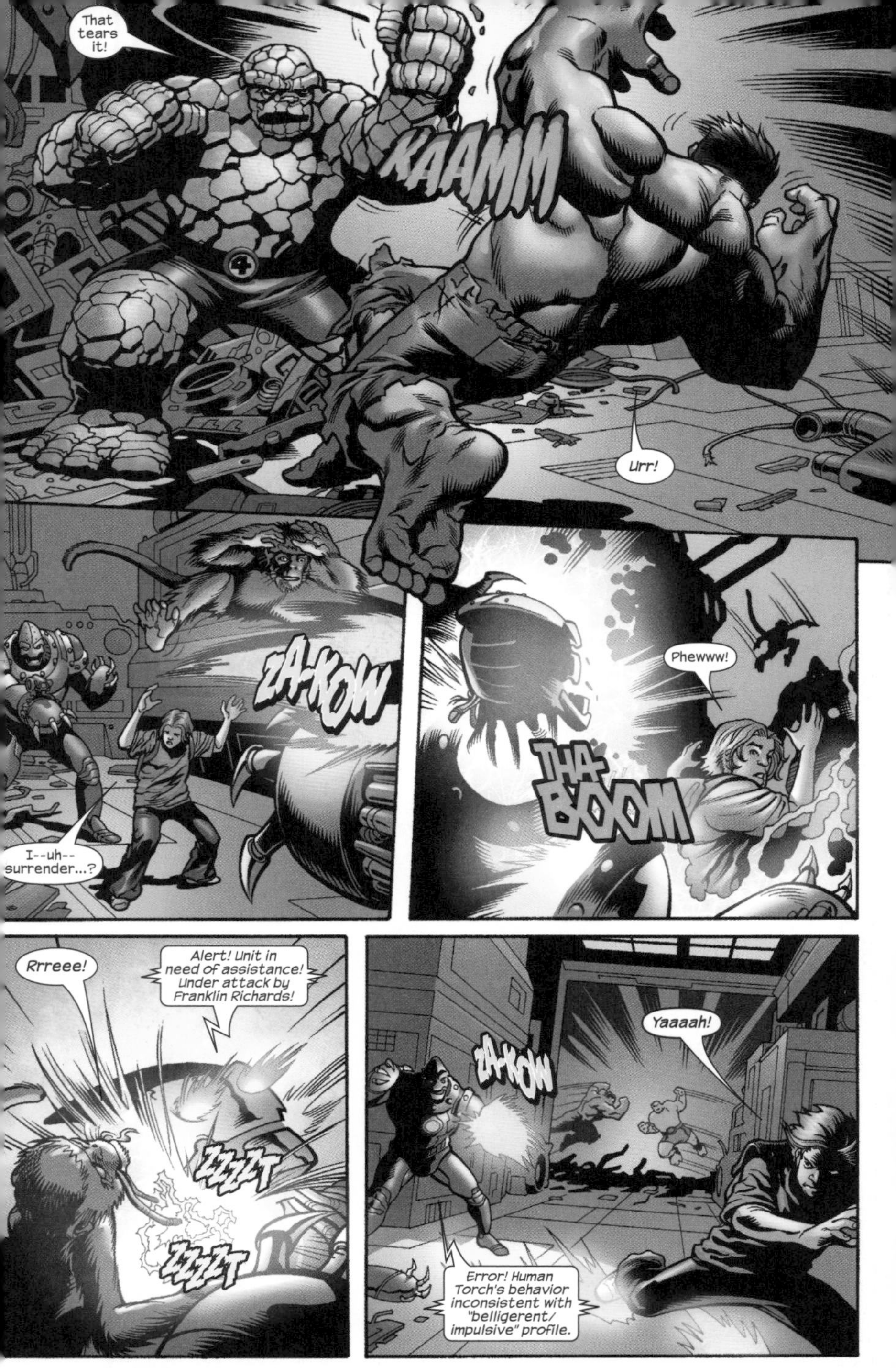
That tears it!
KAAMM
Urr!
ZA-KOW
I--uh-- surrender...?
Phewww!
THA-BOOM
Rrreee!
Alert! Unit in need of assistance! Under attack by Franklin Richards!
ZZZZT
ZZZZT
Yaaaah!
ZA-KOW
Error! Human Torch's behavior inconsistent with "belligerent/ impulsive" profile.

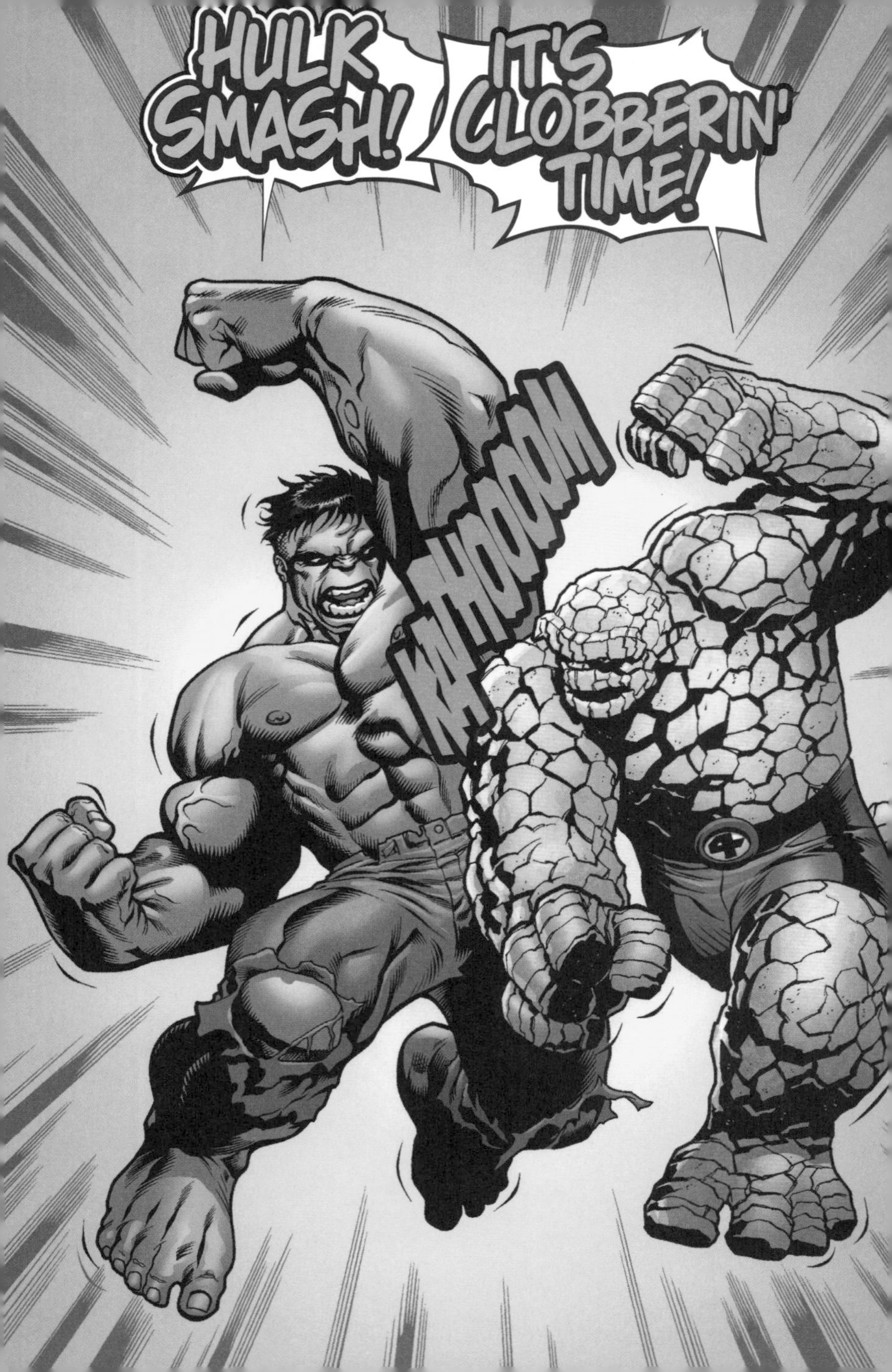
HULK SMASH!
IT'S CLOBBERIN' TIME!
KA-THOOOOM

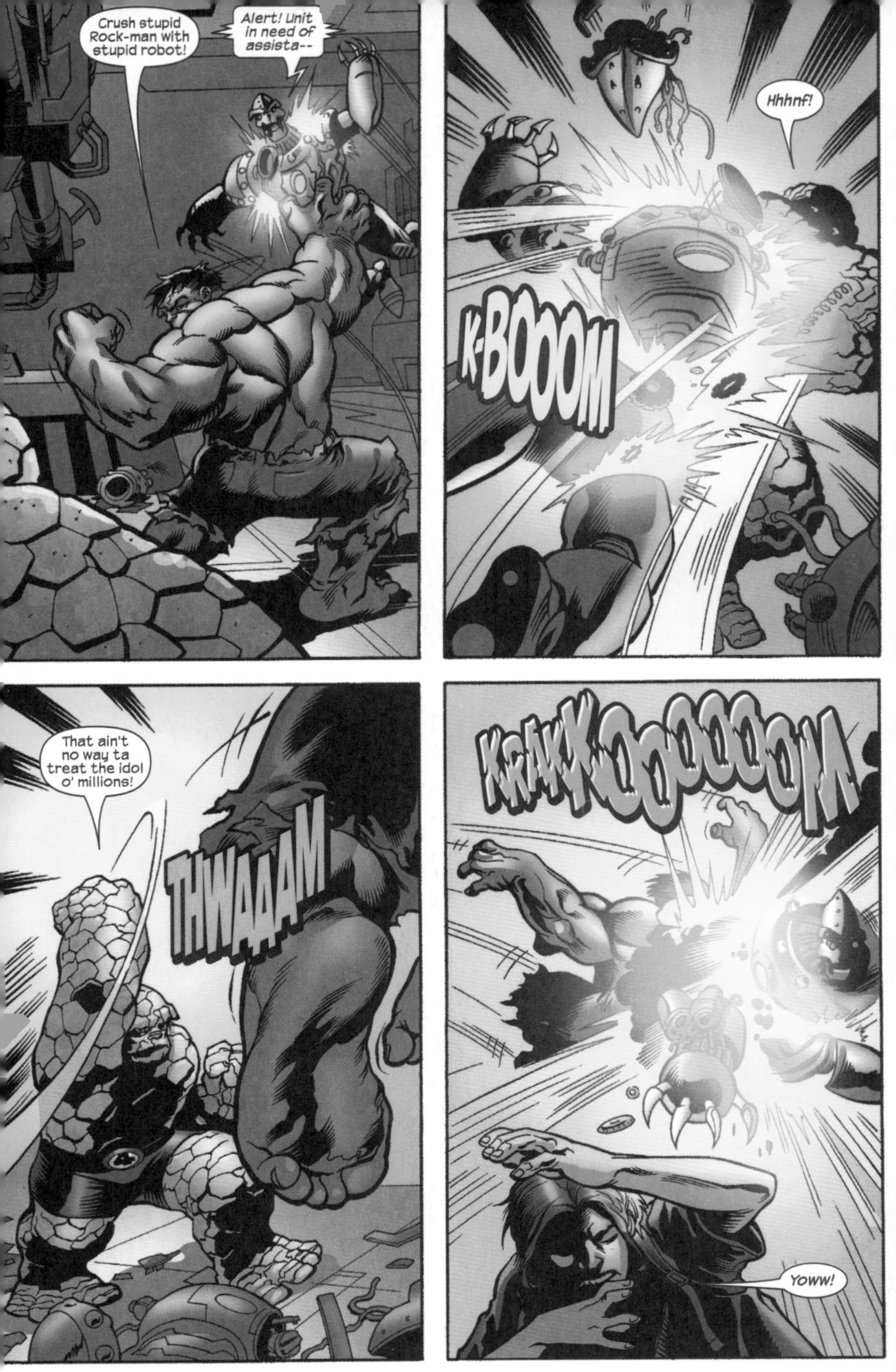
Crush stupid Rock-man with stupid robot!
Alert! Unit in need of assista--
Hhhnf!
K-BOOOM
That ain't no way ta treat the idol o' millions!
THWAAAM
KRAKKOOOOOOM
YOWW!

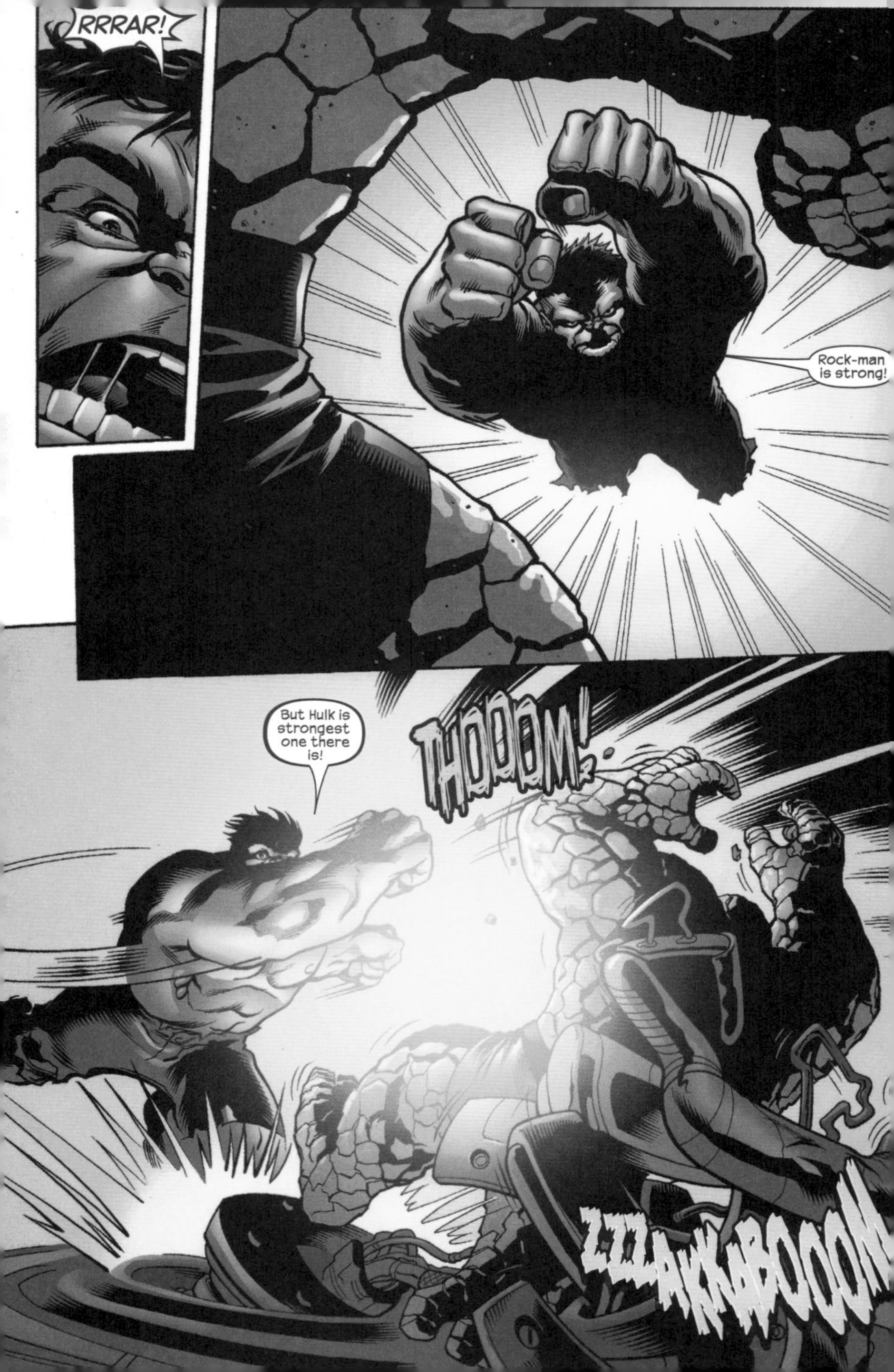
RRRAR!
Rock-man is strong!
But Hulk is strongest one there is!
THOOOM!
ZZZAKKABOOOM

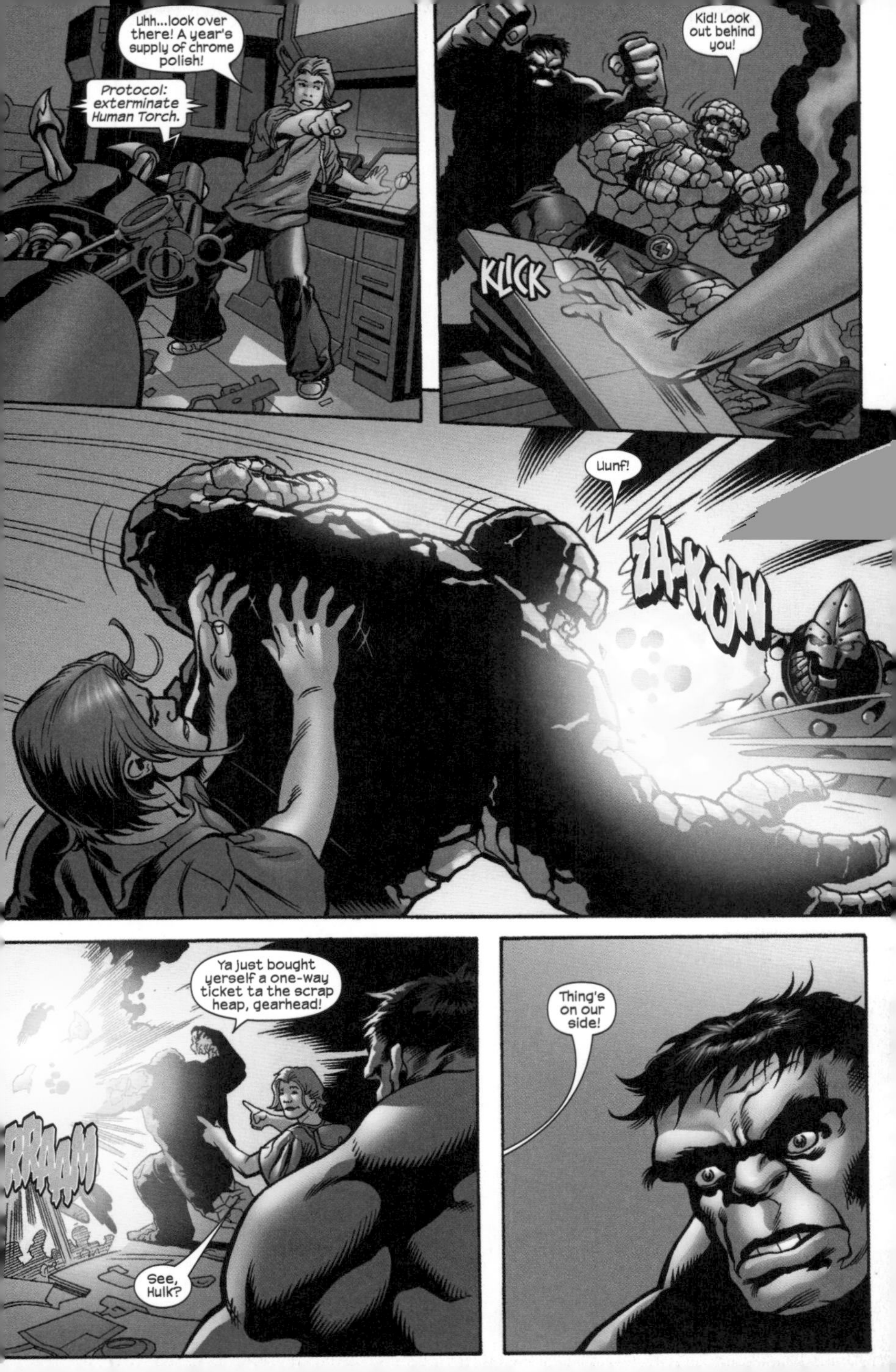
Uhh...look over there! A year's supply of chrome polish!
Protocol: exterminate Human Torch.
Kid! Look out behind you!
KLICK
Uunf!
ZA-KOW
Ya just bought yerself a one-way ticket ta the scrap heap, gearhead!
RRAAM
See, Hulk?
Thing's on our side!

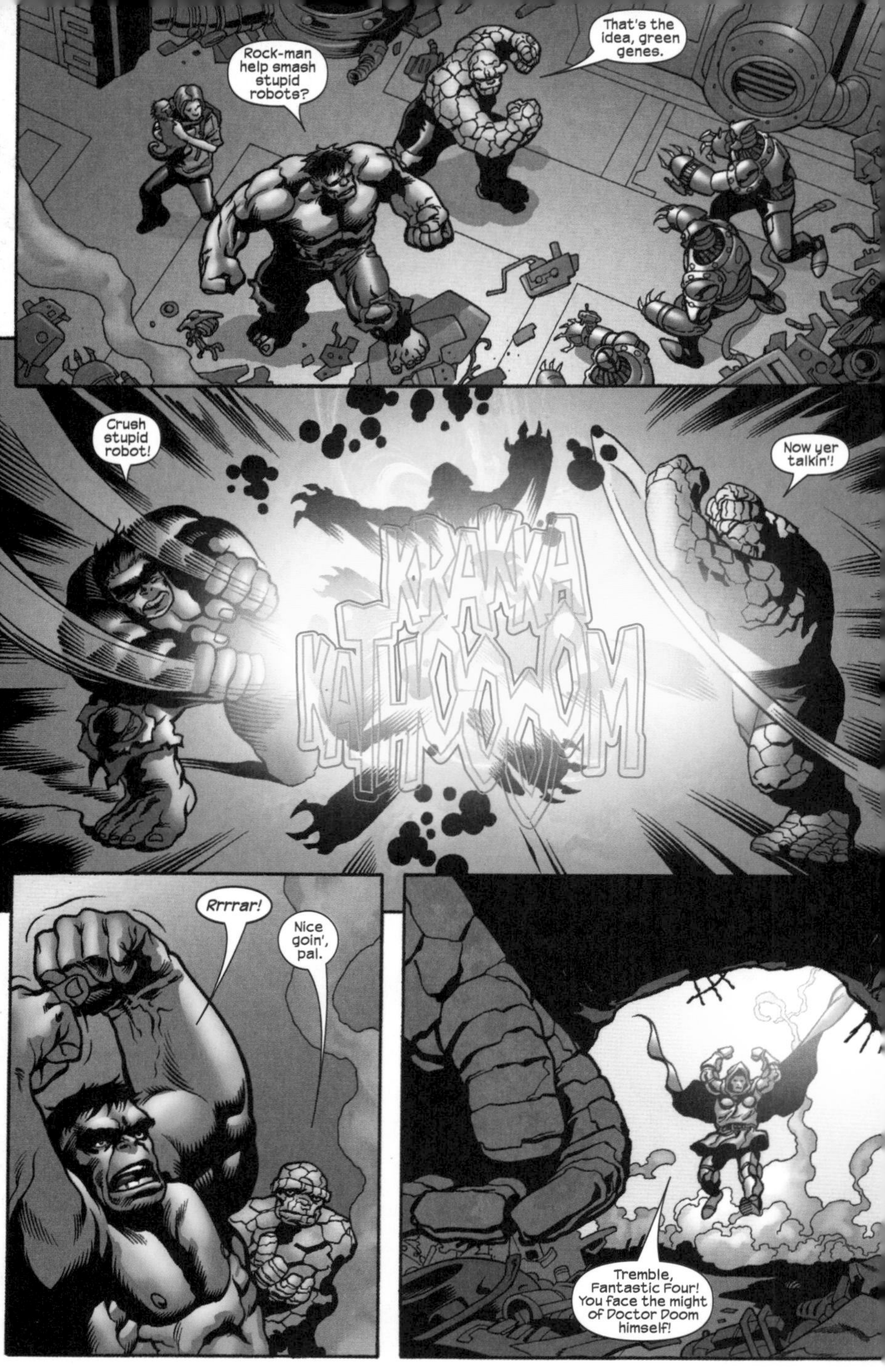

Rock-man help smash stupid robots?
That's the idea, green genes.
Crush stupid robot!
Now yer talkin'!
KRAKKA
Rrrrar!
Nice goin', pal.
Tremble, Fantastic Four! You face the might of Doctor Doom himself!

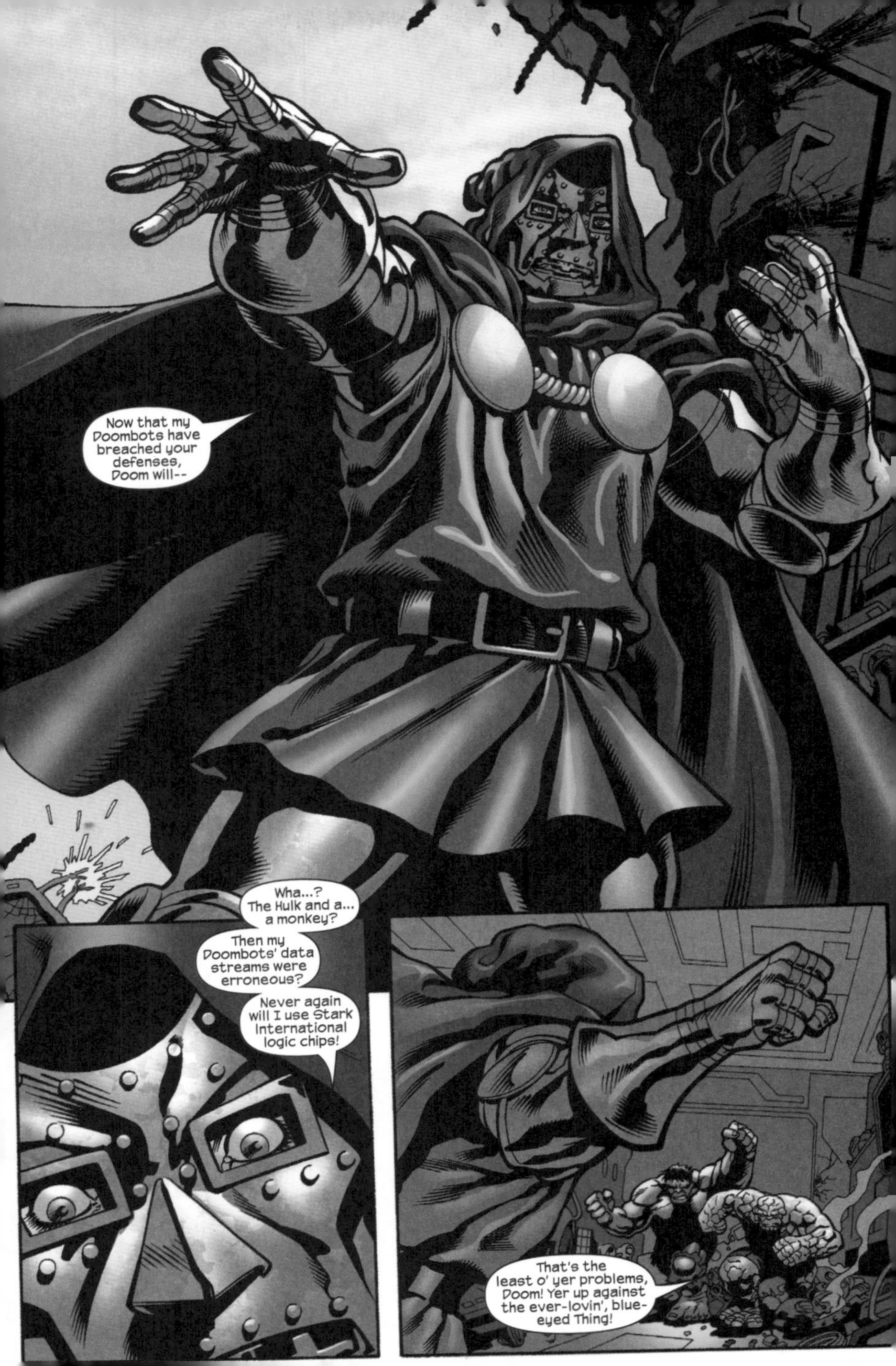
Now that my Doombots have breached your defenses, Doom will--
Wha...? The Hulk and a... a monkey?
Then my Doombots' data streams were erroneous?
Never again will I use Stark International logic chips!
That's the least o' yer problems, Doom! Yer up against the ever-lovin', blue-eyed Thing!

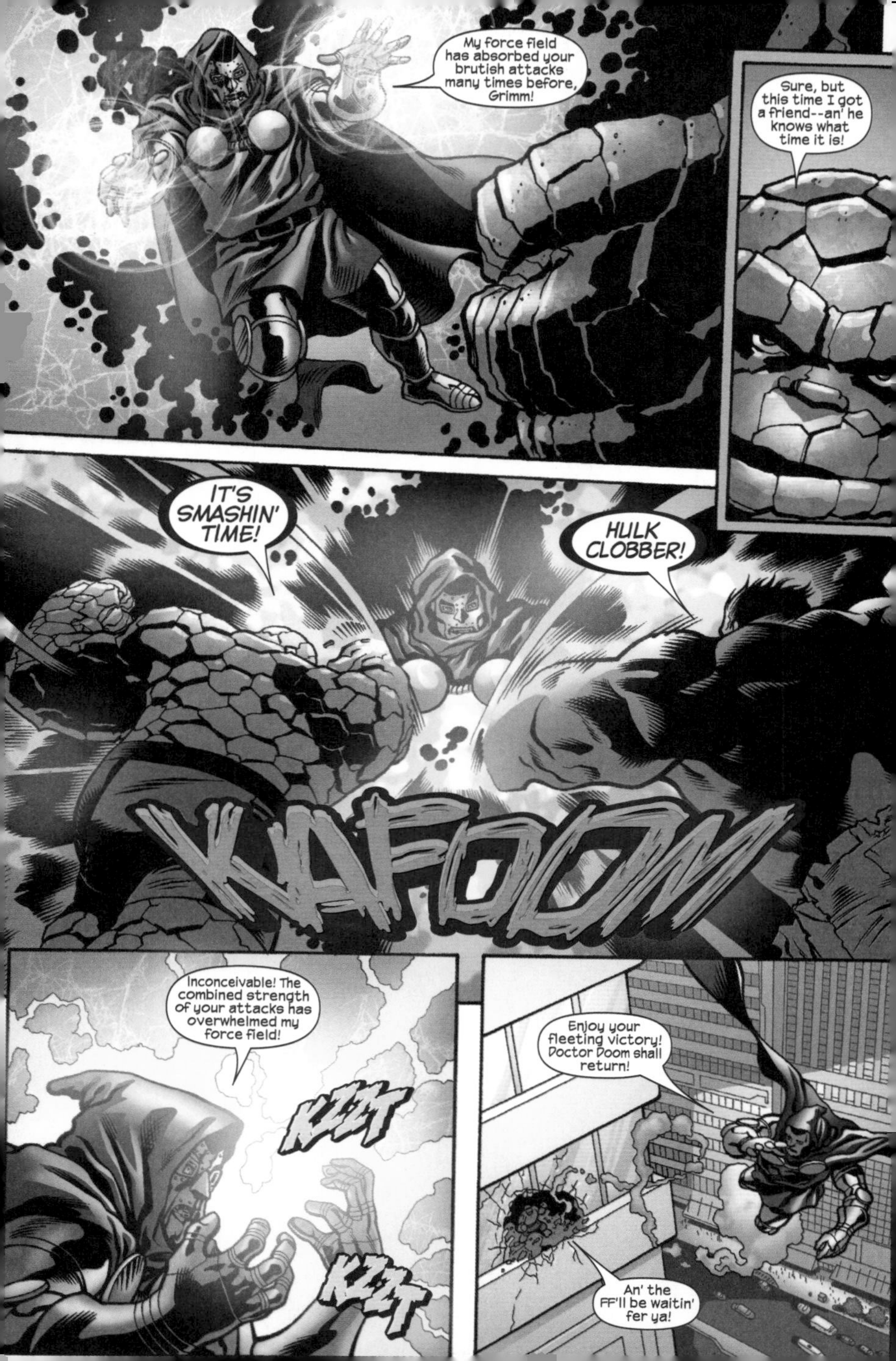

My force field has absorbed your brutish attacks many times before, Grimm!
Sure, but this time I got a friend--an' he knows what time it is!
IT'S SMASHIN' TIME!
HULK CLOBBER!
KAPOOM
Inconceivable! The combined strength of your attacks has overwhelmed my force field!
KZZT
KZZT
Enjoy your fleeting victory! Doctor Doom shall return!
An' the FF'll be waitin' fer ya!

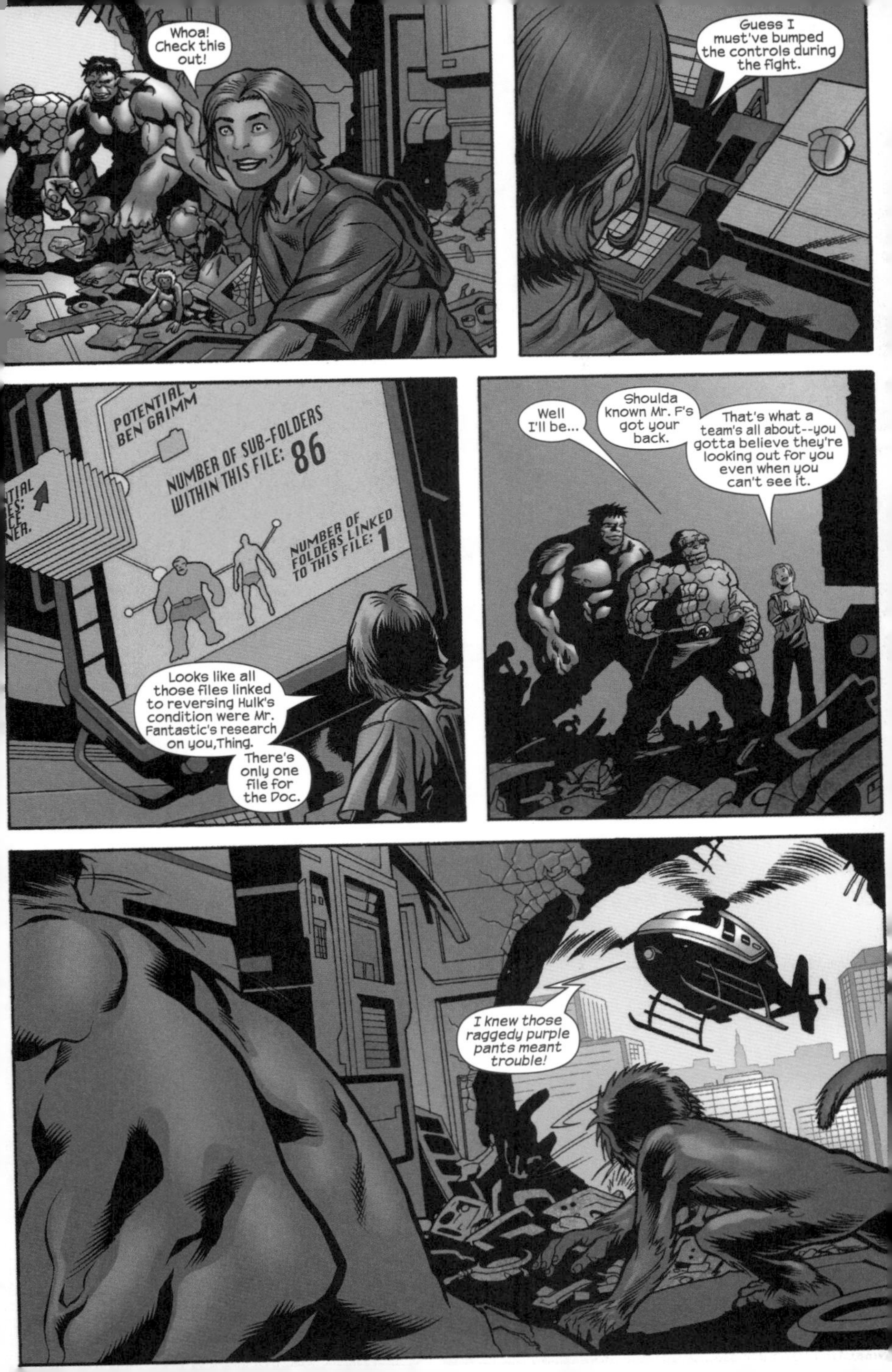
Whoa! Check this out!
Guess I must've bumped the controls during the fight.
POTENTIAL
BEN GRIMM
NUMBER OF SUB-FOLDERS WITHIN THIS FILE: 86
NUMBER OF FOLDERS LINKED TO THIS FILE: 1
Looks like all those files linked to reversing Hulk's condition were Mr. Fantastic's research on you, Thing.
There's only one file for the Doc.
Well I'll be...
Shoulda known Mr. F's got your back.
That's what a team's all about--you gotta believe they're looking out for you even when you can't see it.
I knew those raggedy purple pants meant trouble!

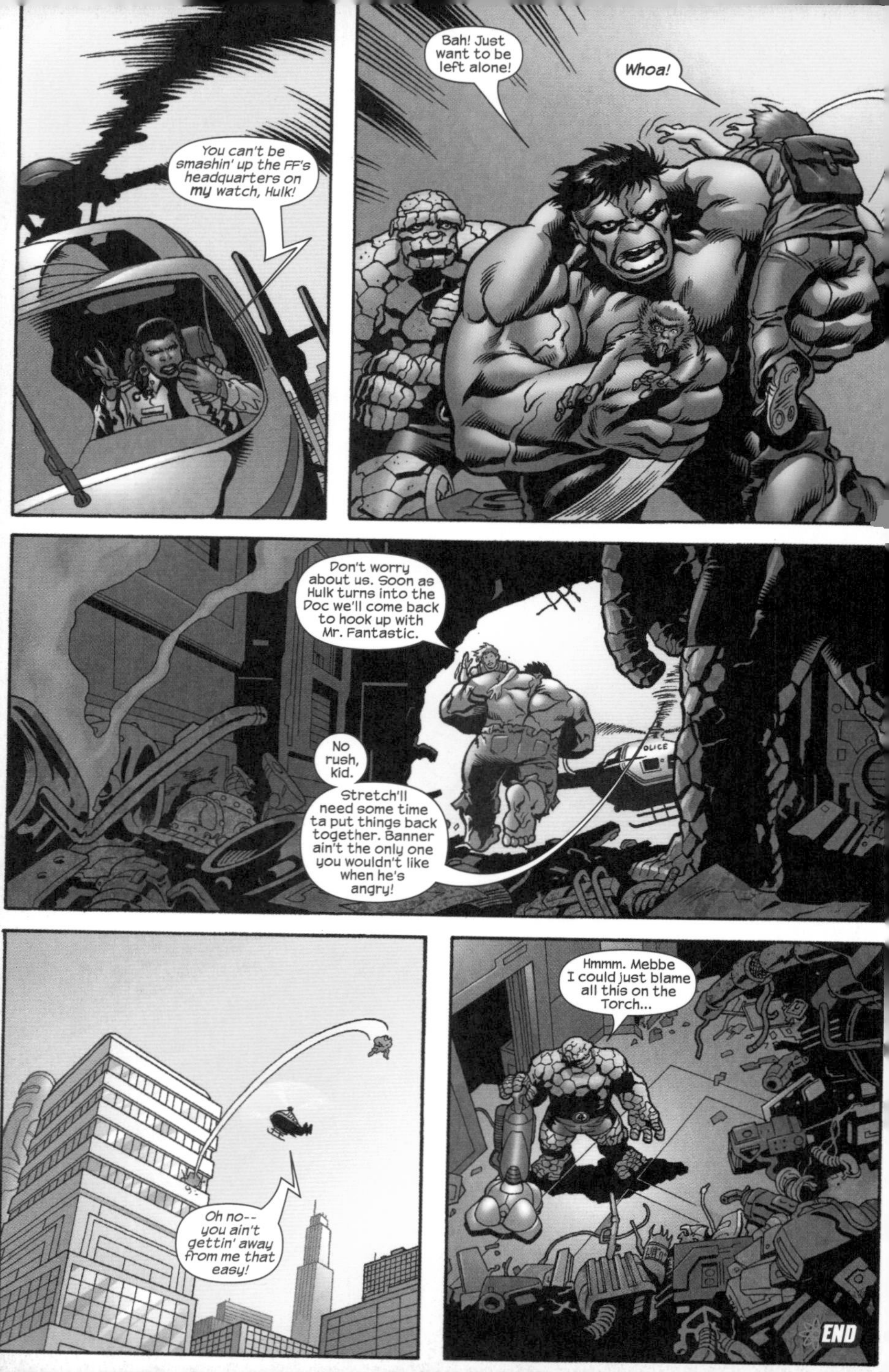
You can't be smashin' up the FF's headquarters on my watch, Hulk!
Bah! Just want to be left alone!
Whoa!
Don't worry about us. Soon as Hulk turns into the Doc we'll come back to hook up with Mr. Fantastic.
No rush, kid.
Stretch'll need some time ta put things back together. Banner ain't the only one you wouldn't like when he's angry!
Oh no-- you ain't gettin' away from me that easy!
Hmmm. Mebbe I could just blame all this on the Torch...
END

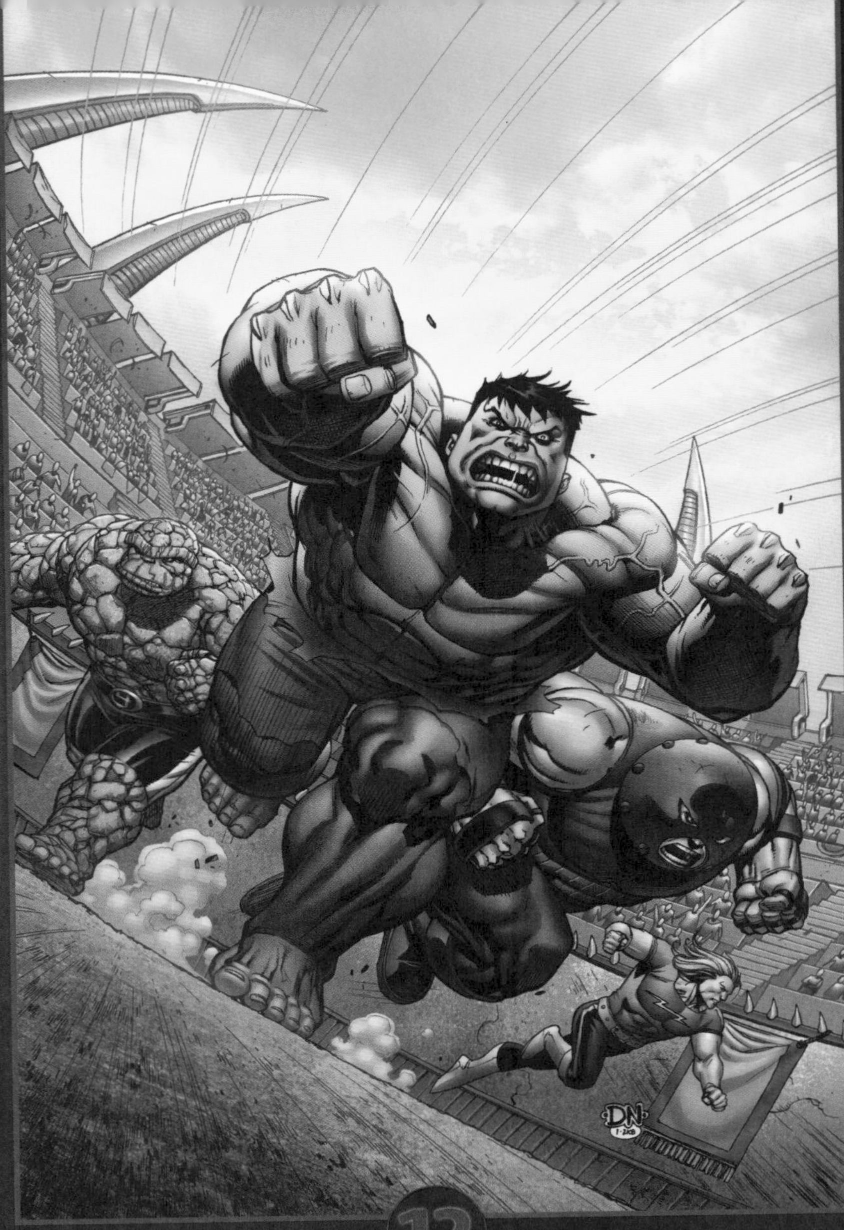

12

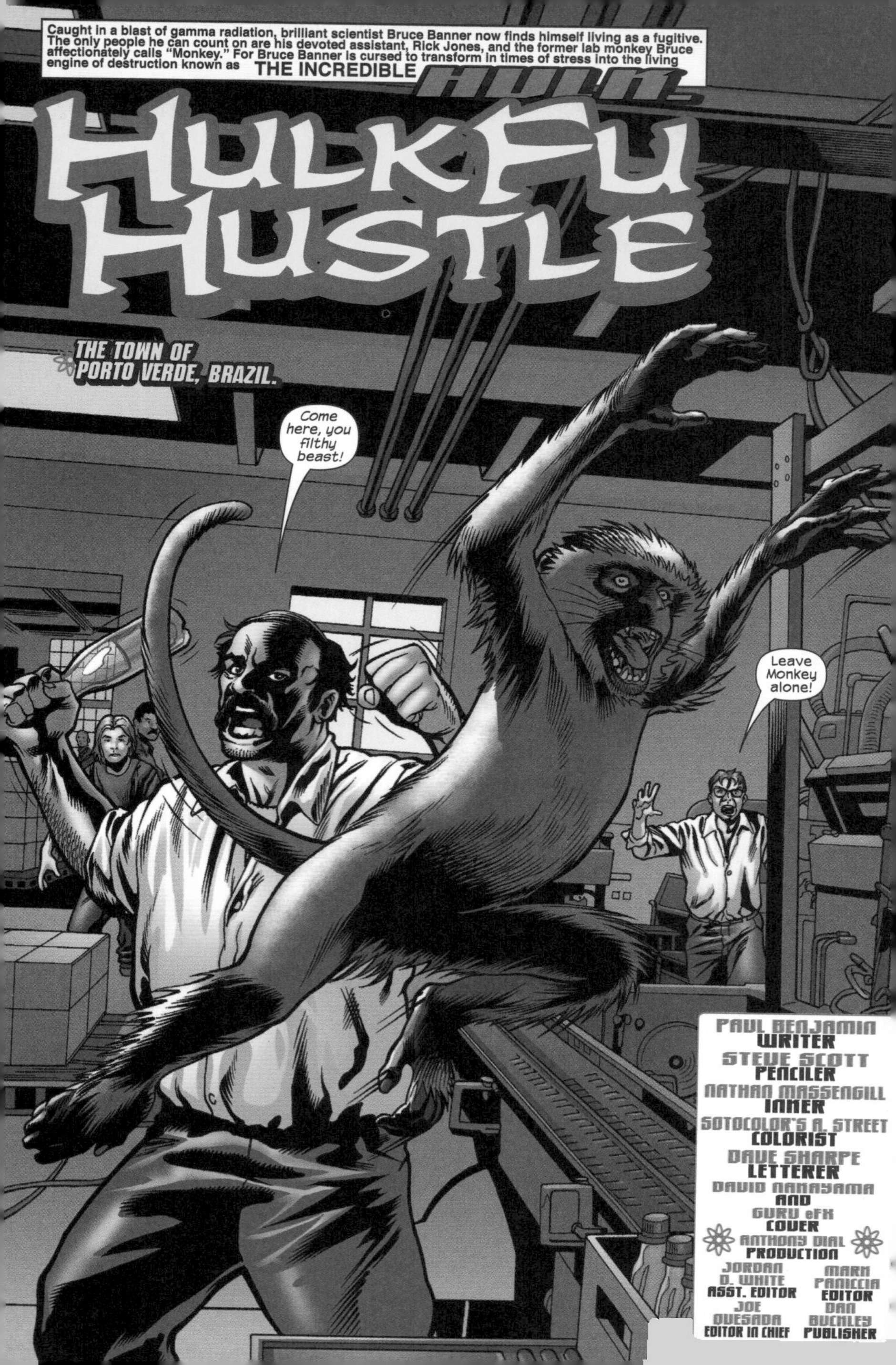

Caught in a blast of gamma radiation, brilliant scientist Bruce Banner now finds himself living as a fugitive. The only people he can count on are his devoted assistant, Rick Jones, and the former lab monkey Bruce affectionately calls "Monkey." For Bruce Banner is cursed to transform in times of stress into the living engine of destruction known as THE INCREDIBLE HULK.
HULK FU HUSTLE
THE TOWN OF PORTO VERDE, BRAZIL.
Come here, you filthy beast!
Leave Monkey alone!
PAUL BENJAMIN WRITER
STEVE SCOTT PENCILER
NATHAN MASSENGILL INKER
SOTOCOLOR'S A. STREET COLORIST
DAVE SHARPE LETTERER
DAVID NAKAYAMA AND GURU eFX COVER
ANTHONY DIAL PRODUCTION
JORDAN D. WHITE ASST. EDITOR
MARK PANICCIA EDITOR
JOE QUESADA EDITOR IN CHIEF
DAN BUCKLEY PUBLISHER

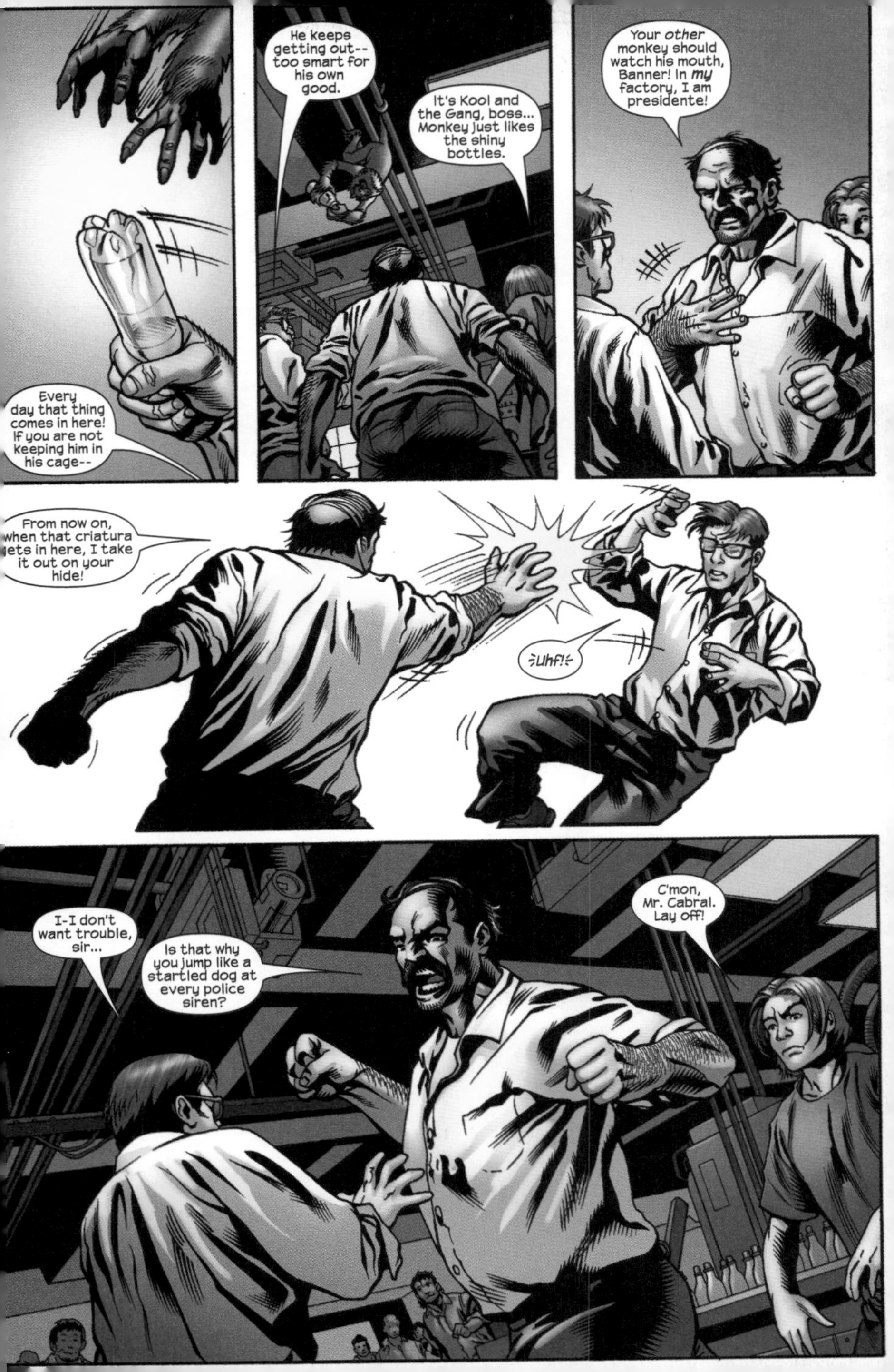

Every day that thing comes in here! If you are not keeping him in his cage--
He keeps getting out-- too smart for his own good.
It's Kool and the Gang, boss... Monkey just likes the shiny bottles.
Your other monkey should watch his mouth, Banner! In my factory, I am presidente!
From now on, when that criatura gets in here, I take it out on your hide!
UHF!
I-I don't want trouble, sir...
Is that why you jump like a startled dog at every police siren?
C'mon, Mr. Cabral. Lay off!

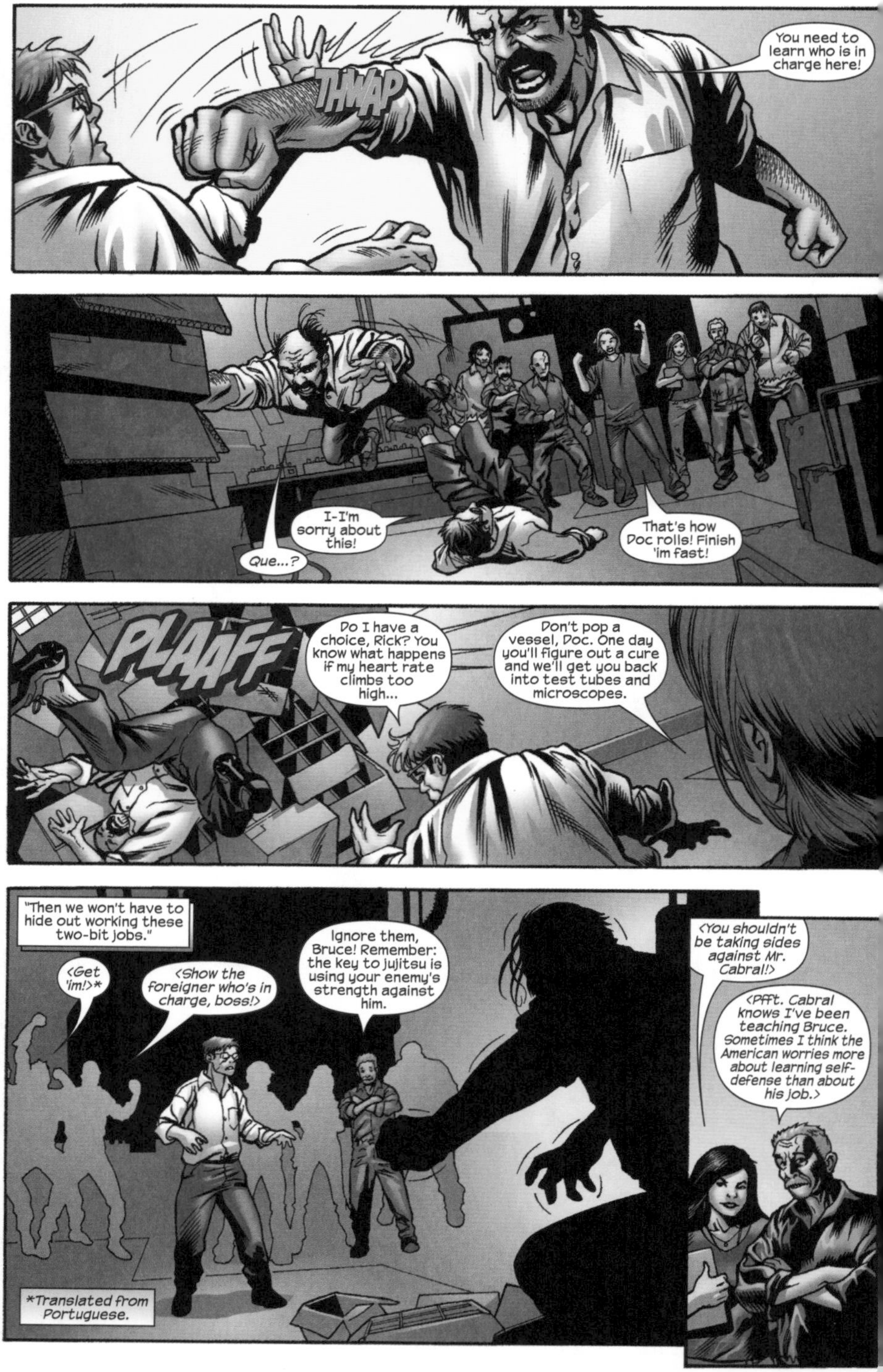
THWAP
You need to learn who is in charge here!
Que...?
I-I'm sorry about this!
That's how Doc rolls! Finish 'im fast!
PLAAFF
Do I have a choice, Rick? You know what happens if my heart rate climbs too high...
Don't pop a vessel, Doc. One day you'll figure out a cure and we'll get you back into test tubes and microscopes.
"Then we won't have to hide out working these two-bit jobs."
<Get 'im!>*
<Show the foreigner who's in charge, boss!>
Ignore them, Bruce! Remember: the key to jujitsu is using your enemy's strength against him.
<You shouldn't be taking sides against Mr. Cabral!>
<Pfft. Cabral knows I've been teaching Bruce. Sometimes I think the American worries more about learning self-defense than about his job.>
*Translated from Portuguese.

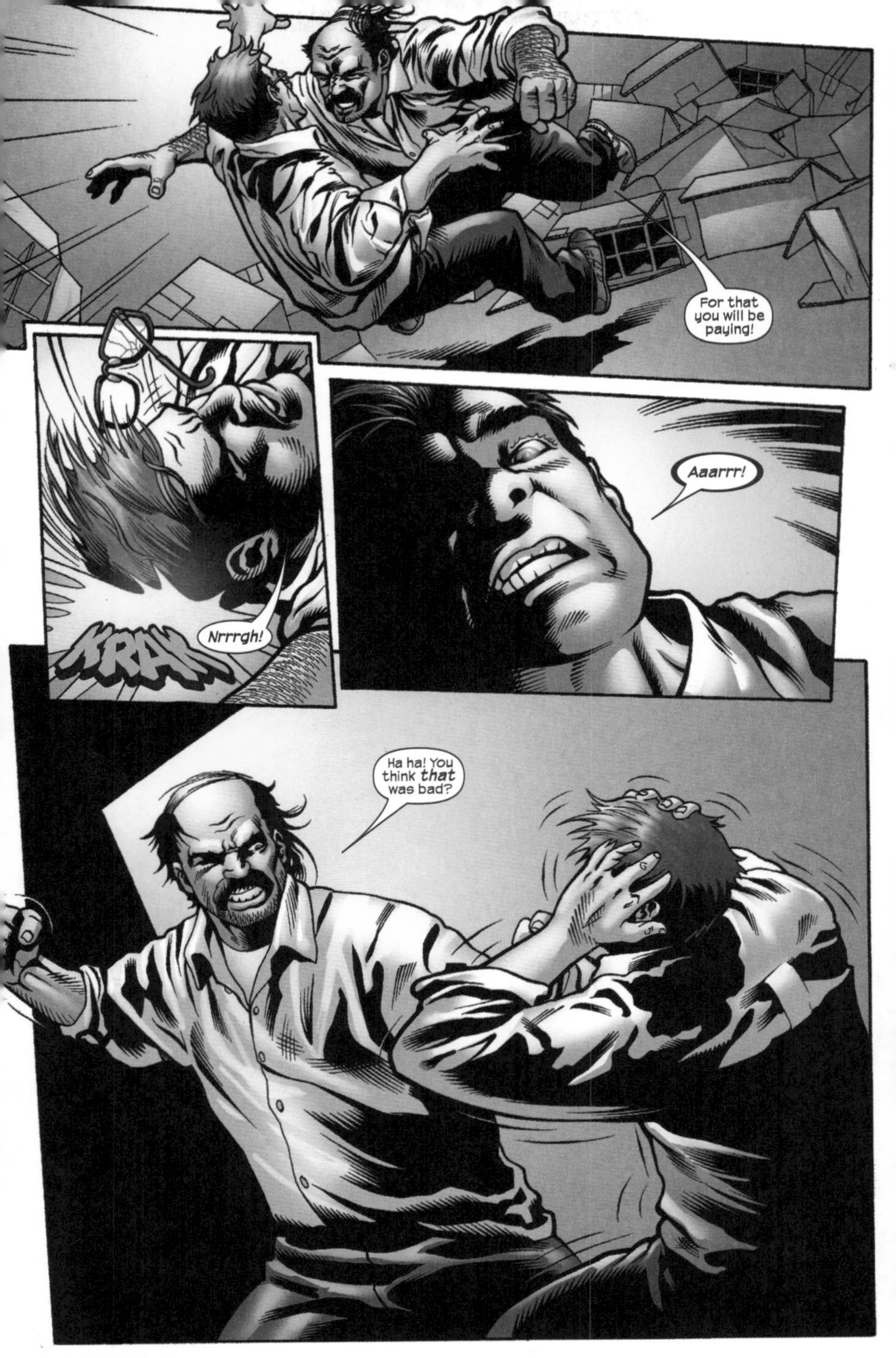
For that you will be paying!
KRAK
Nrrrgh!
Aaarrr!
Ha ha! You think that was bad?

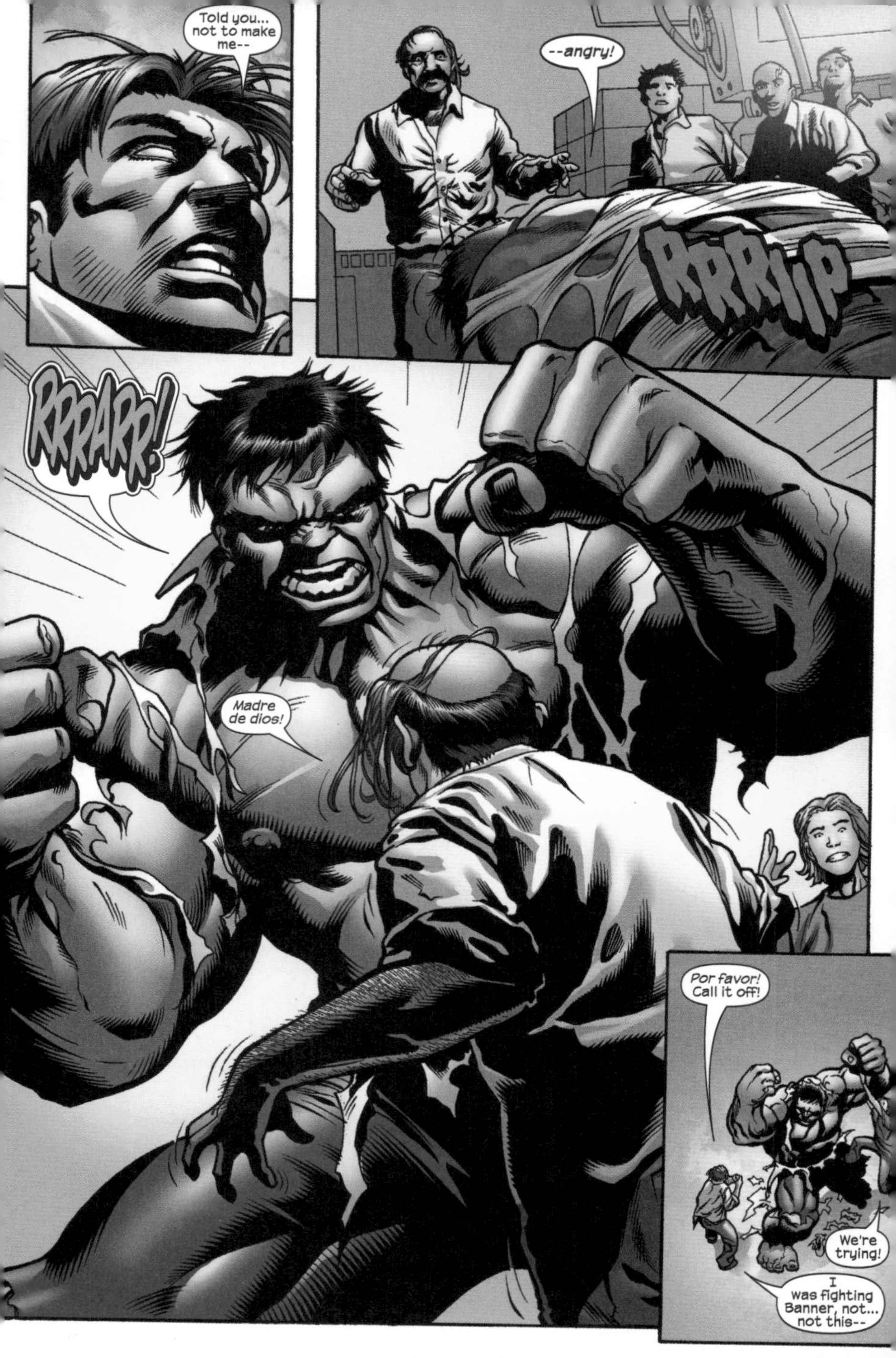
Told you... not to make me--
--angry!
RRRRIIP
RRRARR!
Madre de dios!
Por favor! Call it off!
We're trying!
I was fighting Banner, not... not this--

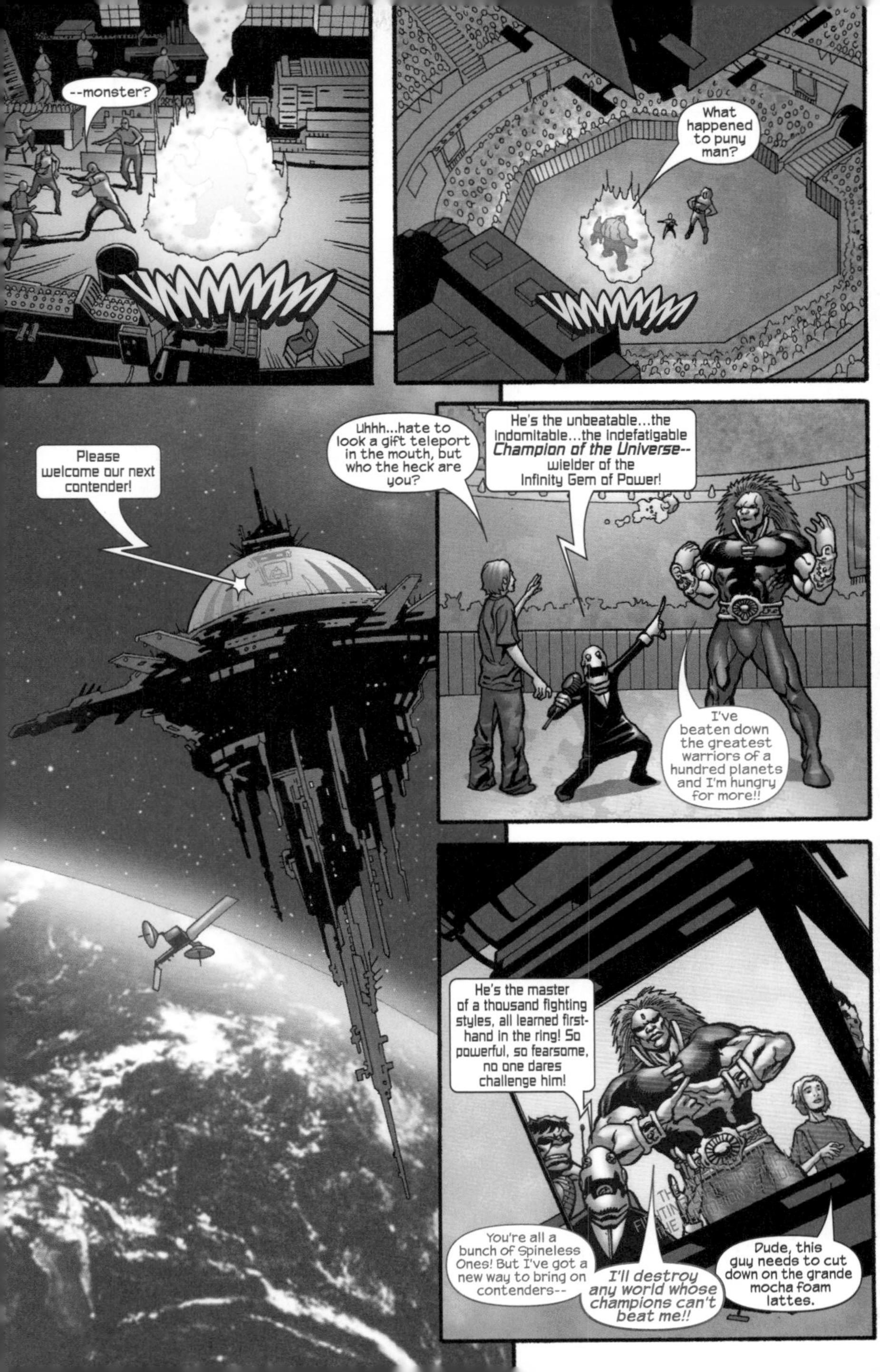
--monster?
What happened to puny man?
Please welcome our next contender!
Uhhh...hate to look a gift teleport in the mouth, but who the heck are you?
He's the unbeatable...the indomitable...the indefatigable *Champion of the Universe*-- wielder of the Infinity Gem of Power!
I've beaten down the greatest warriors of a hundred planets and I'm hungry for more!!
He's the master of a thousand fighting styles, all learned first-hand in the ring! So powerful, so fearsome, no one dares challenge him!
You're all a bunch of Spineless Ones! But I've got a new way to bring on contenders--
I'll destroy any world whose champions can't beat me!!
Dude, this guy needs to cut down on the grande mocha foam lattes.

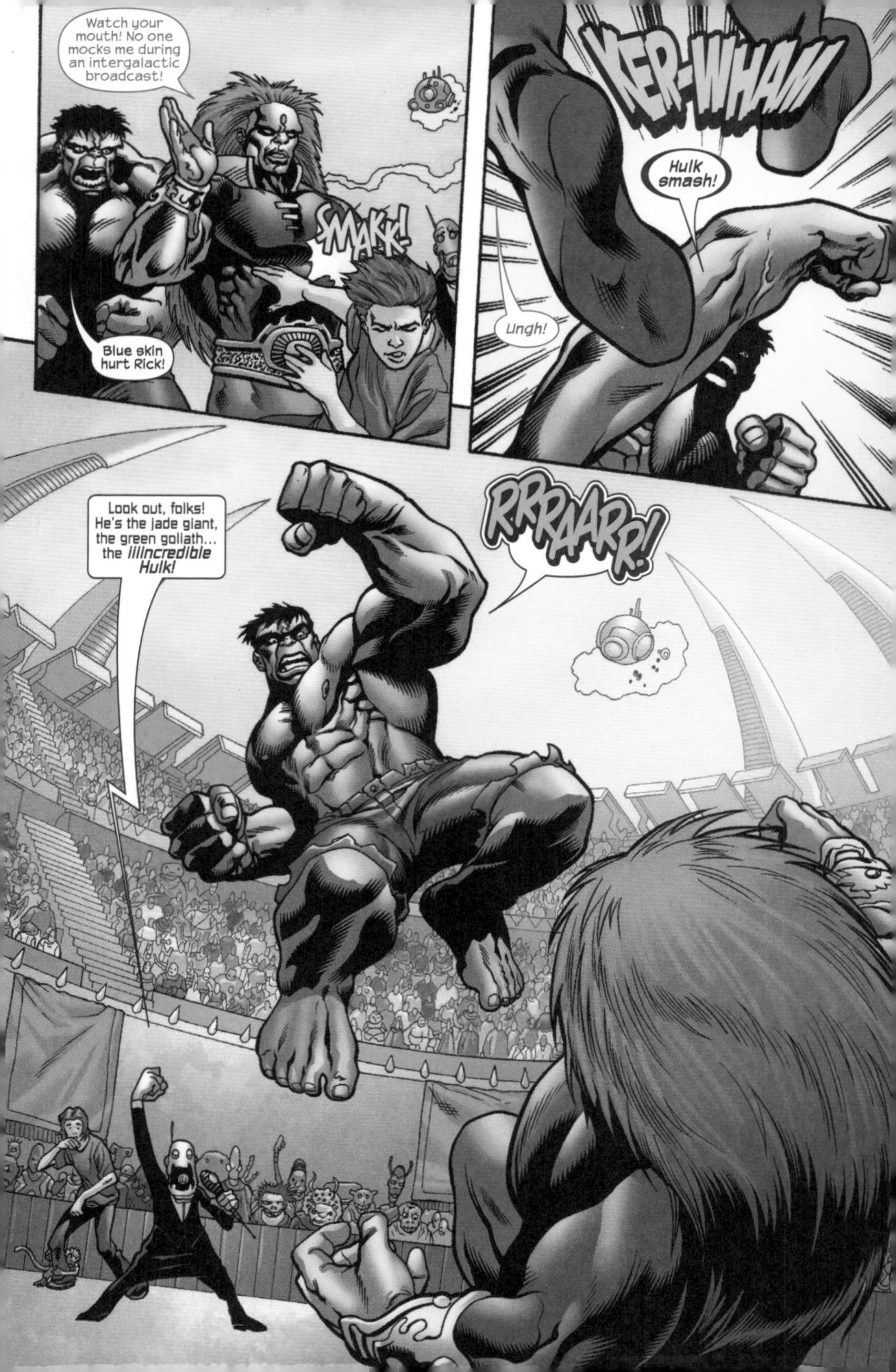
Watch your mouth! No one mocks me during an intergalactic broadcast!
SMAKK!
Blue skin hurt Rick!
KER-WHAM
Hulk smash!
Ungh!
Look out, folks! He's the jade giant, the green goliath... the *Iiiincredible Hulk!*
RRRAARR!

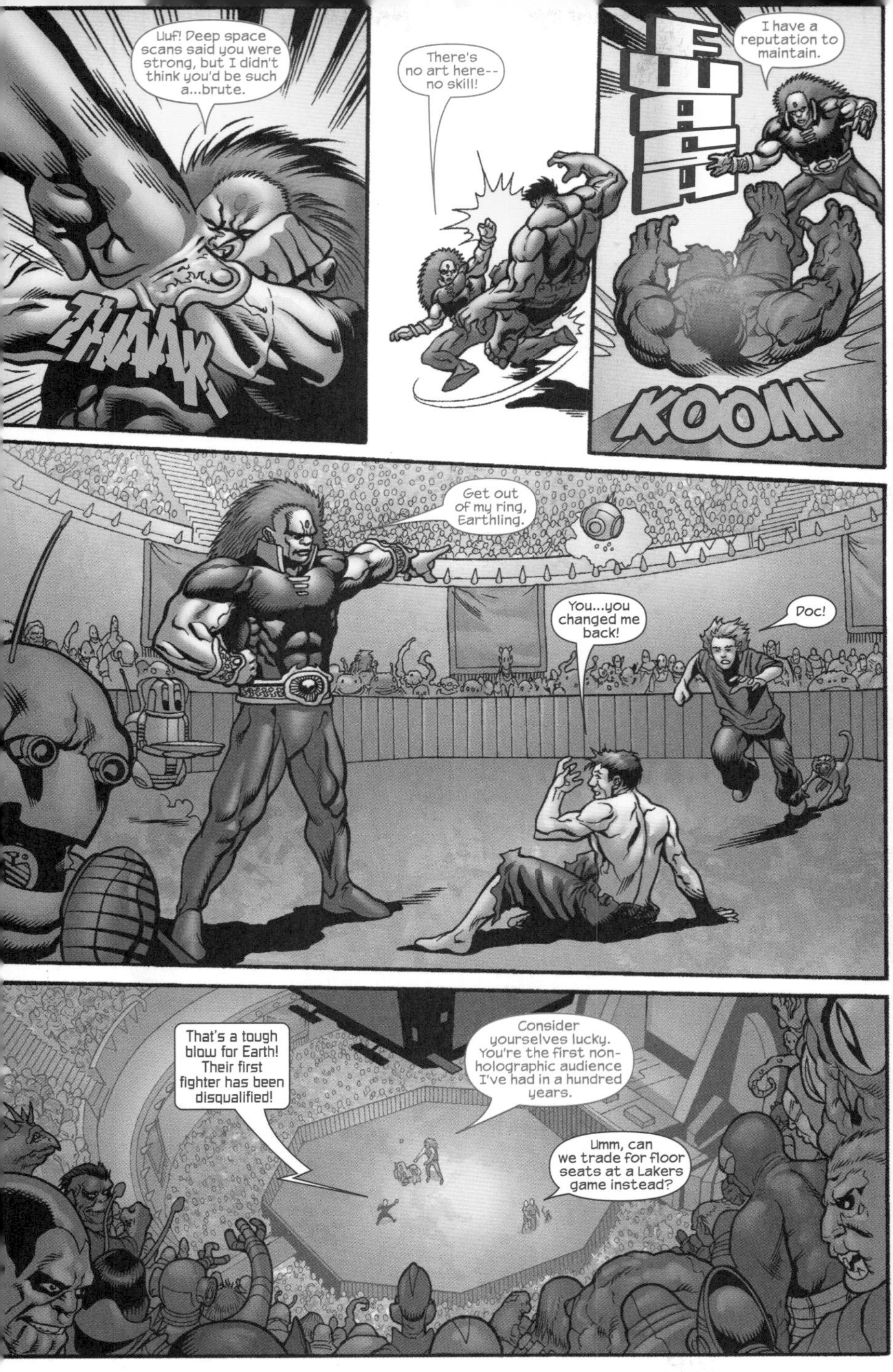
Uuf! Deep space scans said you were strong, but I didn't think you'd be such a...brute.
There's no art here--no skill!
I have a reputation to maintain.
KOOM
Get out of my ring, Earthling.
You...you changed me back!
Doc!
That's a tough blow for Earth! Their first fighter has been disqualified!
Consider yourselves lucky. You're the first non-holographic audience I've had in a hundred years.
Umm, can we trade for floor seats at a Lakers game instead?

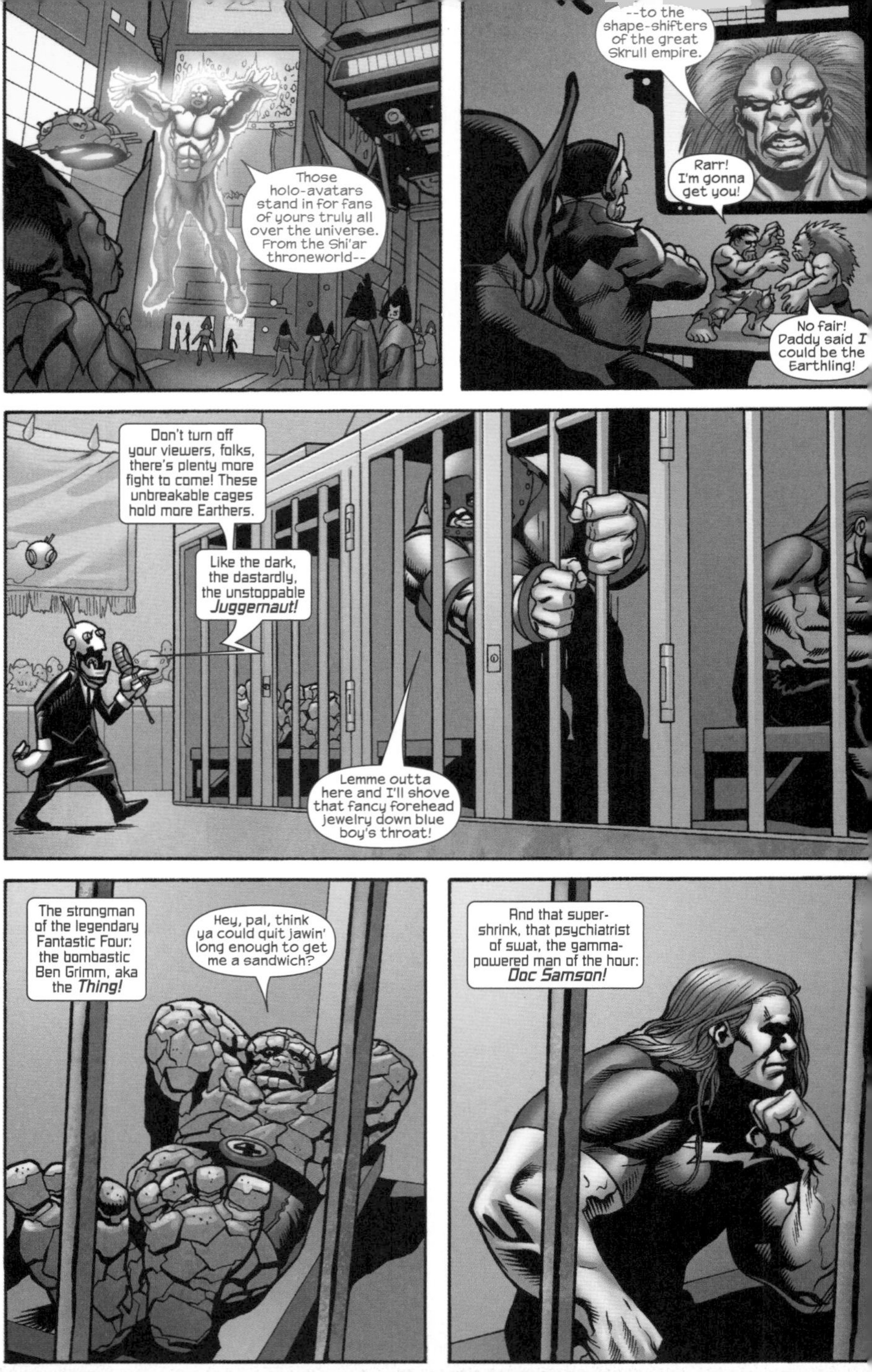

Those holo-avatars stand in for fans of yours truly all over the universe. From the Shi'ar throneworld--
--to the shape-shifters of the great Skrull empire.
Rarr! I'm gonna get you!
No fair! Daddy said I could be the Earthling!
Don't turn off your viewers, folks, there's plenty more fight to come! These unbreakable cages hold more Earthers.
Like the dark, the dastardly, the unstoppable Juggernaut!
Lemme outta here and I'll shove that fancy forehead jewelry down blue boy's throat!
The strongman of the legendary Fantastic Four: the bombastic Ben Grimm, aka the Thing!
Hey, pal, think ya could quit jawin' long enough to get me a sandwich?
And that super-shrink, that psychiatrist of swat, the gamma-powered man of the hour: Doc Samson!

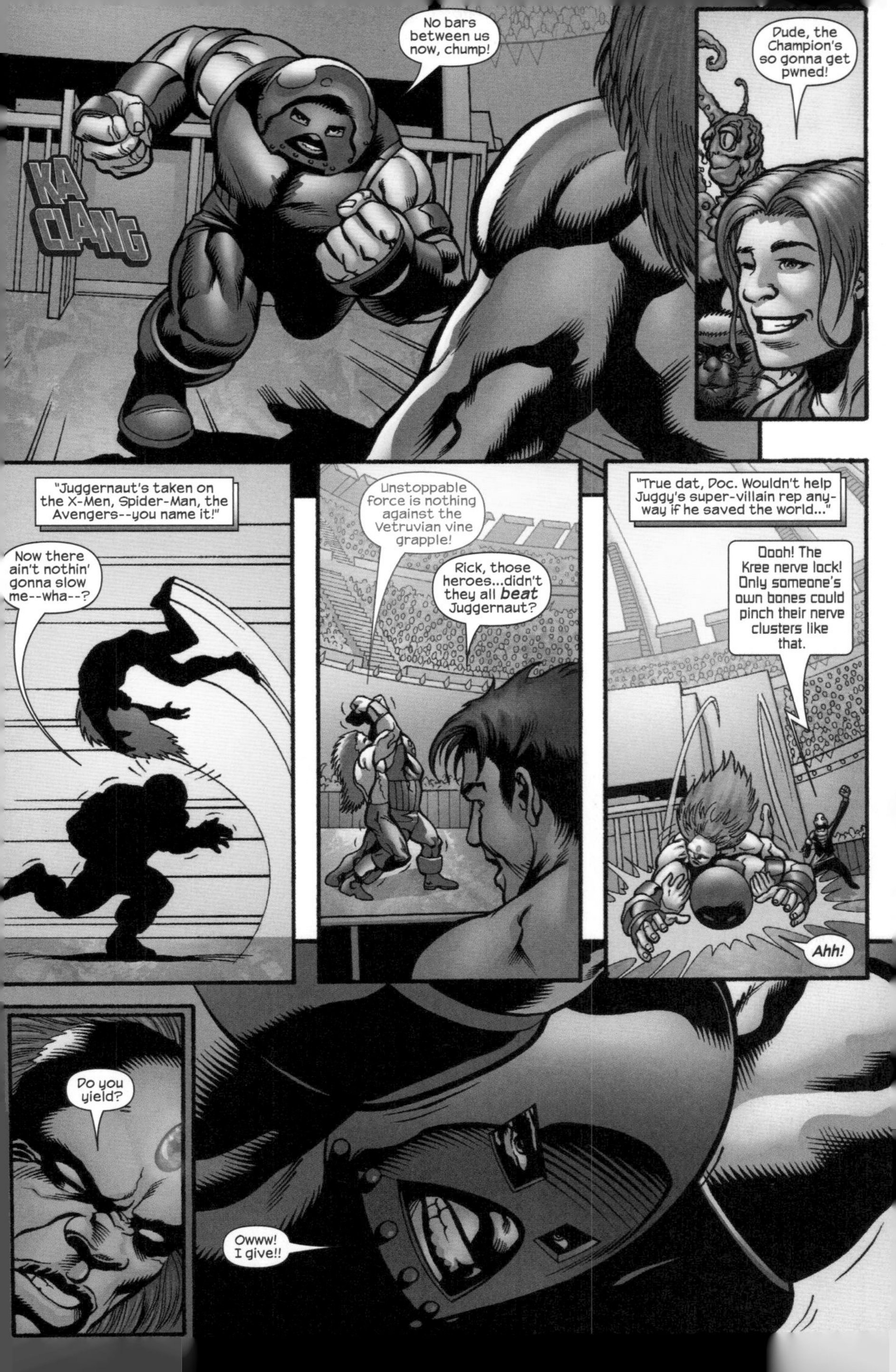
No bars between us now, chump!
KA CLANG
Dude, the Champion's so gonna get pwned!
"Juggernaut's taken on the X-Men, Spider-Man, the Avengers--you name it!"
Now there ain't nothin' gonna slow me--wha--?
Unstoppable force is nothing against the Vetruvian vine grapple!
Rick, those heroes...didn't they all *beat* Juggernaut?
"True dat, Doc. Wouldn't help Juggy's super-villain rep anyway if he saved the world..."
Oooh! The Kree nerve lock! Only someone's own bones could pinch their nerve clusters like that.
Ahh!
Do you yield?
Owww! I give!!

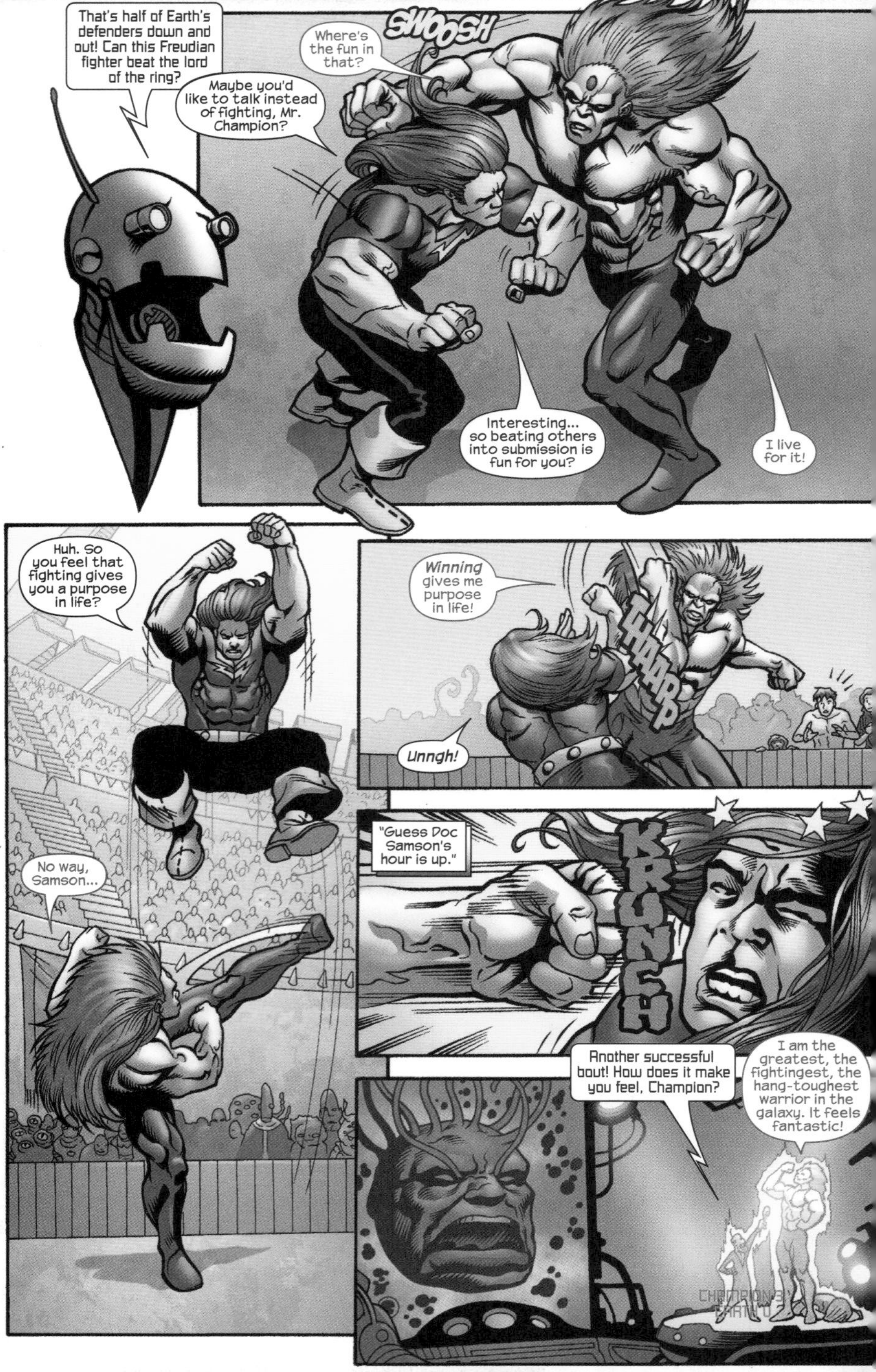
That's half of Earth's defenders down and out! Can this Freudian fighter beat the lord of the ring?
Maybe you'd like to talk instead of fighting, Mr. Champion?
SWOOSH
Where's the fun in that?
Interesting... so beating others into submission is fun for you?
I live for it!
Huh. So you feel that fighting gives you a purpose in life?
No way, Samson...
Winning gives me purpose in life!
THAARP
Unngh!
"Guess Doc Samson's hour is up."
KRUNCH
Another successful bout! How does it make you feel, Champion?
I am the greatest, the fightingest, the hang-toughest warrior in the galaxy. It feels fantastic!
CHAMPION 3
EARTH 0

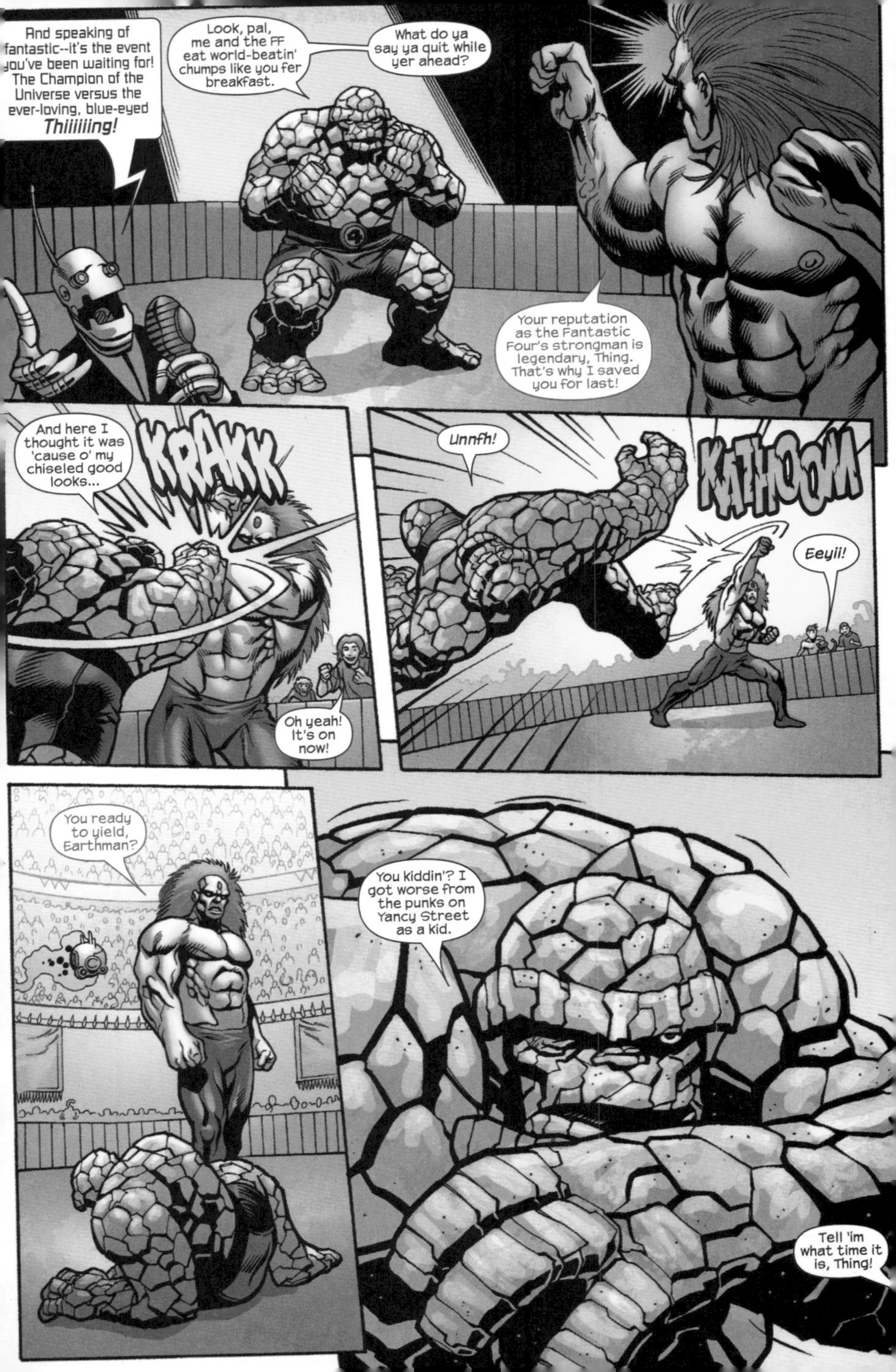
And speaking of fantastic--it's the event you've been waiting for! The Champion of the Universe versus the ever-loving, blue-eyed Thiiiiiing!
Look, pal, me and the FF eat world-beatin' chumps like you fer breakfast.
What do ya say ya quit while yer ahead?
Your reputation as the Fantastic Four's strongman is legendary, Thing. That's why I saved you for last!
And here I thought it was 'cause o' my chiseled good looks...
KRAKK
Oh yeah! It's on now!
Unnfh!
KATHOOOM
Eeyii!
You ready to yield, Earthman?
You kiddin'? I got worse from the punks on Yancy Street as a kid.
Tell 'im what time it is, Thing!

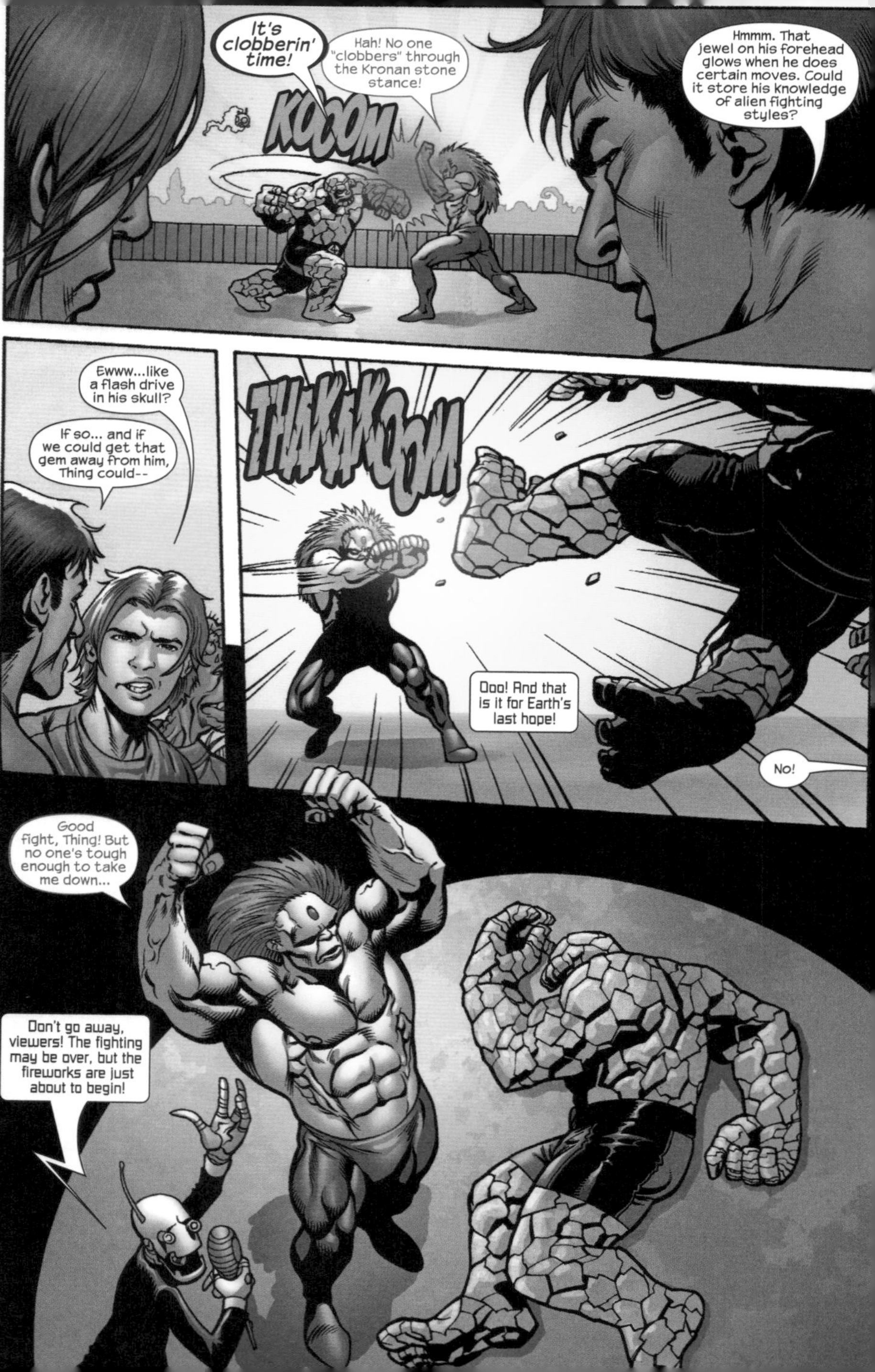

It's clobberin' time!
Hah! No one "clobbers" through the Kronan stone stance!
KOOOM
Hmmm. That jewel on his forehead glows when he does certain moves. Could it store his knowledge of alien fighting styles?
Ewww...like a flash drive in his skull?
If so... and if we could get that gem away from him, Thing could--
THAKAKOOM
Ooo! And that is it for Earth's last hope!
No!
Good fight, Thing! But no one's tough enough to take me down...
Don't go away, viewers! The fighting may be over, but the fireworks are just about to begin!

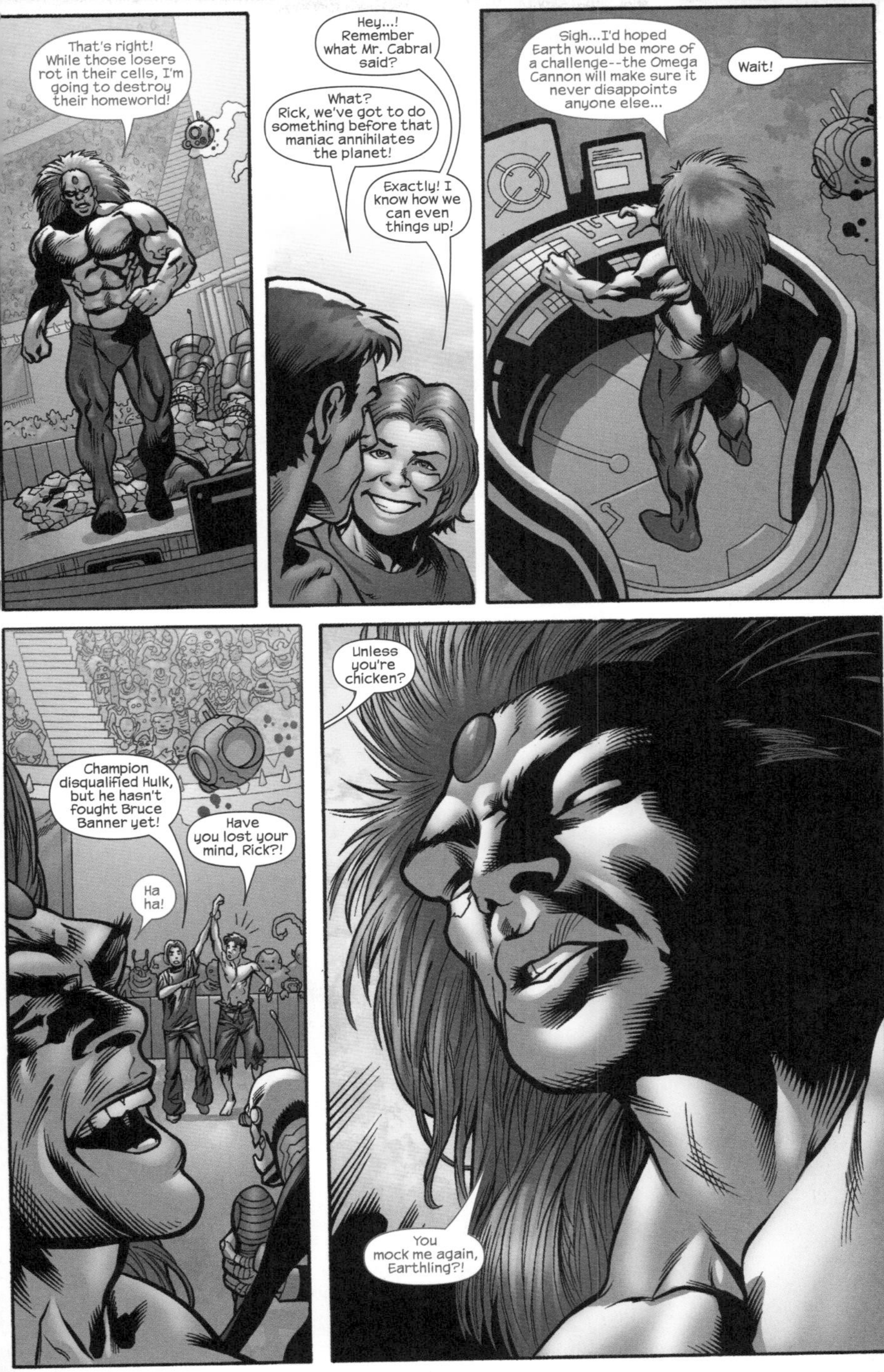
That's right! While those losers rot in their cells, I'm going to destroy their homeworld!
Hey...! Remember what Mr. Cabral said?
What? Rick, we've got to do something before that maniac annihilates the planet!
Exactly! I know how we can even things up!
Sigh...I'd hoped Earth would be more of a challenge--the Omega Cannon will make sure it never disappoints anyone else...
Wait!
Champion disqualified Hulk, but he hasn't fought Bruce Banner yet!
Have you lost your mind, Rick?!
Ha ha!
Unless you're chicken?
You mock me again, Earthling?!

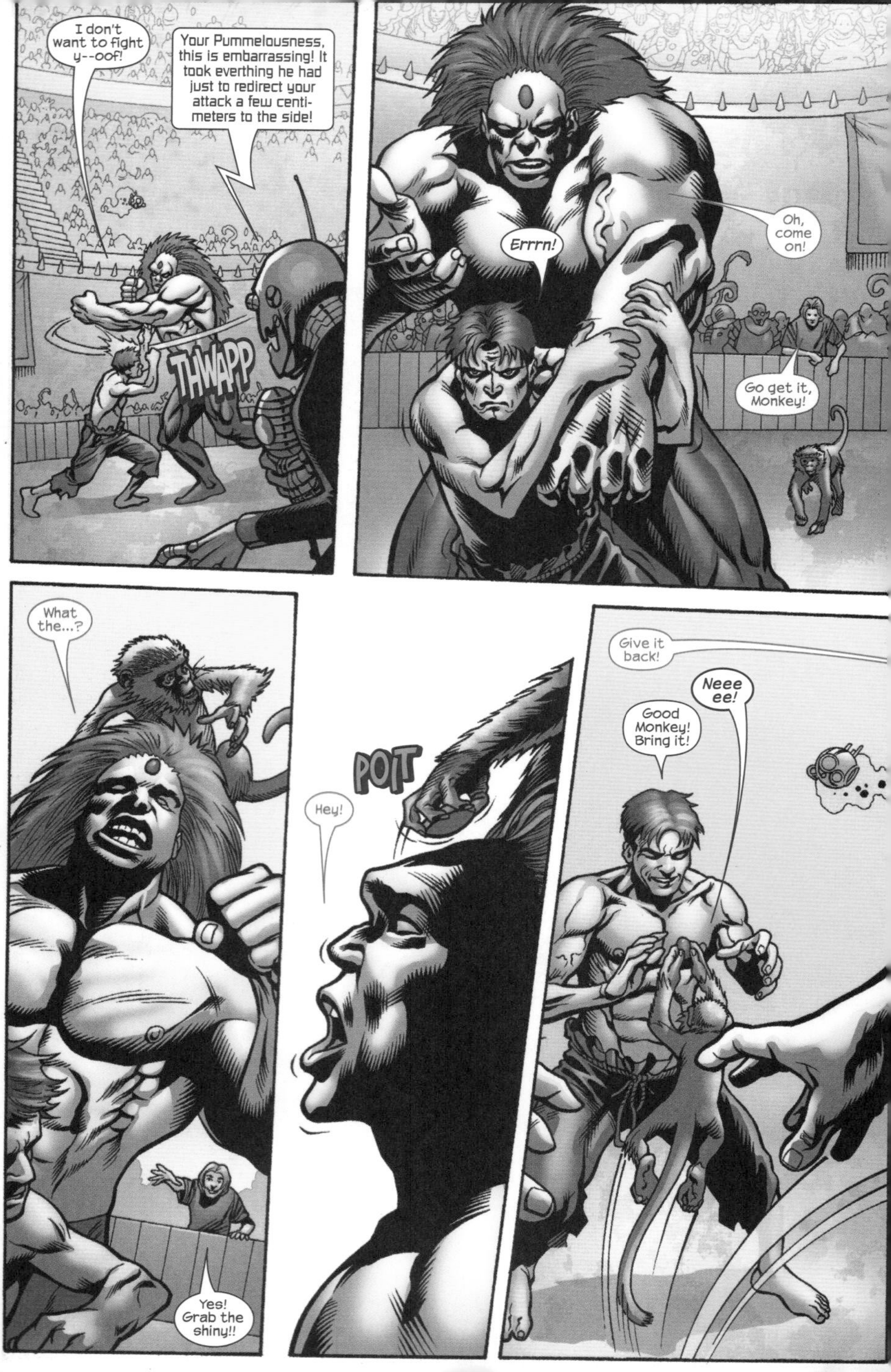

I don't want to fight y--oof!
Your Pummelousness, this is embarrassing! It took everthing he had just to redirect your attack a few centimeters to the side!
THWAPP
Errrn!
Oh, come on!
Go get it, Monkey!
What the...?
Yes! Grab the shiny!!
POIT
Hey!
Give it back!
Neee ee!
Good Monkey! Bring it!

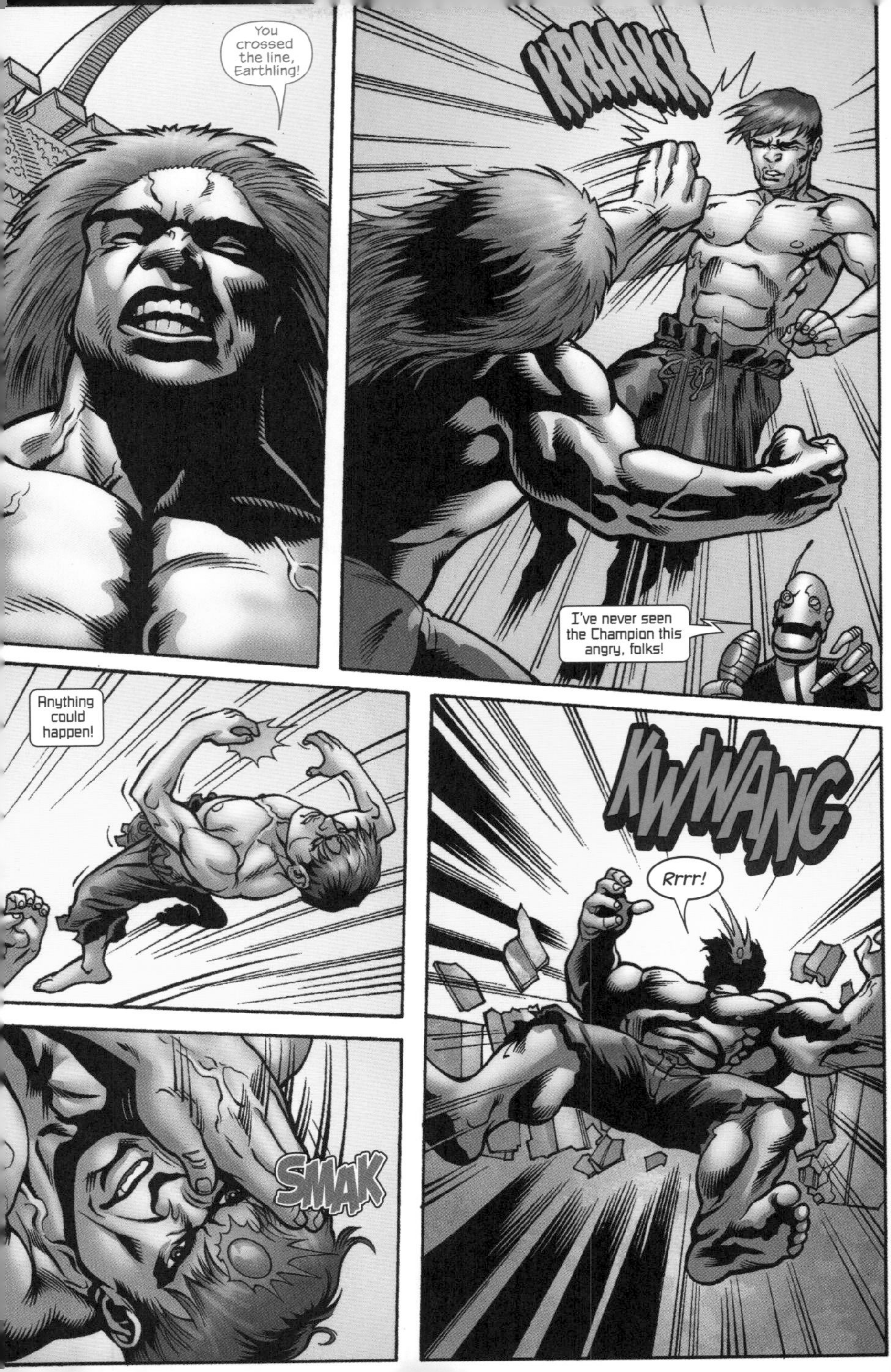
You crossed the line, Earthling!
KRAAKK
I've never seen the Champion this angry, folks!
Anything could happen!
KWWANG
Rrrr!
SMAK

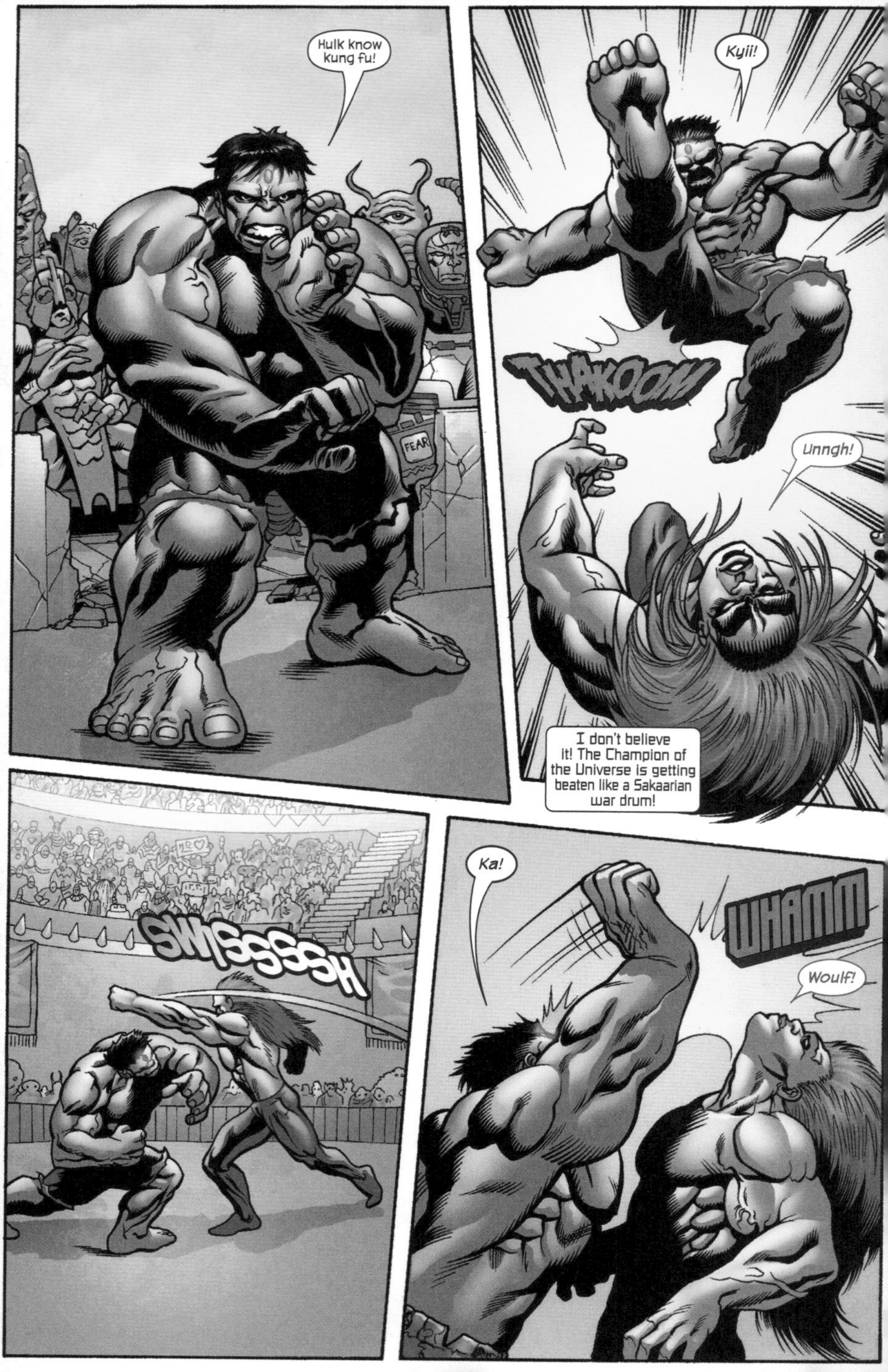
Hulk know kung fu!
Kyii!
THAKOOM
Unngh!
I don't believe it! The Champion of the Universe is getting beaten like a Sakaarian war drum!
SWISSSSH
Ka!
WHAMM
Woulf!

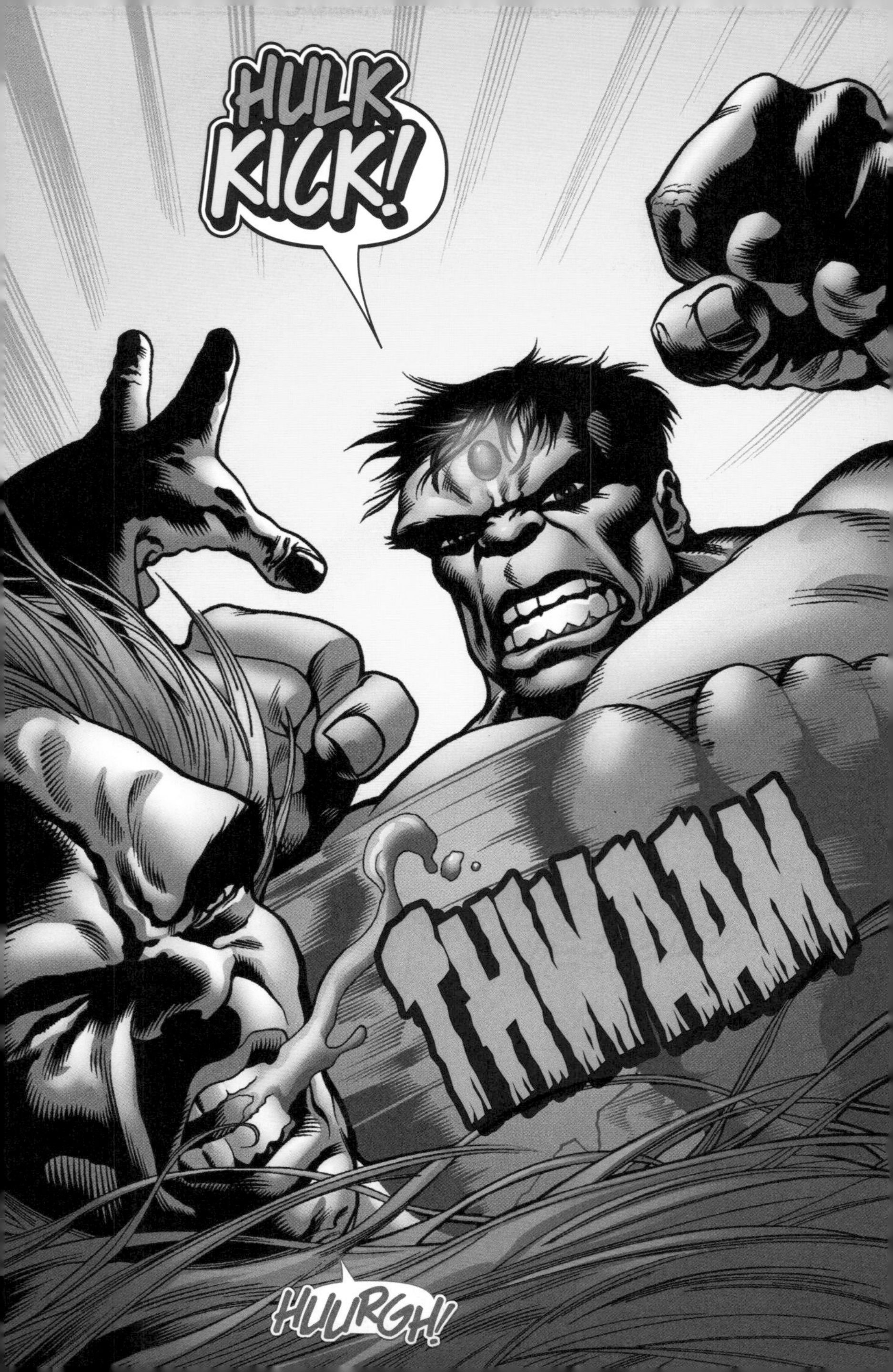
HULK KICK!
THWOOM
HUURGH!

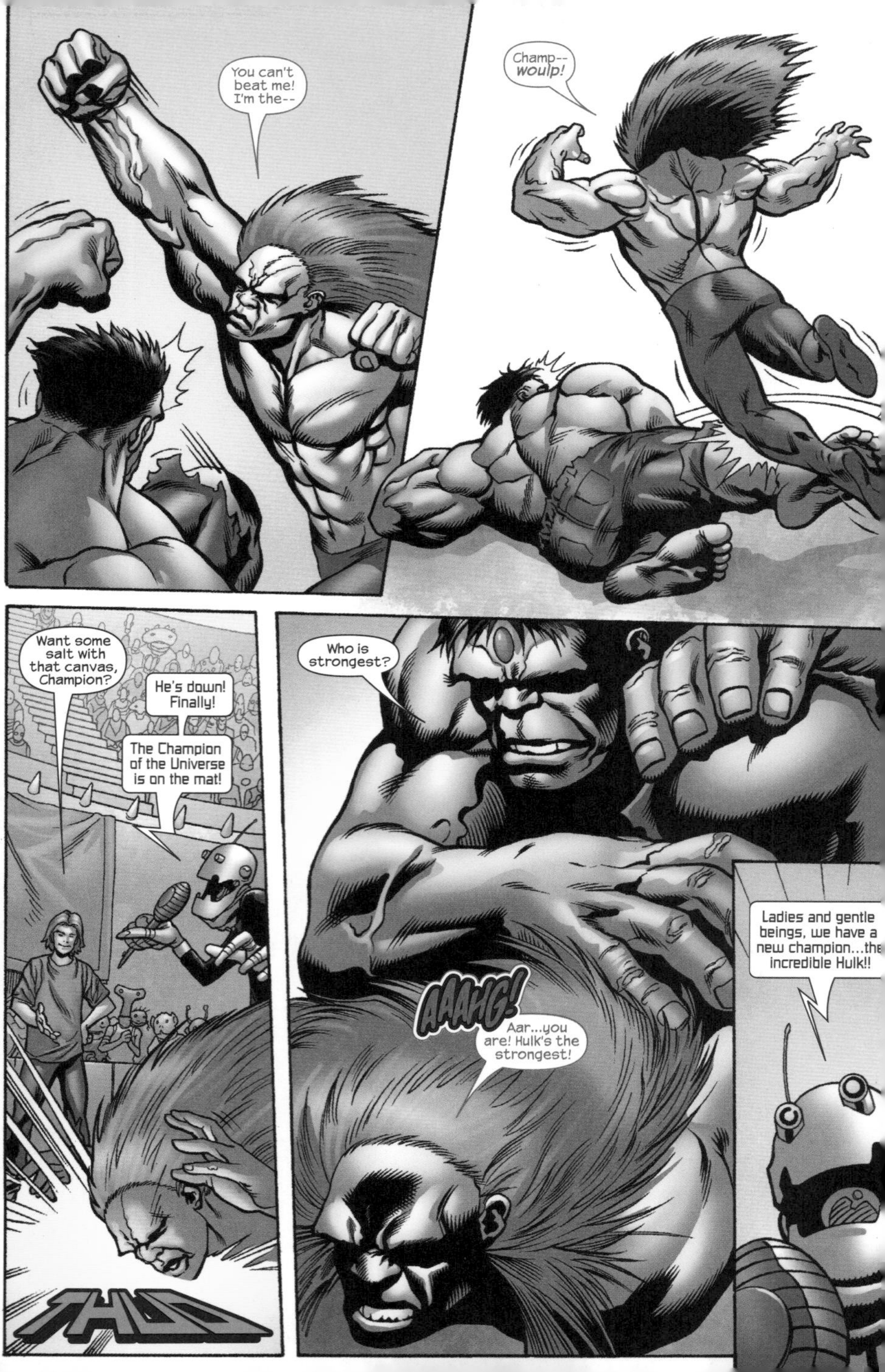
You can't beat me! I'm the--
Champ-- woulp!
Want some salt with that canvas, Champion?
He's down! Finally!
The Champion of the Universe is on the mat!
THUD
Who is strongest?
AAAHG!
Aar...you are! Hulk's the strongest!
Ladies and gentle beings, we have a new champion...the incredible Hulk!!

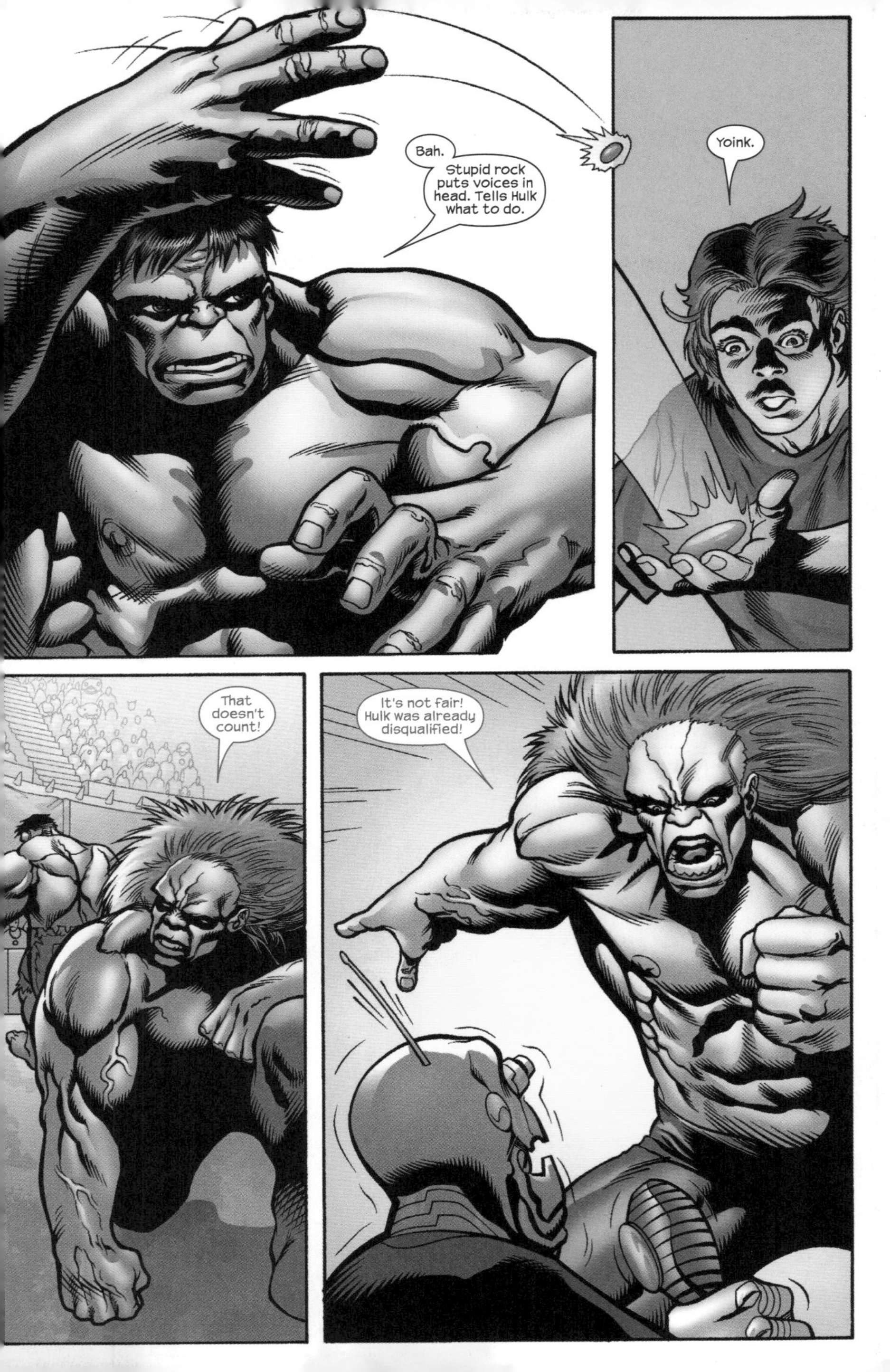
Bah.
Stupid rock puts voices in head. Tells Hulk what to do.
Yoink.
That doesn't count!
It's not fair! Hulk was already disqualified!

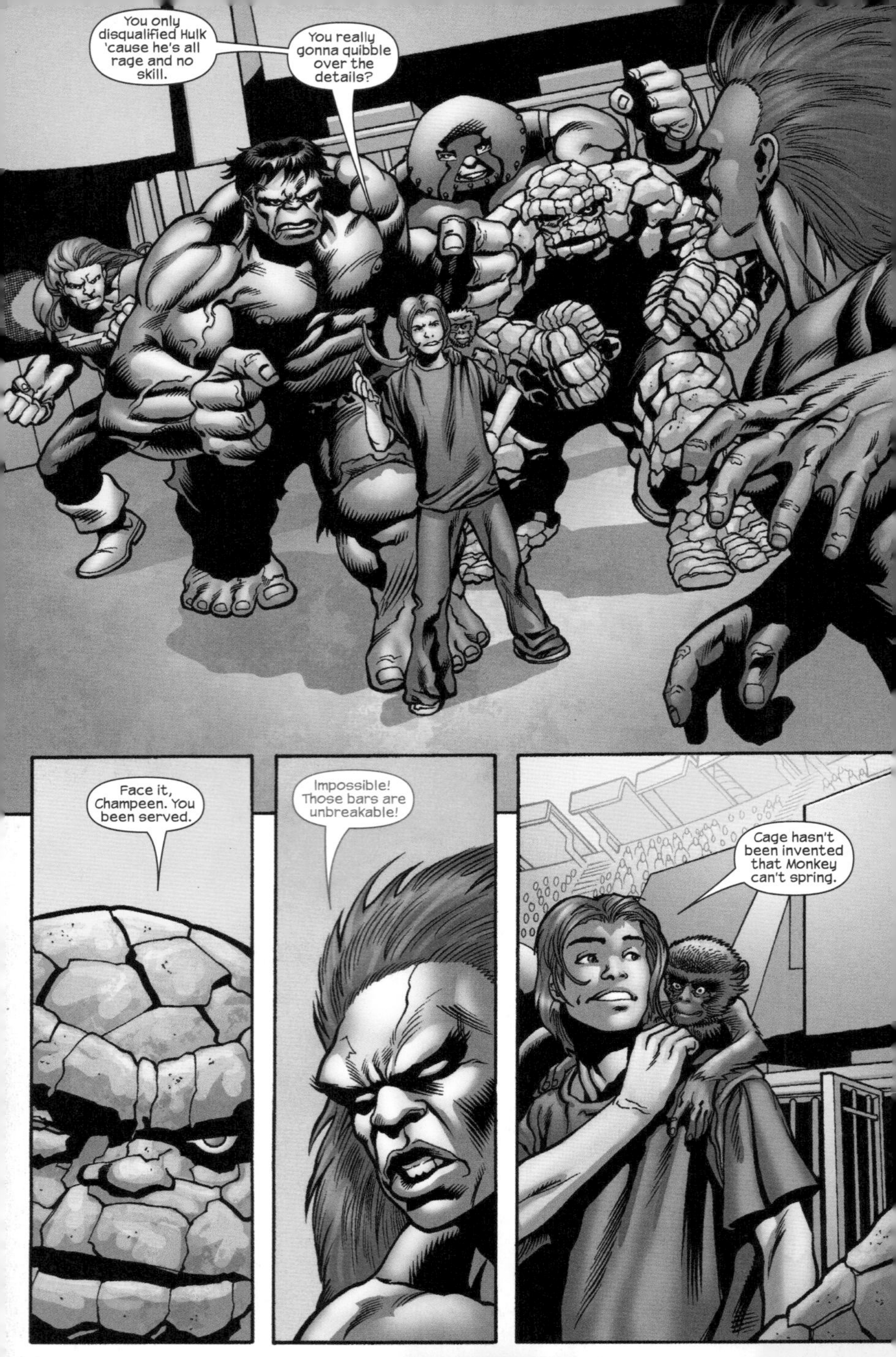
You only disqualified Hulk 'cause he's all rage and no skill.
You really gonna quibble over the details?
Face it, Champeen. You been served.
Impossible! Those bars are unbreakable!
Cage hasn't been invented that Monkey can't spring.

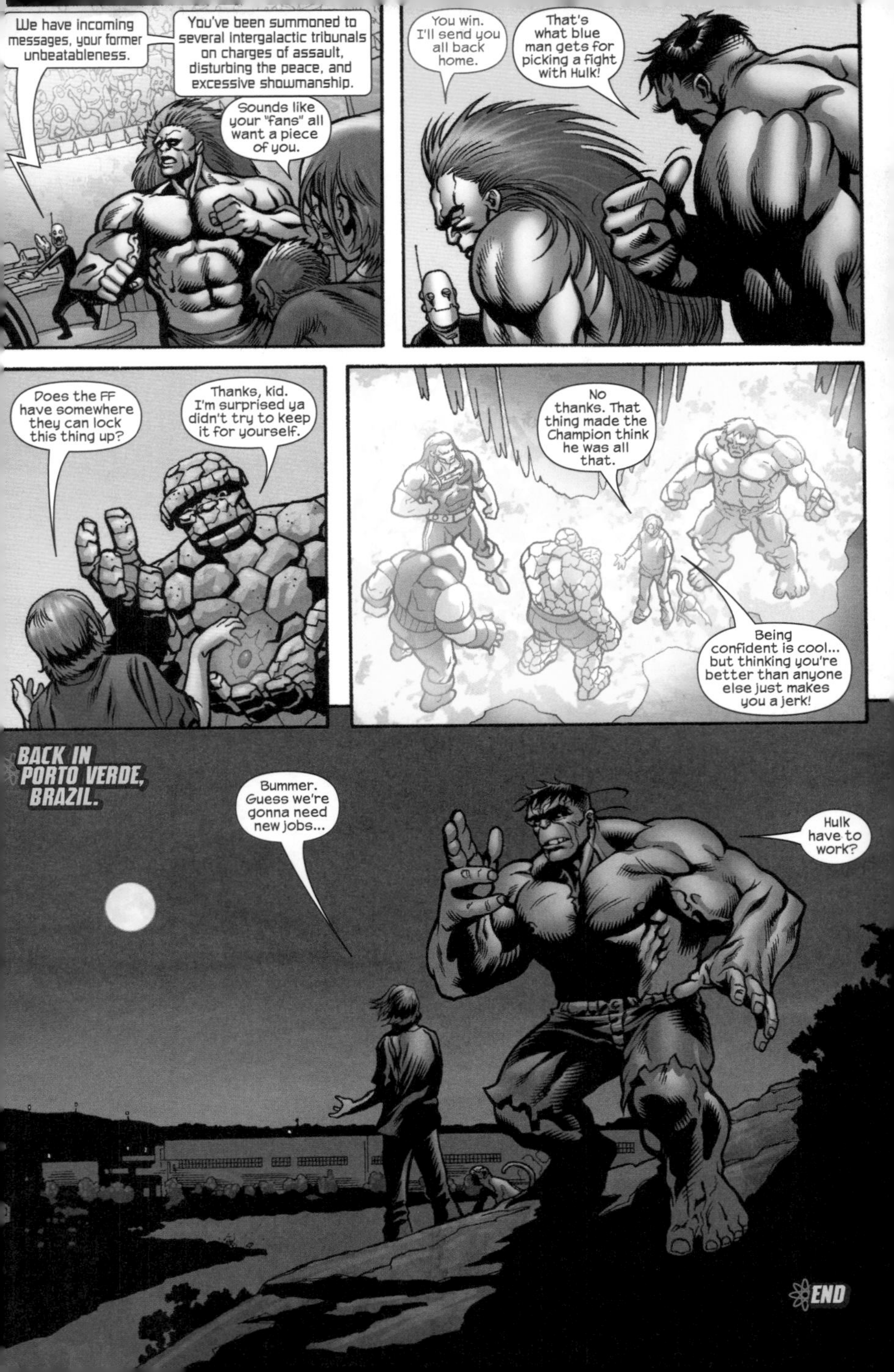

We have incoming messages, your former unbeatableness.
You've been summoned to several intergalactic tribunals on charges of assault, disturbing the peace, and excessive showmanship.
Sounds like your "fans" all want a piece of you.
You win. I'll send you all back home.
That's what blue man gets for picking a fight with Hulk!
Does the FF have somewhere they can lock this thing up?
Thanks, kid. I'm surprised ya didn't try to keep it for yourself.
No thanks. That thing made the Champion think he was all that.
Being confident is cool... but thinking you're better than anyone else just makes you a jerk!
BACK IN PORTO VERDE, BRAZIL.
Bummer. Guess we're gonna need new jobs...
Hulk have to work?
END

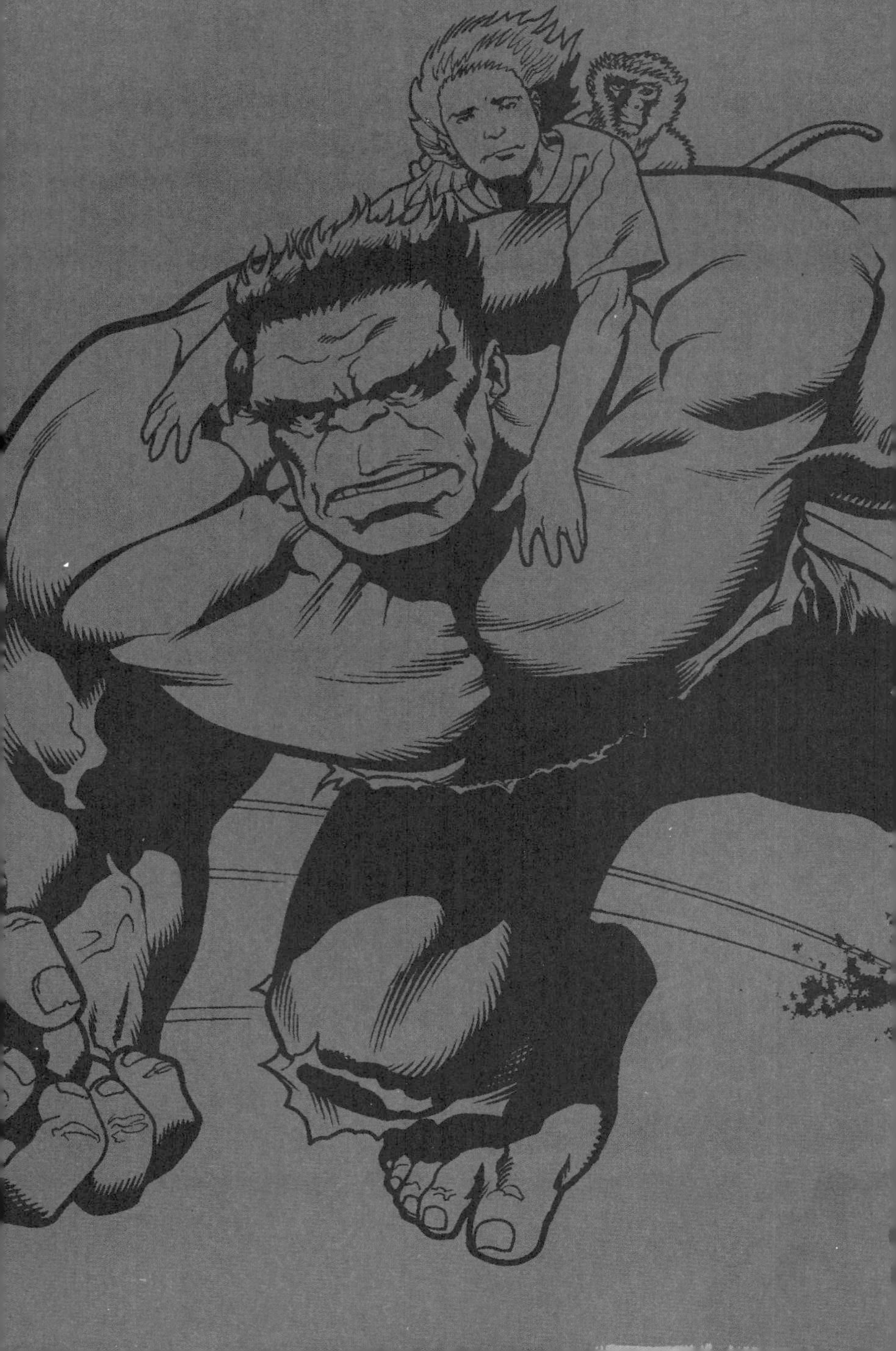